Here's w
Gen

"A saucy combination of romance and suspense that is simply irresistible."
—*Chicago Tribune*

"Stylish...nonstop action...guaranteed to keep chick lit and mystery fans happy!"
—*Publishers' Weekly*, starred review

"Smart, funny and snappy...the perfect beach read!"
—*Fresh Fiction*

"A roller coaster ride full of fun and excitement!"
—*Romance Reviews Today*

"Gemma Halliday writes like a seasoned author leaving the reader hanging on to every word, every clue, every delicious scene of the book. It's a fun and intriguing mystery full of laughs and suspense."
—*Once Upon A Romance*

BOOKS BY GEMMA HALLIDAY

High Heels Mysteries
Spying in High Heels
Killer in High Heels
Undercover in High Heels
Christmas in High Heels
(short story)
Alibi in High Heels
Mayhem in High Heels
Honeymoon in High Heels
(short story)
Sweetheart in High Heels
(short story)
Fearless in High Heels
Danger in High Heels
Homicide in High Heels
Deadly in High Heels
Suspect in High Heels
Peril in High Heels
Jeopardy in High Heels
Deceit in High Heels
Ruthless in High Heels

Wine & Dine Mysteries
A Sip Before Dying
Chocolate Covered Death
Victim in the Vineyard
Marriage, Merlot & Murder
Death in Wine Country
Fashion, Rosé & Foul Play
Killer Among the Vines

Tahoe Tessie Mysteries
Luck Be A Lady
Hey Big Spender
Baby It's Cold Outside
(holiday short story)

**Hollywood Headlines
Mysteries**
Hollywood Scandals
Hollywood Secrets
Hollywood Confessions
Hollywood Holiday
(short story)
Hollywood Deception
Hollywood Revenge

Marty Hudson Mysteries
Sherlock Holmes and the
Case of the Brash Blonde
Sherlock Holmes and the
Case of the Disappearing
Diva
Sherlock Holmes and the
Case of the Wealthy Widow

Jamie Bond Mysteries
Unbreakable Bond
Secret Bond
Lethal Bond
Dangerous Bond
Fatal Bond
Deadly Bond

**Hartley Grace Featherstone
Mysteries**
Deadly Cool
Social Suicide
Wicked Games

Other Works
Play Dead
Viva Las Vegas
A High Heels Haunting
Watching You (short story)
Confessions of a Bombshell
Bandit (short story)

DANGEROUS
BOND

---

a Jamie Bond mystery

GEMMA HALLIDAY

AND

JENNIFER FISCHETTO

DANGEROUS
BOND

CHAPTER ONE

I pulled into the Bond Agency parking lot, stayed seated in my cherry-red Roadster, and used the moment to close my eyes and gather my thoughts. I'd awakened feeling renewed this morning, and I wanted to bask in the new era of Jamie Bond.

Not that the old me was so awful. But recently I'd been framed for murder, nearly killed two—no, three times—seen my best friend shot, and nearly lost my father. Again. It had definitely been one of the more stressful periods of my life. And stress was not pretty.

This had come to me last night while I'd sat in standstill traffic on the 405 and watched two businessmen in tailored suits scream threats to one another over a mild fender bender. Twenty minutes of being stuck would have normally made me scream a few expletives too, but watching the two overgrown children throw their tantrum in the middle of rush hour—arms flapping, faces flushed like maraschino cherries, veins bulging in places nothing should ever bulge—made me realize that it might be time to implement some de-stressing in my own life. Quickly. Before I started to look like a crimson Hulk in heels.

When I'd arrived home, instead of playing my messages or obsessively checking work email, I'd taken a long hot bath, grabbed a bottle of Pinot, and settled down for an evening of *Orange Is the New Black* and a salad Niçoise with seared tuna from a new café up the block.

"This will be an awesome and calm day," I whispered to myself, then opened one eye and inspected the area, making sure no one was watching the crazy blonde talking to herself.

With a smile, I grabbed my purse and stepped out of my car. The early morning sun beat down on my head, but instead of focusing on how hot my scalp was becoming, I said, "At least it's not humid." Was I Zen or what?

I went into the building and pulled on the door marked *Bond Agency* in thick, black lettering. Maya Alexander, the agency's office manager, stood at attention behind her desk, facing me. Her dark hair was swept up in a high bun, and her Bluetooth headset nestled in her right ear. She wore a hot-pink skirt, a cropped-sleeve orange peplum blouse, and cotton-candy pumps. She held a Starbucks cup in one hand and her tablet in the other. She looked impeccable, just as good as when she'd been March's Playmate of the month, and I totally needed to find out where she'd bought that outfit.

"Good morning!" I said in a voice that sounded wildly chipper even to my own ears. Maybe I needed to dial the Zen down just a bit.

Maya, ever professional, didn't seem to notice, thrusting the Starbucks at me. "Morning, Jamie. I have your itinerary." Maya swiped a finger across her tablet. "And—" But before she could finish that thought, the phone rang, and she tapped her earpiece. "Bond Agency."

A door opened, and my two other associates stepped out of their offices. Like Maya, they were both former models. As was I, but that was long enough ago that it felt like a different lifetime. Luckily one good thing that had come out of my teen runway career was my friendship with those two, who had become more like sisters to me than employees.

"'Morning, Boss," said Caleigh Presley—bubbly, blonde, and a distant cousin of the King of Rock and Roll, or so she claimed. I'd never had the heart to actually investigate if it was true. She was a whiz with a computer, could hack into databases even the police couldn't access, and fluently spoke five languages. As an added bonus, the men loved her, which was a plus in our line of work.

"Good morning!" I said, exuding my new uber cheeriness.

The smooth skin between Caleigh's brows puckered for a moment, and Maya's head jerked in my direction, giving me a confused look.

Was "cheery" that weird for me?

When neither verbally commented, I flipped the plastic spout on my cup and sipped my beverage. Yum. A caramel macchiato always hit the spot.

Trailing behind Caleigh was Samantha Cross. With a mocha-colored complexion, thick, dark curls, and legs that put all other models to shame, she was the fourth member of my team. A military-brat childhood and subsequent single motherhood had made her tough as nails when the situation called for it, though I had a sneaking suspicion a healthy layer of compassion lay beneath her tough exterior. Today, however, she looked distracted, her eyes going somewhere beyond my head as she chewed on her lower lip.

I opened my mouth to comment, when Maya hung up and turned to me.

"So, you had an urgent call from Derek," Maya said.

I inwardly rolled my eyes. My father thought every call he made to me was urgent.

Derek Bond had been the "Bond" in the agency for over twenty years, tailing cheating husbands all over the greater Los Angeles basin in his beat-up Cadillac. Lucky me, after my mom had passed away, I'd been the kid in the backseat, reluctantly along for the ride. While it had made for a less than traditional upbringing, I had to admit it had prepared me entirely for taking over the business myself. Not that I'd ever aspired to be a PI myself during those childhood treks, but after Derek's heart attack a few years ago, he'd been forced to retire to his boat, the *Black Pearl*, and I'd been the "Bond" ever since.

Of course, in Derek's mind, I was pretty sure he still saw me as the kid in the backseat. Hence the incessant phone calls. Me? I still saw Derek as the jerk who thought it would be cool to name his daughter James Bond. Seriously. It was on my birth certificate. Hard to forgive a guy for something like that, right?

"What else?" I asked.

"You have a conference call this morning with Mrs. McCanny and her attorney about her husband's beach house…"

A beach house Mrs. McCanny sorely deserved to get after we'd caught her husband and their maid doing things with a feather duster that should not be talked about in polite company.

"Anything this afternoon?"

"You have lunch with Danny at one. And—" The left corner of Maya's mouth lifted, and she whispered, "—there's a celebrity in your office."

Seriously?

I glanced to Caleigh and Sam, who nodded and smiled. Well, Caleigh smiled. Sam just sorta stared into space. Something was definitely up with her.

Beyond curious to see who my new celeb client was, I pivoted on my black patent heels and walked to my office. Just before entering the doorway, I took a quick glance at myself in the reflection of the glass that surrounded my door. I had chosen a navy wrap dress that hugged my body, which was admittedly a bit more curvy than in my modeling days but still not bad. The dress was a bit flirtier than I normally wore to the office, but it had called my attention from my closet this morning.

I stepped over my threshold and greeted my celeb, though I had to admit the woman before me wasn't anyone I immediately recognized. Bummer. There went my dreams of busting a cheating A-lister.

I held out my hand. "Hello, I'm Jamie Bond. I'm the owner and lead investigator here."

The woman stood, and even on four-inch heels she barely came up to my shoulders. Granted, I wore heels also, a modest three-inch, but my height was what had helped me become a fashion model many moons ago…okay, so really less than a decade ago, but after this recent chaos in my life, it felt much longer. The closest I'd come to dying while wearing an itsy-bitsy bikini was of sand inhalation from those giant fans that imitated wind. Nothing like bullets.

"Hello, I'm Bristol Claremont." A fruity scent surrounded her when she moved.

Her name didn't jog my memory. While it wasn't unusual to spot the latest teen star driving through McDonald's off Wilshire or to catch an entourage of glamour and glitz at Spago Beverly Hills, I wasn't totally up on the latest and greatest in pop-culture celebrities.

Bristol Claremont couldn't have been older than twenty-eight. She had long, bright-auburn hair and light-brown eyes. She wore a cream-and-brown paisley silk tunic with a brown miniskirt. A gold chain with a diamond pendant dangled between two high, perky boobs. The kind that didn't move when you walked and that cost mega bucks.

That wasn't unusual in the land of silicone and glitz though. It's what L.A. did best—big dreams, big price tags, and big racks.

I stepped behind my desk and sat in the tall-backed, leather chair. "How can I help you?"

She returned to her seat but sat on the edge of it. "My husband is Roger Claremont."

Still nothing.

"Roger from Hoagies. The submarine sandwich chain. He's their national spokesperson. He lost over a hundred pounds eating their sandwiches."

Finally recollection clicked into place. Dark hair, pale complexion. He appeared on TV holding a sandwich in one hand and his former size gazillion pants in the other, touting the amazing weight-loss properties of ham and cheese on rye.

"From the commercials," I said.

Mrs. Claremont smiled and eased back into her chair. "Yes."

Maya breezed into the room and placed a manila folder on my desk with *R. Claremont* on the tab. She tapped it, and without a word she walked straight out. She had the precise timing of a clock. She was either magical or listened at doors a lot.

I flipped open the file. Maya had already printed the background check she'd run on both the client and her husband. There was also a list of Roger's hangouts, home address, friends, and what he did during his days. He didn't work at a regular job. It seemed as if his Hoagies gig was the Claremonts' only source of income.

Thorough and magical. Maya needed a tiara and wand.

"How can I help you, Mrs. Claremont?" I reached for a pad of paper and a pen.

"Please call me Bristol. I'm very concerned for Roger. He hasn't been himself lately."

If I were to guess, she was about to say she feared he was stepping out. He slimmed down and was now cheating. Unfortunately we'd seen it all too often but usually with couples that were nearing middle age. Bristol was gorgeous and sexually in her prime. What could her husband have wanted elsewhere?

"How so?" I clicked on my pen, ready to write a big *C* for *cheater* on my legal pad.

"I think he's cheating…"

I almost smiled to myself, but that would be rude. This was the business we were in though. The wife always knew.

"…on his diet," Bristol finished

I blinked several times, trying to rewind my brain. "Excuse me? You think he's cheating on his diet?"

She nodded. "Yes. He's been nervous. He's sneaking out at night and not telling me where he's going or where he's been."

Classic signs.

I scribbled her worries down. "What makes you think this has to do with his diet and not…" My gaze involuntarily drifted to her cleavage. "And he's not with another woman?"

Hey, it had to be asked.

She smirked and wiggled her hips ever so slightly. "Trust me. I know. Besides, we have absolutely no problem in that department. No, this is about his health."

"His health?" I scribbled some more.

She widened her eyes, placed a hand to her chest, and caressed her pendant. "Yes. If he's changed his eating habits or isn't walking, he could gain all that weight back. Hoagies would find another spokesperson and…" Her words trailed off.

And he wouldn't be able to buy her diamonds anymore?

I didn't ask but jotted a quick note: *TW?* For possible trophy wife.

"Will you take the case, follow him around, and make sure he's not blowing our future?" she asked.

I smiled and rose to my feet. "We will do our best to find out exactly what's going on with Roger."

She got to her pointy-heeled feet and thanked me. With a fruity puff, she turned and left.

I tore my sheet of notes off the pad, stuck it into the folder, and then walked back into the reception area to fill the ladies in.

Maya sat behind her desk, clicking at her keyboard and talking on the phone. She was the only one there.

I walked across the space to the other offices. The conference room was dark and empty. Sam's office was also empty.

Caleigh, however, was at her desk, staring at her cell phone. She glanced up as I entered. "Hey, Boss, how'd it go? Do we have a new case?"

"Yeah. Roger Claremont. His wife thinks he's cheating on his diet."

She quirked a brow and lowered her phone.

I nodded. "Yeah. We definitely get the weird ones. I think it really has to do with their income. Their cash cow is tied into him maintaining the weight he lost and doing those Hoagies commercials."

Her blue eyes widened. "That Roger? He's kinda cute. In a plain-Joe kinda way."

Which meant she wasn't interested. Caleigh's type was anything but plain.

"Where's Sam?" I asked, remembering her distracted look from earlier.

"She had to run an errand. Something to do with Julio, I think."

Julio was Sam's son. Julio's father, Julio Sr., had been absent for the first couple of years of his son's life, but he'd recently been back in touch, was paying child support regularly, and had been trying to make up for lost time by spending every weekend with Julio Jr. I didn't know the details, but it sounded like things were on the mend in Sam's domestic life lately. Then again, Sam didn't talk much about her private life.

"Is everything all right?" I asked.

Caleigh had glanced back down to her phone. "Oh yeah, I'm sure it is."

While I wasn't 100 percent convinced right now, I had to get working on proving the Hoagies man was still eating Hoagies. How hard could that be?

* * *

Mrs. McCanny's conference call lasted most of the morning as I detailed exactly what Sam and I had caught Mr. McCanny doing. It was uncomfortable, to say the least, my deposition being repeatedly interrupted by Mrs. McCanny's wailing sobs alternated with shouted threats to Mr. McCanny's private parts. In the end, her lawyer sounded fairly giddy at his prospect of getting her the beach house, and I was more than ready for lunch with Danny.

I'd met Danny Flynn on my first photo shoot, when I'd been all teenage gangly limbs and nerves, and he'd been an up-and-coming photographer. He'd stepped into something of a role of big brother at the time, teaching me how to turn gangly into graceful in front of the camera. Over the years Danny had gone from big brother, to best friend, to something that I couldn't quite put a label on now. He had kissed me, and I had liked it. Where that put our relationship now, I wasn't quite sure, but I was looking forward to lunch.

I'd insisted on picking the restaurant, and as soon as I walked through the door, the heady scent of yeasty bread hit me. I inhaled deeply. I was definitely not one of those low-carb girls.

Danny stepped up right behind me and kicked the back of my heels with his sneakers. He whispered in my ear, "What the heck are we doing here, Bond?"

I shivered at his breath against my earlobe. Then I turned around and had to stifle another small shiver.

Danny was a few years older than I was—old enough that fine laugh lines were starting to crease his pale blue-green eyes, giving the look that he was perpetually smiling at some inside joke. But he was still young enough that his little black book was filled with numbers of up-and-coming models and actresses who thought he was "totes hot." In that moment, I had to agree with them. The hotter-than-average summer had tanned his skin to a warm golden brown, and his sun-streaked hair hung just a little too long, threatening to brush the top of his shoulders. He dressed casually in a dark T-shirt and jeans, though there was nothing casual about the way those jeans hugged his athletic frame.

For a moment I completely forgot his question.

Before I could answer, a woman in a brown apron and little paper hat greeted us. "Welcome to Hoagies. What can I get for you?"

I took a quick survey of the small, narrow store. It was empty except for an older man paying the cashier. The glass-enclosed buffet counter of meats and vegetables took up most of the space, but there were four tables crowded by the front windows. There was also another table toward the back. It was surrounded by a red velvet rope—the kind you'd find at a theater. It separated the table from the rest of the establishment.

"Why is that table sectioned off?" I asked the woman, whose name tag read *Debbie*.

Her eyes lit up. "That's a private table. It's for VIPs."

Danny coughed. "Hoagies has VIPs? Who?"

"Well, the company's bigwigs, but they don't visit that often. Usually it's just Roger who sits there. You know, this is the store he ordered from while losing all his weight." She smiled with pride.

Yes, I knew. It was the reason we were here and about to endure cola from a soda machine, instead of frosty margaritas at my favorite Mexican place.

I turned to Danny, pulling out my wide-eyed-and-super-excited look, and hoped he'd play along. "Does this mean I'll actually get to meet a celebrity?"

Danny frowned at me and started to take a step back. But then something shifted in his eyes, and his expression became as zealous as mine felt. He looked to Debbie. "Yeah, that would be neato."

Neato? I clenched my teeth to keep from laughing.

Debbie's smile turned down a notch. "He used to come in for lunch every day, but I haven't seen him at all this week. He's probably busy with traveling all over the world and signing autographs."

She did realize he was a sandwich rep and not the member of a boy band, right?

"Hopefully he'll show up before you leave though. What can I get for you?"

I looked up to the menu hanging on the wall, just beneath the ceiling. There were so many options. This wasn't my first time eating a Hoagies sub, but it also wasn't my regular place. The menu had definitely grown since my last time here.

"What does Roger usually have?" I asked.

Debbie's grin amplified. She grabbed a loaf of bread behind her from a rack. "That's easy. He gets the small turkey and American cheese on our whole wheat bread. It has extra fiber."

"I see."

She cut the loaf in half and started to put the one half back on the rack.

"I'll have the same," Danny said, giving Debbie a wink that had her giggling like a teenager.

I resisted the urge to roll my eyes as I watched her cut each half of bread open. She laid the pre-portioned turkey on the bread and then topped it with triangular cheese slices. She squirted mayo—at least I think it was mayo— from a bottle and then slid the sandwiches down to the veggie section of the bar. She then piled shredded lettuce, thinly sliced tomatoes, red onions, green peppers, and black olives on top.

I was certain the sandwich wasn't going to close, but sure enough, she wrapped it up in yellow-and-green designed wax paper and slid it into a plastic bag.

After paying for both sandwiches and a couple of drinks—I insisted that lunch was on me—Danny and I sat at one of the tables against the window. We didn't say anything as we unwrapped and took our first bites. Although it was mostly a mouthful of lettuce and bread, it was pretty good.

My cell chirped, and I glanced at the caller ID. Derek. It could wait. I changed my settings to vibrate.

"So, why are we here? And what was with the starry-eyed tourist routine?" Danny asked.

I sipped on my soda. "New client. Roger's wife believes he's cheating on his diet."

Danny grinned. A dimple showing up in his left cheek made my heart beat a little faster. "You get all the good cases."

"Tell me about it," I mumbled, and then I filled him in on the details.

When I was finished, he stabbed a finger in the air. "So Mrs. Hoagies sees Roger as her cash cow?"

I nodded. "That's my guess. It doesn't matter though. If the guy is eating junk food, it should be easy enough to catch him in the act."

"Should be a switch from your usual stakeout. Gonna run surveillance on Baskin-Robbins? Krispy Kreme? Cold Stone Creamery?" Danny teased.

I kicked him under the table. "Hey, a celebrity client is a celebrity client. We make Mrs. Hoagie happy, and I'm sure she has lots of D-list friends she can refer our way."

Danny grinned again, munching down on a slice of onion. "Who knows? You get lucky, you might even get a job doing surveillance for Mrs. Jack in the Box."

I narrowed my eyes and sent him a death look. "Very funny."

"Hey, at least you keep me around for comic relief," he said, that dimple making an appearance again.

"And eye candy," I mumbled.

"What was that?"

"Nothing." I took a big bite of my sandwich to avoid saying anything I might regret.

Danny's gaze traveled to my chest and then to my face. "You look nice today. A bit overdressed for Hoagies."

I leaned closer and whispered, "Jeans are overdressed for Hoagies."

He chuckled deeply, causing Debbie to glance our way.

My cell vibrated noisily in my purse again.

"Derek?" Danny asked.

I shrugged, swallowing my bite of turkey and cheese. "Third call today."

"How's he doing lately?" While the tone in his voice was purposely neutral, I could see actual concern in his eyes. Danny and my father had been like oil and water from the very beginning, though I couldn't entirely blame Derek for not being excited about his teenage daughter hanging out with a ladies'-man photographer. However, recently Danny had taken a bullet for Derek, softening the old man's attitude toward him. A bit.

"He's fine," I answered quickly, suddenly feeling slightly guilty for not calling him back.

"Good. Glad to hear it." Danny popped the rest of his sandwich into his mouth. He stared at me thoughtfully while he chewed, before finally speaking again. "And Aiden?"

I nearly choked on my sip of soda.

"Excuse me?"

Danny raised a questioning eyebrow my way. "Internal affairs drop the case?"

I paused, biting my lower lip. The last time I had seen Assistant District Attorney Aiden Prince, he'd been standing over a dead body with a gun in his hand. The dead person in question had homicide on the mind, so in my opinion, Aiden had done the right thing—maybe the only thing. But while the shooting had been completely justified and in self-defense, an internal affairs investigation and temporary suspension had been inevitable.

"Yeah. I think. I guess so."

Danny raised his other eyebrow, doubling the question. "You don't know?"

I squirmed in my seat. "We haven't exactly talked lately."

While my past with Danny was long and varied, my relationship with Aiden had been fast and furious. Emphasis on the *had* been.

Aiden was tall, blond, and handsome in a just-stepped-off-the-cover-of-*GQ* kind of way. He was a straight-laced, by-the-book professional who was a phenomenal kisser. He also happened to still be in love with his dead wife, which had thrown a bit of a monkey wrench into our relationship. Add in the fact that somewhere in the back of his mind, I had the feeling that Aiden blamed me for the fatal shooting and his suspension, and our relationship was not exactly peachy keen at the moment.

"Are you ready to get out of here?" Danny asked, finally taking pity on my discomfort.

"Sure." I folded up my trash and pushed it into the plastic sandwich bag.

After throwing it all away and smiling good-bye at Debbie, I walked out onto the sidewalk just as my phone chirped. I glanced down. It was Derek again. What could possibly be so darn urgent?

Instead of sighing and eye rolling like my formerly stressed self would, I took a deep Zen-filled breath and put on a smile. "Hello, Derek. What's up?"

"It's about time, James. I called you hours ago." His voice sounded gruff and anything but Zen.

"It's been a busy morning. Clients." It was only a half lie, and it was much less stressful to lie than to listen to him yell at me for not doing what he wanted.

A passing car honked so loudly that I had to push my finger into my free ear.

"I'm here now though, so what's going on?" I asked.

He had no misgivings about sighing loudly and clearly. "I've been arrested."

CHAPTER TWO

———

Ouch, talk about guilt. Okay, so maybe this time Derek's needs had been urgent.

When I arrived at the precinct, I expected an officer to lead me to a holding cell, where I'd find Derek seated between a smelly drunk and a dangerous drug dealer. Maybe a small part of me, the old cynical part, hoped that would be the case, simply so he could learn a lesson. I wasn't sure why he'd been arrested yet, but I was certain he'd done something stupid. I wanted to attribute his actions to being retired and having too much time on his hands. But let's face it. He'd always been slightly reckless. As a child, his idea of father-daughter bonding had been hanging in his car eating boxed powdered donuts and listening to the Dodgers game on the radio while on a stakeout.

But—surprise, surprise—I was escorted into the detective division and found him sitting at a desk, talking with an older, plainclothes detective.

I watched for a second. The two chatted and laughed as if they were best of pals. A second officer passed the desk, and Derek drew him into the conversation. I knew Derek still had friends in the LAPD, but this clearly wasn't a man in a lot of legal trouble.

The officer nodded in my direction, and Derek turned. His brows drew together, his mouth hardened, and he had the nerve to look annoyed at me.

When I approached, he snapped, "What took you so long?"

I scoffed and instantly realized why I hadn't grown up to be a rainbows-and-puppies kinda person. "This is L.A. There's traffic. So sorry my magic carpet ride is at the cleaners. What did you do?"

It was his turn to scoff. "What makes you think I did something?"

"Because you said you were arrested. Although by the looks of things, you don't seem to be in any trouble." I turned to the detective seated at the desk. Hopefully I'd get actual answers from him.

The man was paunchy, with a balding head. His brown suit jacket hung over the back of his chair, and a mint-green tie hung crookedly from his neck. He looked like someone had put out a casting call for "typical older cop," appearing a few years older than retirement age and like he had spent one too many days eating donuts and drinking stale coffee. I'd been around enough cops in my lifetime to know that in reality most of the men and women on the force kept in shape. The job demanded it. But every once in a while, like in this guy's case, Hollywood was realistic about something.

"This is Ronnie, my old buddy from when I used to walk the streets," Derek said.

"You were a prostitute?" I asked with a smirk.

He narrowed his eyes. "And this funny lady is my daughter, James." He never refrained from using my legal name. He was so proud that he had named me after one of his heroes. The fact that the hero was fictional had never mattered.

Ronnie raised his brows. "This is little James? Wow, I remember when you weren't much higher than your daddy's knee."

I smiled, not quite remembering back that far.

Derek stared at my outfit and curled his upper lip. "It's a weekday. Why are you dressed like you're going on a date?"

Was this dress really that fancy?

"I just had lunch with Danny," I said. I'll admit my intention might have been to get under his skin at that point. Hey, a girl can only do so much Zen. "What happened?"

"Someone called the cops because I was on a stakeout."

I quirked a brow. Derek no longer took any cases, and we both knew it. Arms crossed over my chest, foot tapping, I looked to Ronnie for the truth.

Ronnie rubbed his chin. "A neighbor called in a suspicious-looking character, and the responding officers arrested him for trespassing."

"Trespassing? That's not a stakeout, Derek. Where were you?"

He shrugged as if he didn't know, but he was simply trying to stall. What the heck was he up to?

"I was just looking inside a window. I needed to see something."

"What window?" If he thought I was letting this go without specific answers, he would be in for a rude awakening.

He huffed. "I was at Elaine's, okay?"

Elaine was the woman he'd been seeing for the past few months. Which in itself had surprised me, because Derek had never been a one-woman kind of man in the past. His philosophy had always been that monogamy was for suckers. Personally, my theory had always been that a lifetime of chasing down cheating husbands had soured Derek on the idea. For as long as I could remember, he'd had a steady stream of girlfriends, none of them serious, none of them lasting longer than a few days, and none of them memorable enough to stick out in my mind.

Only lately, it seemed that Elaine had turned all of that around.

So what was with spying on her?

"We're letting him off with a warning," Ronnie said.

That would explain why he wasn't cuffed in a cell.

Relief flooded my old man's tanned face. "Oh man, Ronnie. Thanks. I really appreciate it."

"I get it," said Ronnie. "We go way back, and I know how it works. But your PI license is expired, and you don't have the same liberties as the licensed investigators do anymore. If you're caught trespassing again, we'll have to book you."

Derek stood and shook Ronnie's meaty hand. "I get it, man. I do. Thanks." With a wink, he led the way outside.

But if he thought this was over, he had another think coming.

When we reached my car, I slipped behind the steering wheel and turned to Derek as he sat in the passenger seat.

"I give up. Why are you spying on your *girlfriend*?" I used that term on purpose, to see if he'd squirm.

But he didn't. Aww, how cute. Dad and Elaine were sitting in the tree.

He ran a hand through his salt-and-pepper hair. For a guy getting up there in age, the color may have changed some, but it was still thick.

"Well?" I prodded when he didn't answer. "What's going on with you two?"

"None of your business," he mumbled, suddenly avoiding my gaze.

But I shook my head. "Wrong, old man. When I'm dragged down to the police station to bail you out, it becomes my business."

"You didn't have to post any bail," he automatically corrected me.

I shot him the evil eye. Giving him the silent treatment. Refusing to turn on the car and let the AC wash over us.

"Fine," he finally huffed. I think he normally might've been able to out-silent-treatment me, but the lack of AC was making him sweat. Either that or the questioning. "Look, I think Elaine might be...cheating on me."

I tried really hard to keep back my giggle. But come on. Ladies' man Derek Bond afraid that *he* was being cheated on? The irony was killing me.

"I'm so glad you think this is funny."

Satisfied enough with his confession, I turned, stuck my key into the ignition, and brought my car to life. "More like irony coming to bite you on the butt. Tell me—how does that shoe feel?"

He glanced down at his worn-in Converse.

I rolled my eyes. "The proverbial one. As in the shoe being on the other foot."

He tossed a glare my way. "I'm serious, James."

I cleared my throat and pushed the snark from my brain as I pulled out of the parking lot. "Okay, so tell me why you think she's being unfaithful."

"She doesn't always take my calls."

"I don't take your calls."

"Yeah, but that's because you're my kid and a pain in the butt."

I grinned. I couldn't disagree. "Continue."

He sighed. "She's been acting different, distant. A guy just knows."

"And you thought peeking in her windows would be the solution?"

Derek shrugged, sighing again. "I don't know! Look, I gotta do something. I can't just sit around and wonder who this guy is. At the very least, I gotta know what I'm up against."

Leave it to Derek to look at his relationship as a competition.

"Fine," I acquiesced.

Derek shot me a questioning look, one bushy eyebrow going up into his hairline. "Fine?"

"Fine. I'll look into it for you." I took a right at the next corner.

"Wait—you? Oh no. No way, James," he snapped.

"And why not?"

"Kid, I've been tailing cheaters for as long as you've been alive. There's no way I'm having my *daughter* do my dirty work."

I glanced at him, and his brows were furrowed.

"Do I need to remind you that you're not a PI anymore? You were almost just arrested."

"It doesn't matter. This is my business, and I'll handle it."

I shook my head. "Derek Bond, I forbid you from looking into this."

He turned his head and stared out the window, ignoring my demand. I expected him to yell at me and tell me he was the parent in this relationship. But he didn't. So far my expectations with him had been far off today.

"I'm serious," I added. "If you get arrested again, I'm disowning you and letting you rot in jail."

He still didn't answer or even acknowledge my words.

This was not good.

I knew we were both thinking the same thing. That no matter what I said, there was no way Derek was going to walk away from this. And that left me only one choice: I needed to find out what was up with Elaine before he ended up behind bars.

* * *

I dropped Derek off at his car, which was still parked across the street from Elaine's small bungalow. After he drove off, I waited a few minutes just in case he was circling the block to double back. I took the time to scan through my new celebrity client's husband's itinerary, which Maya had forwarded to my phone. It showed that Roger was normally at home this time of day. In fact, according to what Maya could find out, he generally spent his afternoons at home unless he was making a commercial or speaking at a Hoagies sponsored event.

I called the office and had Maya put me through to Sam and then Caleigh. Some surveillance seemed to be the best way to keep an eye on our cheating dieter.

"Great," I said to Caleigh after she agreed to be ready. "I should be there in a few minutes."

We hung up, and I took a quick glance around for Derek's car before leaving.

As soon as I got to the office, I approached Maya's desk just as she was hanging up the phone.

"Hey, Boss. How was lunch?"

I thought of the turkey sandwich and how the taste of black olives and tomatoes still lingered in my mouth. "It was actually good." I paused. "I need you to do something for me."

"Shoot."

"This something is a bit delicate and on the down low."

Maya raised one eyebrow in my direction, her eyes twinkling mischievously. "This sounds like a fun something."

"Could you check into Elaine's recent cell activity?"

Maya grabbed a sticky pad and jotted down my request. "The one your dad is dating? Looking for anything in particular?"

"Possibly. We're looking for any sign that she's been seeing someone."

"Oh." Maya sounded disappointed. "As in someone other than Derek, right?"

I nodded. I sincerely hoped Derek was wrong. I didn't know Elaine well, but from the few interactions we had, she'd seemed to be a stand-up woman. One who miraculously had Derek doing a one-eighty on his entire view of relationships. But as much as I hoped Derek was wrong, I'd been in this business long enough to fear he was right.

"Poor Derek," Maya said, sitting behind her computer.

It wasn't normally a sentiment I had about dear ol' Dad, but today I had to agree.

I stepped into Sam's office. She was on the phone and held up her index finger when she saw me.

"Okay, sweetie, you can go to Chad's after your homework is done. I'll be checking it when I get home. Yeah. Okay, bye." She hung up and smiled at me.

"Is everything all right?" I asked.

She stood and walked around her desk. "Oh yeah. Julio's bored and wants to spend the night at his friend's house so they can play Minecraft."

"Are you ready to go?" I asked.

"Yep." She picked up her purse and followed me to Caleigh's office.

Caleigh stood in front of her desk, swiping a tube of red lipstick across her mouth. She smacked her lips together, then clicked her compact mirror shut. "Ready, ladies?"

* * *

We hopped into Sam's car (which had a backseat, unlike my Roadster), and pulled up to Roger's address in Orange County, just south of Los Angeles down the 5. It was a Spanish-styled mini-mansion with light-pink stucco and a tiled roof. A tall wrought iron security gate prevented us from driving to the front door without being noticed. From our vantage point though, it wasn't hard to make out the large arched windows that ran the length of the first floor. Squat, round manicured shrubs dotted the walkway. Despite Bristol's appearance and Roger's notoriety, I'd expected something more modest. Did the guy really have the money for this place just from eating sandwiches?

We were only there for a couple of minutes when the front door opened and Roger stepped out. He wore light-colored slacks, a blue shirt, and brown loafers. He headed to the shiny white brand-new BMW and peeled out of the driveway straight toward us.

I didn't have time to get out of the way, so we all slunk down in our seats. The sound of the metal gate sliding and then his engine filled my ears. Surely he'd wonder why a car was parked outside his property. Our luck, he'd pull to the side, get out, examine our car, and find us folded into human pretzels. How would we explain that?

No, a little voice in my head shouted. *Think positive.* That was right. *Okay, visualize him not being suspicious and just driving off.* Unfortunately, I was about as good at visualization as I was about being Zen, and my stomach grumbled, and my mind wandered to the Hoagies sandwich from earlier.

Caleigh peeked up over the seats and said, "He's getting away."

This snapped me out of my delicious daydream of mayo and lettuce. I straightened up, and Sam threw the car into drive and took off.

He hopped onto the 55 going west toward Costa Mesa, and ended up pulling into the South Coast Plaza Mall parking garage. We watched him back into a parking space in the south parking structure.

We parked a row away and quickly got out to follow, but his steps were quicker than ours, and we lost him after he rushed inside. The clicking of our heels was masked by a concentrated sound of voices. It was more than typical mall chatter. A small crowd was gathered in front of a store several yards down. Was Roger there?

We hurried over and quickly recognized the trademark yellow-and-green logo of Hoagies. Next to it was a banner that read *Grand Opening*. Of course.

Caleigh and Sam moved toward the left of the crowd, while I took a spot near the back, right where I could see the front of the store. Roger stood behind a long, yellow ceremony ribbon that had been strung across the store's opening. To his left was a short, pale man wearing a gray suit and a big cheesy smile. He held an oversized pair of scissors and was looking at Roger like a kid looks at Superman. Clearly Roger was Hoagies royalty.

Off to the King of Sandwiches' right, two African American men stood. Not smiling. If sandwich shops had bouncers, I'd say that's what these two were. The taller guy was not only broad shouldered but thick around the middle. He wore black jeans, black high-top sneakers with neon-colored laces, a long-sleeve red T-shirt, and a black puffy vest. Dark sunglasses covered his eyes, and a gold cross dangled mid-chest.

The man beside him appeared vastly different in a black suit and silver tie. He too wore dark sunglasses, but instead of flashy neckwear, a thick gold link bracelet wrapped around his left wrist, with a wide-faced gold watch. I wasn't well versed in men's jewelry, but they looked expensive.

Something about the pair raised my internal radar, along with the hairs on the back of my neck. Roger's bodyguards? I hadn't noticed the two men leaving the house with him, but maybe they were his public protection?

The portly man with the big scissors, who I gathered to be the store's manager, went on to announce the new opening, and then he handed the scissors over to Roger.

Roger flashed the crowd a big grin. "I now officially declare this Hoagies franchise open for business. Let the deliciousness begin!" Then Roger cut the ribbon.

A small round of applause circled. Sam and Caleigh joined in, blending in easily with the lunch groupies.

After a few minutes of talking, the scissor man handed Roger a wrapped sandwich and waved the crowd in. Roger turned and said something to the two guys in gold behind him. The taller of the pair nodded, and they followed him back in the direction we had come.

I waited a beat before signaling Sam and Caleigh to follow him. At a safe distance, pretending to window-shop (which wasn't very difficult because the window-shopping was good here!), we followed him back to the parking garage. Not once did he turn around.

Once we got to the parking garage, the two shady-looking guys split off from Roger, heading left while he headed right. As curious as I was about the two guys, Roger was our only objective here. We followed him just far enough to see him get into his BMW before we got back into Sam's car as well.

Twenty minutes later we tracked him to his dry cleaners, where he picked up several items that looked like suits. Then he stopped at the post office and walked inside holding a single envelope. Next, he was on to the barber for a trim. We knew this because Caleigh peeked inside, pretending to be lost. She "played blonde" very well.

When she returned to the car with a big grin, she pointed down the street. Across from the barber and several stores down was a Hoagies.

They sure were everywhere once you noticed them.

Without a word, I dug into my wallet for a twenty, handed it to Sam and said, "Small, turkey, Roger's style. It's on me."

Neither of them had to be told twice. They scrambled off to get our food like kids in a candy store. I kept my eye on the barber, but they returned before Roger emerged. I managed one yumified bite before Roger came out, with a slightly shorter do, and we were back on the road. We ended up where we'd started—in front of his mini-mansion.

He parked in his garage and went inside, leaving the garage door open. Other than his car, it was empty. Bristol Claremont must've been out. Not only was their property quiet, but the street we were parked on was also. No cars passing by, no people outside walking their dogs. Other than a black SUV parked up the road, it appeared most residents weren't home.

I turned my attention back to the Claremont estate. I hated being this far away from a subject, but at least my dinner was as perfect as I remembered. There was something about the mayonnaise mixed with the tomatoes and olives that really took the deliciousness over the edge. Who knew mayo could be so magical?

"This turkey is amazing," Caleigh said around a bite.

Sam nodded in agreement. "They should have a drive-through window. It would be great for stakeouts."

Caleigh widened her eyes. "Oh my gosh, yes." She paused. "You don't think I could lose a couple of pounds eating this stuff?"

"Roger did," Sam said around a hunk of turkey and cheese.

"Best. Diet. Ever," Caleigh responded, diving in for another large bite

It didn't take long for the sandwiches to disappear and for us to get antsy. Sam yawned, Caleigh studied her manicure, which was a pretty pale pink, and I tapped my hand against the dashboard, strumming out some beat stuck in my head. I silently cursed ad makers who used old songs in their commercials.

"This is boring," Caleigh finally announced.

"This is tedious," Sam agreed.

"This isn't that bad," I said, trying to maintain some positive outlook.

Caleigh and Sam both stared at me.

"What?"

"Since when do you enjoy stakeouts where nothing is happening?" Sam asked, shooting me a look full of attitude.

"I'm just trying to reduce my stress by focusing on the positive. I'm being Zen."

Caleigh glanced up to Sam and raised her perfectly arched brows.

Sam leaned toward me and used her mom voice. "James Bond, snap out of it. You are not a positive person."

I bit the inside of my cheek to stop from laughing at her tone. "Hey. I can be."

They both gave me *you're crazy* looks.

Sam patted my shoulder. "You are cynical and sarcastic. You don't look at rainbows and puppies and think the world's okay, because it's not. It's dark and cruel, and we just have to survive."

Now it was time for Caleigh and I to exchange concerned glances about Sam.

She must have caught them, because she quickly amended, "So maybe it's not *all* cruel. There are bright spots and beauty and joy and stuff. But the point is we love you the way you are. There's no need to change."

While I appreciated her sentiment, I still got the impression that something was going on with Sam. Was it my imagination, or was she more tightly wound than normal?

"How about we turn in for the day?" Caleigh suggested, and rotated her ankles. "These shoes are pinching my toes." Encased around her slender feet were black pumps with extremely pointed toes.

I nodded to Sam, who grabbed the key dangling from the ignition. "Sure thing. There isn't much else to see here anyway."

Suddenly a loud sound shot through the still evening, causing each of us to flinch.

Caleigh slid down into her seat. We looked to one another. Holy crap. There was no mistaking that.

It was a gunshot.

I opened my purse, grabbed my Glock, and hightailed it out of the car. Luckily, the gate wasn't fastened. I ran past the round shrubs to the front door. I pressed down on the handle. It was unlocked. I glanced over my shoulder. Sam and Caleigh were right behind me, with their weapons drawn as well.

With my arms extended, gun aiming straight ahead, I pushed the door open with my shoulder. We stood in a two-story foyer. My gaze was focused on danger and didn't take in the surroundings. There was time for that later.

I circled toward the back of the house and entered the kitchen. Sunlight spilled into the room, making it super bright. I blinked several times adjusting to it and then inched further into the room, where I circled the long center island and sucked in a breath.

Roger was lying on the floor, unmoving. A deep red hole sat in the center of his chest, and it was quickly spreading across his pale-blue shirt. I ran to him and pressed two fingers to the vein in Roger's neck. When I couldn't find a pulse, I looked up and shook my head.

Damn. Our mark was dead.

CHAPTER THREE

It didn't take long for the estate to be crawling with emergency vehicles and personnel. Sam pointed out that if Roger had been poor and living in a different neighborhood, we'd probably still be waiting. Sadly, she was right. I wasn't sure I'd ever seen so many emergency responders in one place.

The police had ushered us outside to an area beside the front door while they'd checked the house and dealt with the body. The house and land were vacant, which meant the shooter had come and gone through a back entrance. But as far as I could see before the cops ordered us out of the kitchen, the backyard looked fenced in.

A man who'd identified himself to us as Detective Myers placed a stick of gum into his mouth and immediately began popping it. I flinched a couple of times at the loud sound.

He rubbed his protruding stomach and popped some more. "Sorry. I'm trying to not snack in the middle of the day, and the gum helps. Doc says something about an oral fixation."

"I know exactly what you mean," Caleigh said with a gleam in her eyes. I doubted they were referring to the same fixation though. "You should eat at Hoagies. They have great sandwiches, and it's how Mr. Claremont lost all his weight."

The detective leaned closer. "I saw pictures of him before. He was my size, maybe a bit bigger. Do you think I should try that? Do you think it would work for me?"

Caleigh widened her baby blues. "Totally. And the sandwiches are super yum."

Sam wasn't paying us much attention. She seemed lost in her own world, staring down at her pointy black boots.

I was about to ask her if she was okay, when I spotted a black SUV pull through the gates. I sucked in a breath. I knew that SUV. It was Aiden Prince's. Since when did he show up to murder investigations? Normally the DA's office would assign an assistant to a case, but the ADA would wait until the police came to him. Then it hit me. He was here because of Roger's celebrity status. The district attorney must want this wrapped up quickly.

Instantly butterflies swarmed my belly, and I wished I had time to check out my hair and makeup, but I'd left my purse in the car. I was grateful my gut had told me to wear the blue wrap dress though.

Aiden walked directly to us, cutting Caleigh and the detective's diet conversation short.

"Good evening, everyone," Aiden said with a curt nod, but his gaze lingered solely on me. It was intense but totally unreadable as to whether it said *I still blame you for my suspension* or *dang, you look hot in that dress*. My new positive self hoped for the latter, but my realistic self suspected the former. Aiden lived life by the rules. He would never drink on the clock, he'd never run personal errands on the government's time, and he'd never flirt over a dead body.

Before I had a chance to say anything in response, he and the detective stepped inside the house. The detective glanced back at us and said, "Please stay here. I'll be right back."

And then we were left standing there. Waiting.

Normally I wouldn't have minded. Stakeouts made a person develop patience. But I had quite a few questions of my own that needed answering, and staring at the round shrubs wasn't going to cut it. I took a few deep breaths, trying to be Zen-ish.

I saw Caleigh's and Sam's heads turn toward me from the corner of my eye. They didn't comment on my meditation sounds as I inhaled through my nose and exhaled through my mouth. Several more seconds later I started to get dizzy. Maybe I was doing it too fast. I returned my breathing to normal just as the detective came back.

He lumbered through the doorway again, then turned to us. "Now, where were we?" he asked.

Caleigh answered, "Talking about ham and cheese versus turkey and avocado."

The detective smiled at her as if wishing that really was all he had to talk about. "Maybe we should go over exactly what you all were doing here when you found Mr. Claremont's body?"

"Uh…" While we'd been 100 percent within our rights to stake out Roger's place, I wasn't totally comfortable spilling all until I'd had a chance to talk to my client.

Luckily, I was saved by the sound of tires and squeaky brakes. I turned to find a Channel 4 news van had just pulled up.

Detective Meyers sighed. That would definitely make his job harder, but he had to have expected them eventually, given Roger's celebrity.

"Miss Bond?" the detective prompted.

Dang. Maybe I wasn't *totally* saved.

"Well, we were…" I considered lying. I wasn't totally accustomed to sharing PI business with the cops. They weren't always approving of our methods, and I liked to keep them in the dark about slightly less than legal behavior. But we hadn't done anything wrong. This time. Just the same, that didn't mean I needed to blab all.

"We had come by and heard shots. The front door was unlocked. We went in and found Mr. Claremont in the kitchen. Then Sam, um, Ms. Cross, called 9-1-1."

The detective raised his brows in surprise. "Most people run away from gunfire, not to it."

Caleigh flashed a dazzling smile. "We're not most people."

Aiden appeared in the doorway. He leaned on the frame and smirked. "That's very true."

He'd been listening.

The detective pointed to each of us. "You're all licensed PIs?" When we nodded, he said, "Then your fingerprints are on file. We'll need them to eliminate them against the others we find."

Something niggled in my stomach. A part of me that still somehow feared becoming the prime suspect in another murder. But this time I had Caleigh and Sam as my alibi. Unless the police wanted to accuse the three of us as working a conspiracy, I was just being paranoid. I tried to take a deep breath, but this wasn't the place. Something in the way Aiden stared at me made me almost wish he'd look away. That was crazy though. I normally didn't mind his eyes on me.

I feared our first interaction since the shooting would be awkward, but I'd never imagined it would be over another dead body.

"And why were you here again?" Detective Meyer asked. "Are you all friends with the Claremonts?"

Sam and Caleigh looked to me. I was surprised Sam was even paying attention. Her unusual silence had made me forget she was with us for a moment.

"We were hired by Mrs. Claremont to find out if her husband was cheating on his diet," I finally said.

The detective patted his belly, and Aiden laughed. We all turned to him.

He raised a brow. "Sorry, that was insensitive. I just wasn't expecting that."

I knew how he felt, but I was more unnerved by his actions. Since when was he anything less than professional? His professionalism usually bordered on militarism.

"Continue, please," Aiden said.

"That's it. We were watching the house, and that's when we heard the shot."

"Did you see anyone enter or exit the house?" the detective asked.

We all shook our heads together.

"Anyone in the neighborhood?"

I shook my head, remembering how quiet it had been. "There was a black SUV parked down the street, but no one was in it."

"Did you see anyone inside the house, perhaps through a window?"

We thought about that. To be honest, I just remembered watching Caleigh and Sam inhale their

Hoagies. It wasn't something I wanted to share, so I shook my head. "I didn't see anyone."

"How did the killer get out?" Caleigh asked.

"The back door was unlocked as well," Detective Meyers said.

"It's unlikely Mrs. Claremont left and didn't lock up behind her. But why wouldn't Mr. Claremont lock the front door when he came home?" I asked.

"He'd been out?" Aiden asked.

Oh yeah, I guess I hadn't mentioned that part. I told them about tailing Roger to the mall and the opening of a new Hoagies store.

Aiden gave me a momentary look of disapproval. There was the old by-the-book I knew.

"And he came back alone?" Meyers asked.

I nodded.

"Okay, ladies, if I have any more questions, I'll be in touch." He stepped back into the house, pushing past Aiden.

Sam and Caleigh looked to one another and then headed down the walkway to Sam's car.

I faced Aiden. He hadn't moved, still leaning in the doorframe, and he didn't look like he was going anywhere.

I paused, unsure whether I should say something or just go. I bit my lip. The longer I froze there, the more awkward it was becoming.

"So, how are you?" I asked, the words coming out stilted even to my own ears.

But Aiden just smiled back, the corners of his mouth turning up in a slow, almost sensual movement. "Busy. A guy just got shot." He nodded back toward Roger's kitchen.

The casual way he was talking about the shooting unnerved me, and I cleared my throat. "Yeah, that's…terrible…" I trailed off. "I guess your suspension has been lifted?" I asked. Then immediately wished I hadn't. Why did I have to bring up the sorest subject I could?

But Aiden's smile didn't falter. "Yep. All clear."

"Uh, good. Nice. Glad to hear it." Okay, this was more painful than trying to chat up the cute guy in seventh period freshman English. "I, uh, should get back…" I pointed toward Caleigh and Sam over my shoulder, desperately looking for an out.

"Don't you want to know what they've found?" Aiden asked, nodding his head toward the house.

I paused. Aiden voluntarily sharing information with me? That was definitely not by-the-book.

"What did they find?" I asked, curiosity getting the better of me.

"A shell casing under a cabinet," he said.

"What type of weapon?" I asked and took several steps closer, just in case he decided to lower his voice. I didn't want to miss a syllable.

"Forty-five caliber."

That didn't narrow it down much. There were a lot of guns of that caliber, including my own.

"I'll be informing the wife soon," he said.

Unless she heard about Roger's death on her car radio before she returned home. That would not be the way I'd want to find out this horrible news. Especially not while driving. Was it possible she already knew though? Did Mrs. Claremont kill her husband? No, that didn't make sense, with everything I knew about her. She clearly loved this lifestyle. If Roger had saved a nice little nest egg, then she wouldn't have hired me to make sure he wasn't cheating on his diet. She needed him to stay thin and alive.

Unless… What if she'd gotten fed up or caught him nibbling on Hostess snacks in their football-field-sized master bathroom? (Yes, I'd peeked while waiting for the cops. Someone had to make certain the killer wasn't still in the house.) If she'd learned he was cheating with Ho Hos, maybe she snapped. There could be a hefty life insurance policy in play. I made a mental note to have Maya look into it.

Then it hit me like a ton of Twinkies.

It had been less than 24 hours, and I'd already lost our first and only celebrity client.

Damn.

* * *

Instead of heading back to the office or home, Caleigh, Sam, and I decided to go out for a drink to decompress.

The club Caleigh recommended took swank to a whole 'nother level. The walls were painted white, and full-length mirrors in geometric shapes hung in various places. The floor was black tile so shiny I could see my reflection. The bar spanned the entire length of the room, rimmed in neon lighting with a clear, Lucite top. The stools were silver and white, and the wall behind the bar was all mirror. The whole place looked like an art project, something that deserved to be in a museum. It had a nice, fresh vibe about it though. The music was loud, and the staff was dressed in skintight white leggings and sleeveless tops. Their laundry bill must've been outrageous. And there were just enough bodies drinking and gyrating at this time of day to make this place "happening."

We approached the bar and ordered three cosmopolitans.

Caleigh looked to her left and her right and then pouted. "There's no one to flirt with." If I de-stressed with a drink, Caleigh de-stressed by flirting.

I glanced around. She was right. Everyone here seemed to be a part of a couple. It had to be our timing.

"Sorry you had to see Roger like that," I said to Caleigh. While I knew she was tougher than she seemed, I also knew the sight of a dead body was enough to unnerve anyone. And I had the feeling Caleigh hadn't seen many.

"I'll get over it. Eventually," Caleigh said, taking a deep sip from her drink.

I nodded. "You will," I agreed, trying to keep up my positive attitude. "Vodka helps." I raised my glass with a grin.

She smiled at my joke, then glanced over to where Sam had been silently sitting, once again staring at the lack of spit shine on her boots. "What's up with her?" Caleigh asked. She sat between Sam and me, but she'd pushed her stool out a few inches so Sam and I didn't have to look around her to see one another. She was considerate that way.

I waited for Sam to notice Caleigh was referring to her, but Sam's thoughts were still someplace far, far away, and she didn't respond. I shrugged. "I don't know, but she's been like this all day."

"Has she? I didn't notice." Caleigh stuck her pink tongue out of her mouth and used it to find the red stirring straw in her glass. Every time she pushed toward it, the straw rotated in the glass. She finally latched on to it and pulled it in to sip her drink.

"Yep, ever since this morning when I first got to the office. And especially so while we were talking to the detective and Aiden."

"Hmm, Aiden," Caleigh said with an all-too pleased smile on her face. "He looked extra yummy today, no?"

The left side of my mouth twitched. "Yes, he did. Did he seem different to you?"

She thought about it for a second and then shook her head. "Nope. But other than noticing his yumminess, I didn't pay him much attention."

Exactly how it should be.

"I was too busy noticing our glum friend here," she added.

Sam looked up and met our gazes with a deadpan expression. "You know I can hear you, right?"

I grinned. "We hoped so," I said. "And you know you can tell us anything, right? We're more than just coworkers. Associates. We're your best friends. Comrades. Sisters."

Caleigh nodded furiously.

I had to lay a hand on her shoulder to get her to slow down. She sipped her drink and eventually stopped.

Sam looked away, toward the dance floor. I expected her to clam up and change the subject. But instead, she took a deep breath and let it out slowly. "I totally think of you guys and Maya as my sisters too."

"Yay!" Caleigh said, causing a man on the other side of Sam to turn and glance at us.

"Okay, fine," Sam said. "I really hate doing this, but this seems as good a time as any." The skin between her brows puckered and lined.

I held a swig of drink in my mouth, anticipating whatever she was about to say.

"I was wondering if I could get an advance on my paycheck this week." She said it so low I almost didn't hear it over the music.

I swallowed hard. That was it? She'd been worried all day because she didn't want to ask? "Yes, of course. Is everything okay though? This isn't for something like an emergency or anything, right? You and Julio are fine?"

She smiled, and I realized it was the first one I'd seen from her all day. "Yes, we're good. Julio Senior, however, hasn't paid child support this month."

I had no idea about their arrangement, but I assumed that money was essential for a single mother. It was essential for this single gal with a shoe fetish too, but I knew feeding a child never compared to the latest Jimmy Choo.

"Do you want me to find him and shatter his kneecaps?" Caleigh asked.

I held back a chuckle. Caleigh was all mint julep and bubblegum-colored lip gloss until you got between her and her money. She was far from a gold digger or materialistic. She came from a family of laborers and hard workers. So when someone tried to interfere with her livelihood, she became a grizzly. This applied to interfering with her friends' livelihoods too. Plus, Auntie Caleigh adored Julio as much as I did.

"No. He'll need both of his kneecaps to keep working and sending me child support," Sam reminded her with a half smile.

I waved over the bartender and pointed to our near-empty glasses for another round.

Sam knocked back the last of hers. "It's not like Julio to do this. He's never missed a payment, and I'm actually a little worried about him."

My PI radar switched on and began beeping and flashing in neon pink. Pink was so much prettier than red. "Why?"

"I've called him a few times, and the calls keep going to voice mail."

"Is that unusual?" Caleigh asked.

"Kinda. I mean, he has his own life. Whatever that is. But he always gets back to me right away. He's been trying to be a good father lately. He's been there for Julio every weekend without fail."

The bartender set three new drinks down.

I tossed a few bills onto the bar and traded my empty glass for a full one. Caleigh and Sam reached for their new ones too.

Sam took a long sip and then shrugged, as if everything was truly fine. "It's probably not a big deal. He's probably off chasing a new skirt. Hopefully he'll come through next month."

It didn't sound very reassuring to me, but Sam seemed lighter.

My cell rang. I glanced at the caller ID. Maya.

I slipped off my stool and walked closer to the front door to get farther from the speakers. "Maya?"

"Hey, Boss. I thought you'd want to know that I got Elaine's cell records. She's meeting up with a friend named Suze in twenty minutes, and it looks like she's planning for a hot night out."

CHAPTER FOUR

———

Sam dropped Caleigh and I off at the agency, where I promptly hopped into my car and sped just slightly over the speed limit to the Van Nuys address Maya had texted me. When I got there, Maya was parked in the lot of a dive bar called The Happy Hour.

I pulled up behind Maya's Jetta and put my Roadster in park. After locking my car, I slid into her passenger seat. "You didn't need to follow her here, but I appreciate it. Thank you."

Maya shrugged. "I didn't have plans tonight. Brandon is working late."

Brandon Duke was Maya's ex-fiancé, who had resurfaced in her life when his most recent wife had suspected him of cheating on her. Maya had run the investigation, which hadn't gone at all the way the wife had planned. In the end, Maya had busted a crime ring, and Brandon had ended up asking her out. Again. I wasn't exactly sure what the current status of their relationship was, other than complicated, but the fact that she was referring to him as her usual evening plans was promising.

"Anyway, Elaine went inside with a couple of girlfriends. I thought about going in, but I wasn't sure what to do," Maya said.

While Maya had played undercover while on Brandon's case, she wasn't technically licensed as an investigator. And even though that one time had been a success, she had been a nervous wreck. Unlike the rest of us, Maya was perfectly content to limit her investigations to those she could do at her desk.

"You've done great. Thanks." I paused, almost hesitating to ask… "Did you see any other red flags in her cell history?"

Maya shrugged. "Hard to tell. But the only name that jumped out as obviously male was an Ira Steingarden."

I raised an eyebrow at her. "And he is…"

"Gynecologist in Chatsworth. She's got an appointment Monday."

TMI territory was an occupational hazard. "Thanks. Why don't you head home. It's been a long day." After we said our good-byes, I slipped out of the car and walked inside the bar.

Dim, ridiculously loud, and smoky, this was far from the place Caleigh, Sam, and I had just left. The dark, dusty floors and woodwork and the deep-teal-colored walls didn't help the lighting situation. Luckily, the bar was only a couple of yards long, and there were only a handful of tables, so it didn't take long to scan the area. Plus, it wasn't that crowded, which was surprising for the end of the week.

I didn't see Elaine, and I wondered if Maya had got the location wrong. No, Maya was too efficient to make that kind of mistake. Then I heard that over-the-top smoker's laugh of Elaine's and turned to spot her by the pool table. She was talking to two women in their forties. I assumed they were the friends Maya'd mentioned.

Both were as tiny as Elaine, but neither of them sported the double Ds she did. The blonde friend wore mom jeans with brown cowboy boots and a white-and-brown cow-print blouse. She was only missing the hat to complete her *yee-haw* ensemble, which had her fitting in with the decor of the place perfectly. The other friend had long, shiny black hair and wore a powder-blue jumpsuit, a bright-pink fake feather boa, and white pumps.

I stared longer than what would be considered polite. I just couldn't understand the outfit. Elaine, however, looked the most out of place in a long-sleeved, silver-sequined minidress with matching strappy heels. She had teased her light-brown hair so full that I wondered if she'd thought they'd be spending tonight traveling back to the days of fanny packs and Aqua Net.

Despite their adventurous fashion sense, they didn't seem to attract much attention. Cowgirl aimed her cue stick and knocked the ball into another, shooting that one into a corner pocket. The three of them raised their arms and cheered.

Jumpsuit turned to a passing server and ordered a round of drinks. I couldn't hear their exact words over the song about big trucks and hot girls streaming through the speakers. But when the server—a petite blonde woman in a brown skirt and apron and teal blouse nodded and walked toward the bar, I assumed Jumpsuit was ordering beverages.

I found a seat at the end of the bar in a dark corner. It was far enough from them that Elaine wouldn't be able to spot me, but I could still make out their actions. The bartender was a slender guy with long bangs that had been dyed neon blue. Despite wearing brown pants and a teal T-shirt, his personal style suggested he wasn't a big truck owner. I ordered a coffee, having had enough vodka for one night.

An older man around Derek's age with a similar build moseyed up to the pool table and started talking to the women. He had the same salt-and-pepper hair, and if it wasn't for the way he bowed during their introductions, I would've thought it was my father.

Elaine and Jumpsuit laughed at something the man said, and then Jumpsuit went to take her turn with the cue stick, leaving Elaine and the man to talk by themselves. And boy did they talk.

I dumped more sugar into the bitter coffee and sipped while watching Elaine's and the man's mouths move at Road Runner speed. Elaine liked using her hands when she talked, and there were moments when it looked like she was signing for the hearing impaired. I hadn't a clue what two strangers could get on so well about…unless they were flirting. That thought filled me with dread on Derek's behalf. But honestly, from my vantage point, they seemed to be only talking and laughing. Neither of them was in each other's personal space. Elaine's body faced her friends straight ahead, and she turned only her head toward the man, so they weren't leaning into one another. Maybe there was hope.

As the evening wore on, the man joined their game, I suffered through another cup of coffee, and Elaine and her friends started singing a country song. This one was about a cheating man and a woman only too eager to get her revenge.

Another man walked over to their group, which had gotten rather loud with their chatter and laughter. This guy was older, shorter, and rounder than the first. He approached Cowgirl, who was all smiles and coy looks. They chummied up quickly, and he didn't give Elaine and Jumpsuit much attention. This seemed to bother Jumpsuit, who slid her way between them to whisper into Cowgirl's ear.

Round Man frowned and looked annoyed. He wrapped his meaty fingers around Jumpsuit's upper arm. I assumed he was going to pull her away, but before he got the chance, Jumpsuit turned her head, glanced at his probably unwelcome hand on her bicep, and glared at him. Her lips moved, but unfortunately I couldn't hear the manhandling beatdown I hoped she gave him. Some guys didn't understand that touching a woman without their permission wasn't endearing or charming. It was simply too much.

Round Man let go of Jumpsuit and took a step back. I smiled and wanted to cheer at her standing up for herself. Before I got a chance to see how they reacted next, a tall, lanky guy in jeans and a plaid shirt sat at the corner of the bar in front of me. He completely ruined my view.

Seriously?

I softly scoffed, wondered why he couldn't choose one of the other four empty bar stools, and looked up to the man's face. I expected to see a scruffy dude with a down-and-out expression to his weather-beaten face. I sounded like a country song. But instead he was tanned, clean shaven, and had a twinkle in his hazel eyes. Too bad Caleigh wasn't here. His red-and-white plaid shirt didn't make him "bad boy" material, but he was definitely adorable.

He ordered a Guinness on tap, then turned and looked behind him to the rest of the room.

Dude, not even a glance my way?

I wasn't conceited, but come on. Hadn't I been told all day how sexy my dress was?

He turned back around when the bartender placed his beer down. He set money on the smooth wood bar top, took a sip, and then looked behind him again. I couldn't tell who he was looking at, but when he faced his beer again, he made a *tsk* sound. Something wasn't kosher.

"You okay?" I asked.

Finally he looked my way, but his gaze immediately shifted to his beer. It didn't travel up and down my body the way most did. My ego decided he was either severely depressed or gay.

A slight smile tugged one corner of his mouth. "Do I not look okay?"

"You look upset."

He didn't answer but jutted his chin out at my coffee. "Not exactly bar beverage."

"Drinking and driving do not mix."

He nodded, then brought his glass to his mouth. "They sure don't. I'll be calling a cab."

"Good for you." I pushed my stool back so I could get a better viewpoint of Elaine. There was only so much space before I hit the wall though.

"Do I smell?" Plaid Guy asked with a soft chuckle.

I grinned and straightened my legs. The tips of my shoes touched the side of the bar. "No, just stretching." It was pretty lame, but I didn't want to admit I was stalking my father's girlfriend.

He pointed his thumb over his shoulder. "My boyfriend and I got into an argument, and I followed him here."

Bingo. I knew my gaydar.

"Oh yeah? Which one is he?"

"He's talking to the woman in the silver dress."

I bit my lip to keep from laughing. Derek had nothing to worry about tonight.

Ten minutes later, Plaid Guy left with a disgruntled sigh. He never went up to his boyfriend or even tried to catch his attention, which was perfect for me. Elaine would've spotted me for sure. Ten minutes after that, Elaine kissed the cheeks of her friends, waved good-bye to the boyfriend, and headed my way.

Oh shoot!

I turned to my left, faced the deep-teal wall, and prayed she didn't look my way.

Once I heard the door click shut, I threw a couple of fives onto the bar and ran out. When I reached the sidewalk, I spotted the back of Elaine. She was walking to her Honda Civic, parked a few storefronts ahead. I ran across the street to my own car and waited for her to pull onto the street, before making a U-turn and following her.

My cherry-red Roadster was too familiar to go unnoticed, so I had to stay several vehicles behind her. I almost lost her a couple of times, but once she hit the 101, I knew she was headed home. But just to be sure, I followed her three more exits before she turned off into her neighborhood in North Hollywood.

As she pulled onto her street, I headed to my apartment. The coffee had done nothing to perk me up. My bones felt tired, and I simply wanted to kick off my shoes and crawl into bed. Was it possible to become immune to caffeine? Maybe I needed to up my dosage. I could switch to espressos.

When I reached the front steps of my building, a woman rushed toward me. I tensed, not a huge fan of a person flying at me at night on the street. I reached into my bag for my gun, just in case, and wrapped my fingers around its handle. But I didn't pull it out just yet, as I didn't want to scare an innocent woman simply out for a nighttime jog.

But this person wasn't in yoga pants and sneakers. She wore a black miniskirt, leopard-print blouse, and four-inch platform heels. Clearly this was no jogger. That was when I realized it was Bristol Claremont. She sure loved her animal prints.

I released my hold on my pistol and withdrew my hand from my bag. "Bristol, are you okay?" The real question was what was she doing here? How the heck had she found out where I lived?

"No, I'm not!" she cried, flapping her arms up and down. "The police questioned me all evening. They think I had something to do with Roger's death!"

I had to admit that the thought had crossed my mind as well. "What did they say?" I asked.

"They kept asking where I was at the time he…" She trailed off, her face scrunching up into a tearless sob. "This can't be happening. I loved my husband. I didn't want him dead." Her voice was even higher pitched than when we'd first met, if that was possible. I thought I heard a dog bark next door in response.

"I'm so sorry, Bristol. But it's customary for the police to talk to the victim's loved ones. I'm sure you have nothing to worry about." Unless, of course, she'd actually killed him.

She shook her head violently, causing several tendrils of hair to fall loose from her low bun. "No, you don't understand. They truly think I did it. They want me to surrender myself tomorrow with my lawyer. And I need your help. You have to help me prove who really killed Roger. Please, Miss Bond."

I would've loved to think that a spouse wouldn't hire a PI if she'd been guilty, but I knew the world was full of dishonest people. And that wasn't me being negative. Simply a fact. I'd been in this business too long to know otherwise. Plus, I was raised in the backseat of Derek Bond's Bonneville. I'd seen infidelity, lies, and betrayal up close and personal.

Tears gathered in the corners of Bristol's eyes. "Roger was my world. Now I have to figure out how to move on without him. I can't have this hanging over my head too."

I had assumed she was just a simple trophy wife, nothing more. But now I began to wonder if my judgment had been wrong. In order to take on her tweaked case, though, we'd need to check into several things—like her alibi at the time of Roger's death.

"I'll need to know a few things first," I said. While Maya would carefully check the facts, I needed to get Bristol's side of the story.

She widened her eyes. "Yes, anything."

"Where were you this afternoon when Roger was shot?"

She sniffled and glanced away. Then she laid a hand at the side of her head. "I was at Lucerne's, a new hair salon on Rodeo Drive."

Well that seemed easy enough to check out. Which made me wonder just how solid it was…or manufactured. It would be handy to have been seen in public by several people at the exact time you had your husband bumped off.

"I had no reason to kill my husband. I loved him," she said is if reading my thoughts. "I had nothing to gain by his death and everything to lose."

"How so?" I asked, figuring the more I kept her talking, the more I'd get a feel for if she was lying or not.

Bristol looked down at the pavement. "It's not a secret that I like living…a certain type of lifestyle."

I stifled an unladylike snort. "You mean the one that Roger's money afforded you."

She straightened her spine. "Roger wanted me to be a stay-at-home wife. He liked taking care of me, and he loved showering me with gifts. Now I'll have to…" She hiccuped. "Get a job or something."

Since I'd been working since I was fifteen, my empathy was a little low, but that didn't mean I couldn't sympathize with her plight. If I was suddenly faced with starting over… Heck, I knew exactly how scary that was. Going from modeling designer swimwear on the beach was worlds different from trailing cheating husbands and sitting in my car for hours. That wasn't to say that modeling couldn't be a tough gig too. I just hadn't expected how much my life would change. I definitely felt for Bristol.

"What about life insurance?" I asked. "Surely someone as well off as Roger had a policy." And a hefty one at that.

She lifted and lowered her bony shoulders. "I don't know about that sort of thing. I assume so, but he never told me about any of the finances. He handled all of it. It was his money, after all."

I had a hard time believing he hadn't at least discussed it with her, but I let it go.

"And I never wanted to discuss life insurance," she continued. "It's so morbid." Her voice lowered to almost a whisper.

If she truly hadn't had a hand in his death, she must've been going through hell right now, and I felt for her in that aspect as well. Grief was an ugly part of life. One that I'd had to experience young when I'd lost my mother. But if she was pulling one over on me, I'd make certain she spent the rest of her attractive years in prison.

"What about enemies? Do you know if Roger had any?" Though, who could possibly hate a sandwich guy enough to kill him?

"I don't think anyone was angry with Roger. He never mentioned anything like that."

I suddenly got the impression they hadn't talked much.

"But I know who you should talk to."

"Who?"

"You should check out this rapper guy. He's Roger's new *celebrity* friend," she said on a sneer. "They've been hanging out a lot recently."

Roger hadn't struck me as the hip celebrity type. "Do you have a name?"

"He calls himself Heavy Cash."

I assumed that wasn't on his birth certificate. Then again, on mine was the name James.

"He's tall, big, wide, African American, and he wears black sunglasses all the time. Even when it's cloudy out," she told me.

She had to be referring to the guy that the girls and I had seen with Roger that afternoon at the mall. "You think he knows something about who'd want to hurt Roger?" I asked.

She shrugged. "Maybe *he* would want to."

"Why do you say that?"

"One afternoon at our house, Heavy Cash bent over to pick up something, and I noticed he had a gun tucked into the back of his pants."

That didn't mean he killed Roger, but I was definitely interested in why these two were friends. Roger seemed about as tame as a suburban food-chain spokesperson could be. I didn't see anyone writing rap songs about his life.

I nodded. "Okay, I'll look into it."

She gasped, pulled me forward, and embraced me in a quick hug. "Thank you so much." Then without another word, she ran two cars down to her silver BMW and hopped in.

I watched her drive off and then went up to my apartment and slammed the door behind me. After kicking off my shoes, I did exactly what I'd planned. I walked into my room and flopped onto my bed. This day had definitely been up there on the interesting scale.

CHAPTER FIVE

The next morning, I opened my eyes and was greeted by blinding sunlight and loud banging. It took me a few seconds to realize the banging was someone knocking on my door. I flipped my covers off and shuffled to the door, seriously in need of the bathroom. I opened the door to find Danny.

He was clean shaven, dressed in dark jeans, a pale-green T-shirt that offset his eyes, and his good sneakers. He looked alert and like he'd been up for hours. His brows shot up as he took in my appearance.

I glanced down at myself, hoping I was fully dressed, and remembered I hadn't changed when I'd got home last night. Still in the blue wrap dress, which was slightly askew, I assumed my hair had some serious bedhead action going on, because the nape of my neck felt naked.

"Good morning to you, sunshine," he said and stepped inside.

"What time is it?" I turned my back to him and rubbed my eyes. The taste of stale coffee lingered in my mouth, and I could only imagine how vile my breath smelled.

"It's time for breakfast. My treat."

I groaned at the idea of not being able to go back to sleep.

"You may want to run a brush through your hair though. You're looking pretty rough."

I groaned louder and hurried to the bathroom.

Over a spinach-and-mushroom egg white omelet (my choice) and pecan pancakes with bacon and hash browns (Danny's choice), I filled him in on Bristol's late-night visit.

"So you haven't lost your client at least. That's good," he said.

I sipped my steaming hot coffee and nodded. "Yeah, swell."

He lifted a packet of sugar to pour into his cup of coffee. "Okay, so it's not *ideal*."

I shot him a look. Finding a client's husband dead was never ideal.

"But it could be worse."

"Exactly how could it be worse?"

Danny opened his mouth to speak, but then he quickly shut it with a click. "Yeah, sorry. I don't know."

"Thanks a lot," I grumbled.

"Geez, what happened to your Zen?" Danny asked, turning away from the scowl I could feel on my face.

"Someone woke her up too early," I mumbled.

Danny sipped his coffee, his mouth quirking up in a half smile. "You know, you're kinda cute when you're all grumpy like this."

Damn, it was hard to hold on to a scowl when a hot guy was calling you cute. I turned to look down at my omelet instead, stabbing a mushroom like it had done me wrong.

"So, you going to check on Mrs. Hoagies' alibi today?" Danny asked.

I nodded, grateful for the subject change. "Among other things. I've got Maya running background on his buddy, Heavy Cash."

Danny smirked. "Let me guess—he's related to Johnny Cash?"

I smiled. "Long-lost cousins," I joked.

"So what's after Mr. Cash?"

I glanced up. "What do you mean 'after'?"

"Do you have plans later?"

I paused, my fork in midair. While his tone was causal, his eyes were shifting nervously around the table, as if the answer meant something deeper to him.

"Nooo…" I slowly drew out the word. "Why?"

He did a totally-trying-to-look-causal shrug, eyes still on the table. "I thought maybe we could go out."

"Go out where?" I pressed

His eyes finally moved up to meet mine, locking on like a homing device. "Out on a date."

The mushroom stuck in my throat. The only word my brain could quickly form was, "What?"

"You know, wine, dinner, me, you. Maybe some slinky lingerie."

I stammered and stared for several seconds. Mostly because I didn't altogether hate the lingerie idea. But this was Danny. My pal, my friend. Somehow I knew once we crossed that line of seeing each other naked, that would change forever. And I wasn't sure it was a change I was ready for.

"It's not a difficult question, Bond." His words jolted me from my thoughts.

"I think I have to work." As soon as the words flew out of my mouth, I realized what a crappy excuse that was. Didn't the boss set her own hours? "I mean, you know my schedule. I, uh, don't know what the police have yet on Bristol, and there's the rapper to talk to, and I might have to go to a cowboy bar with Elaine again, and that could take a while." I was totally babbling now. I shut my mouth to keep the words from spewing out.

"Right." Danny's eyes went back down to the table, his jaw tensing. He knew I was making excuses.

I shook my head, suddenly feeling really guilty. "Let me think about it. Right now I need to get to the office."

Danny nodded on. "Sure, I understand."

But I knew that was a lie. How could he understand when even I didn't?

* * *

As I stepped into the agency, I still had Danny and his slinky date on my mind. The more I thought about it, the more I got annoyed at his mention of lingerie. As if one date would equal sex. As if I was like all the girls who had graced the pages of his little black book in the past. I mean, if he thought I was that easy, there was no way I was going out on a date with him!

Yes, I was totally trying to come up with reasons not to go. Because deep down I knew that if I did, there was a good chance we wouldn't even make it through the appetizers before he'd be getting a peek at my lingerie.

I passed by Maya's desk, not really paying attention to my surroundings. I vaguely heard her call my name, but I was walking too fast and was too preoccupied to stop. When I reached my door, I realized my office wasn't empty. Derek was seated in one of the leather chairs that faced my desk, waiting for me. As if my morning couldn't get more stressful.

I paused, took a deep breath, and tried really hard to find a smidgen of that Zen I'd been so friendly with yesterday morning.

Derek turned on me, his complexion pink and irritated, and gritted his teeth. "I told you to stay out of it."

I wasn't in the mood for this. I walked around my desk, threw my purse into the bottom drawer, and then sat down. "What is *it*?"

His brow furrowed, and he flapped his arms like he was about to take off in flight. "Me and Elaine. You said you were going to stay out of it. I was going to take care of it."

"You're clearly paranoid and clearly worried Elaine is cheating. So what is the big deal? I followed her to get answers for you." And then it hit me. The only way he knew I was following her last night was if *he'd* been following her too.

I jumped up and nearly smacked my knee into the side of my desk. "You followed her! You're not licensed!"

"I can handle this." His words were still gruff, but his tone had lost its angry edge.

"Next time the cops catch you nosing around, they'll arrest you. No buddy warning this time. Is that what you want?"

Something flickered in his eyes. It was a moment of fear or sadness, and my heart gave out. Well, not literally. But I sat back down and calmed down as well. "Elaine is not cheating on you." At least I was pretty sure.

Derek stood and walked out the door without another word. Had I gotten through to him? I wasn't sure. Knowing his stubbornness, I hadn't. But I had bigger fish to fry today.

I pressed the intercom, reaching Maya's desk.

"Yes, Boss?"

"I want a full rundown on Roger Claremont today. Court records, financial records, etc. Anything you can get your hands on."

"On it!" Maya chirped, sounding way more chipper this morning than I was. "Anything in particular that I'm looking for?"

"Anything even resembling a grudge or a reason to want him dead."

"Got it. Looking for enemies."

I nodded even though I knew she couldn't see me. "Right, and I'll be checking out his friends. Specifically his celebrity rapper friend."

"You shouldn't go alone." The voice wasn't Maya's.

Sam stood in my doorway, leaning in the frame.

"Oh?" I asked, leaning back in my chair and really wishing I had a caramel macchiato.

Sam shook her head. "I actually know Heavy Cash, or at least of him. Julio Senior shot one of Heavy's first music videos back when Julio and I were still together."

"And?" I led.

"And the guy is totally scary. Not the type you want to upset, if you know what I mean."

"You didn't mention this yesterday at the mall."

She shrugged. "I didn't think anything of it then. I figured he was just at the opening for his fifteen minutes of fame. He didn't strike me as the type to actually know Roger personally."

That made two of us. "What do you know about him?" I asked.

Sam thought about it for a second as she sat in a chair opposite me. "I only met him once—the one time Julio helped him. Back then he was younger and thinner. Much thinner. He was a scrawny guy who was hard. You know the type. Always expecting the other shoe to drop, so he puts up walls. He's probably seen way too much crime and negativity in his time, and he probably caused a lot of it too."

I knew the type. The actual bad boy. Not the kind who has a heart of gold and just needs the "right woman" to keep him from diving too far over the line. No, this was the kind who had lost sight of "the line" so long ago it was no longer even in his rearview mirror.

"Sounds like an awesome suspect to me."

Sam displayed a wide grin. "Want company?"

* * *

According to Maya, Heavy owned a studio called Big Stuff Productions in Inglewood. Which ended up being a small set of offices with a coat of dingy off-white paint and cracked tile at the entrance. Graffiti in a variety of colors decorated the parking lot, and I suddenly had a small niggle of fear for my Roadster's wheels. This looked like the sort of neighborhood where tires went mysteriously missing. It didn't get much better, as we climbed a rickety wooden staircase to the second floor and something sticky attacked my palm on the banister. I grimaced at the clear substance and fished a bottle of hand sanitizer from my purse. There was just enough left to do the job. I seriously rubbed my hands together as we entered the Big Stuff Productions. Then I tossed the empty container in a wastebasket beside a metal and fake-wood desk. It was obvious the wood wasn't real, because there was a corner missing, and the exposed part looked like corkboard.

"Can I help you?" asked a young blonde woman in pigtails, a blue halter, black booty shorts, and platform wedges. She was adding a clear coat of polish to her neon-green nails and snapping gum like machine gun fire.

But it was okay because I refused to let a little gum popping bother Zen me. I would remain calm and not grimace or roll my eyes with each pop. No matter how annoying it became.

"We're here to see Heavy Cash," Sam told the girl.

"Yeah, you and every other hopeful comin' through that door." The girl paused to give Sam and me an up-and-down. "Honey, you in the wrong neighborhood if you think you can get a recording contract dressed like lawyers." She snorted.

I looked down at my knee-length black pencil skirt and cream-colored silk sleeveless top. While it was a few notches more professional than Halter Top, I didn't think I looked *that* bad.

"We're not here for a recording contract," Sam said.

Halter Top popped her gum. I took a deep breath and thought Zen—calming ocean sounds, chanting Tibetan monks, and lavender incense.

"Whadda ya want with Heavy then?" she asked. "He owe you money or something?"

I raised an eyebrow, suddenly wondering if Heavy Cash was having a cash flow problem.

"We want to ask him a few questions," Sam responded.

The young woman looked Sam up and down again, then went back to her nails. "He's busy."

Sam narrowed her eyes and cocked her head. "Aren't we all?"

The girl grunted and blew on her nails.

Sam started down the hall, and the girl jumped up and used her body to block my associate.

"I don't think so," Halter Top said.

Sam pushed up the sleeves of her blouse and looked like she wanted to deck the young woman. Not that Sam would. At least, I didn't think she would.

"Look, just tell him that we need to talk to him about Roger Claremont," I jumped in. While I would've enjoyed watching Sam make the girl stop popping that gum, I didn't want handling an assault charge added to my day's to-do list.

The girl rolled her eyes very dramatically, huffed, and walked down the short hall. She disappeared into a room and shut the door behind her. In a moment the door opened again, and the big man from the mall walked toward us. He wore a black tracksuit, white sneakers, the same cross at his neck, and black sunglasses. Bristol had been right. He didn't even take them off indoors.

He stopped a couple feet away from us and crossed his arms over his massive chest, staring down at us. While he seemed like a rough character when I spotted him at the mall, up close and in the confines of the dingy office, the effect was amplified. He had bad news written all over him, and I suddenly understood Bristol's immediate suspicion of him. I could totally see him shooting someone over a sandwich, and the weight of my Glock in my purse suddenly felt very comforting. "Who are you?" he demanded, taking a wide stance.

"My name is Jamie Bond," I replied, trying my best to match his intimidation level. Or at least not cower under it.

"So, what's that to me?" he asked.

"We're from the Bond Agency, and we're inquiring about Roger Claremont's death. I hear the two of you were friends."

He rubbed his chin. "You a cop?"

Ah, so now we were at the uncooperative portion of our conversation. I couldn't say I was exactly surprised. People didn't always want to talk to a PI. People who usually had something to hide.

I placed a hand on my hip. I may not be able to bench press a Buick, but I had a streak of tough-girl in me. I was used to people underestimating the blonde girl. Once.

"No, but I have the assistant district attorney on speed dial. Shall I call him?"

This would've been the perfect moment to see if any fear registered in his eyes. Darn glasses.

"All right. Fine. Let's talk." He waved a beefy hand and turned to reenter the room he'd come from.

Sam and I hurried after him. For a big guy, he walked pretty fast.

The room we entered was a recording studio. Halter Top was seated at the console, with her feet up on a chair beside her. And next to that was the other guy from the mall. The recording side of the room behind a glass partition was empty except for some hanging microphones.

Heavy swatted at the girl's platforms. "Get back up front."

She rose, made a big pink bubble with her gum, and then popped it just as she passed me.

Zen, Jamie. Zen.

"Sit," Heavy told us and dropped himself into the black leather chair the girl had just vacated.

A small, brown leather sofa was pushed up against the back wall. The room wasn't large, and the furniture was worn, but the equipment looked well taken care of. Sam and I sat down on the couch.

The thinner guy wore a black suit with a silver-and-white pinstripe tie. Though he was sporting a lot of jewelry as well. I noticed two huge diamond earrings in his ears, and a lot of rings on his fingers. "Who are they?" he asked Heavy.

"They're from the Bond Agency." To us, Heavy asked. "Are you private dicks?"

He and the other guy grinned and chuckled.

I wasn't nearly as amused. "Yes, we are. Can you tell us…"

"Who hired you?" the other guy asked.

Weren't we the ones asking the questions?

"Who are *you*?" I asked, turning the tables on him.

"This is my manager, Edwin Johnson," Heavy said. Johnson nodded in my direction.

I gave him a curt nod back before turning to Heavy again.

"Mr. Cash," I said, feeling just a little silly calling him by his obvious stage name, "we just want to know what your relationship with Roger was."

He tilted his head back. "We didn't have no 'relationship.' I don't swing that way."

I did a mental eye roll. "I mean, I was told you were *friends* with Roger. Is that correct?"

"Yeah. So?"

"We know you and Mr. Johnson were at the mall at the opening of the Hoagies store with Roger just a few hours before he died. Where did you go after the mall?"

Heavy leaned back in his chair and nodded. Then he turned to his manager and said, "These girls are good. And cute. A little too skinny, but nice T&A."

I looked to Sam. "They are aware we're sitting right here, aren't they?"

Sam narrowed her eyes at the two men. "Oh yeah."

I turned back to the pair. "So where were you?"

Heavy shook his head. "What makes you think I'm gonna tell you?"

I shrugged. "You can tell the ADA if you like…" I trailed off, picking up my phone.

"Wait a minute," Johnson said, sitting up straighter in his seat. "No need for that. We haven't done anything wrong here."

I raised an eyebrow. "Answering my question would go a long way toward convincing me of that."

"We came straight here after the Hoagies opening. We threw down some tracks," Johnson said. He looked to Heavy for confirmation.

The big guy nodded slowly. "Yeah. We were here. Cool?"

Not cool. Heavy had an alibi. Assuming his manager could be trusted, this made my suspect list fold in half, and the only one remaining was the wife. Had she killed Roger after all?

The young woman popped—no pun intended—her head back in. "Heavy, there's a call from George."

He sprung up as fast as someone his size could spring. "I gotta take this."

When he and Halter Top left, I turned back to his manager.

"How do you know Roger?" I asked, still not seeing the sandwich king and Heavy Duty there as besties.

Johnson narrowed his eyes. "Like Heavy said, they were friends."

"How did they meet?"

Johnson's eyes went from me to Sam and back again. He was hiding something.

I turned to Sam. "You want to know what I think?" I asked her, taking a turn at talking about him as if *he* weren't in the room.

"What do you think, Jamie?" Sam asked, playing along.

"I think these two had something on Roger." I glanced at Johnson out of the corner of my eye. "Blackmail, debts. Or maybe they were just shaking Roger down for sandwich money to finance their next record."

"It's nothing like that!" Johnson protested, shaking his head vehemently.

"Then tell me what it is like," I demanded, crossing my arms over my chest.

The manager leaned toward us and lowered his voice, one eye on the doorway Heavy had exited through. "Listen. Heavy needs to lose some weight if he wants to go on tour again, okay? His health isn't great. He's got diabetes. So we hired Roger to be his personal weight loss coach."

I blinked at him. "Wait—Roger isn't a personal trainer. He just sells sandwiches."

Johnson nodded. "I know. That's Heavy's kind of diet."

Sam snorted beside me. "And how has that been going?"

"He's been eating subs for every meal," Johnson said proudly. "Just a matter of time before the pounds start falling off."

I didn't even try to hide the eye roll this time.

The door opened, and Heavy returned. I thought about asking him what kind of subs he'd been eating, but I figured his weight was his business. Plus, I really didn't want to get on the wrong side of this big guy.

"Tell me about Roger," I asked the rapper instead.

Heavy looked to Johnson as if asking permission to speak. I saw Johnson give him a small nod of the head. Clearly the guy in the suit was the brains of the operation.

"Roger was a cool dude," Heavy finally answered. "He wasn't all pompous like some of those celebrities get."

Maybe because he wasn't really a celebrity, unless you were a mayo groupie. But I bit back the smart remark, letting Heavy continue.

"He was a laid-back cat. Had a thing for Guinness. Boy, that man could down a pint like nobody's business." He chuckled, and his belly shook. Then he got serious. "I didn't kill him."

No one had asked him that. Was he feeling guilty about something?

"Did he ever discuss his personal life? Ever mention any enemies?" I asked.

"Nah," he said, lowering himself into an office chair. It groaned under his weight. Clearly it didn't believe Heavy was slimming down by eating hot pastramis any more than I did.

"What about any issues at work?" I pushed.

Heavy shook his head. "None that he mentioned. Those Hoagies dudes took care of him right. You know what I mean?"

The man couldn't have led a charmed life. If he had, he wouldn't have been dead.

"Had he been getting along with his wife?" Sam jumped in.

Heavy leaned back in his chair and smiled. "Yeah, it was great, when she wasn't spending all his money and robbing the dude blind."

That was exactly what I was afraid of.

"Anything else you can tell me about Roger?" I grasped, feeling like I was losing our audience.

Johnson and Heavy shook their heads in unison. Heavy crossed his arms over his chest.

"We done?" While it was ostensibly a question, the tone in his voice didn't leave much room for argument.

I nodded, and Sam and I left before we overstayed our welcome. I wasn't sure what happened to people who overstayed in Heavy's world, but I was sure I didn't want to find out. Plus, I wanted to get out of there with four tires.

"You believe that alibi?" Sam asked as we made our way back out into the blaring sunshine.

I shrugged. "Hard to say. Johnson could have easily been lying for him."

Sam nodded. "That's what I was thinking too."

"Though, I'm not sure why he'd want Roger dead. I mean, if he was counting on him as a weight loss coach, it's better to have him alive, right?"

"Unless Heavy *wasn't* losing weight," Sam pointed out.

I glanced back up at the building. Honestly? Heavy seemed like the kind of guy who'd kill over a couple of pounds without any qualms.

"So," Sam asked as we walked back to my car (which was thankfully untouched except for a small offering from a pigeon), "what now?"

I fished my phone out of my bag and checked the time. "I figure Bristol has surrendered herself and is in police custody right now. Might be a good time to ask the ADA how solid her alibi is."

CHAPTER SIX

I dropped Sam off at the office and headed across town in midafternoon traffic to the DA's. That wasn't an easy feat to accomplish without stress. Let's just say that by the time I pulled up to the government building, my chanting monks and soothing lavender had turned to thoughts of a martini with a Rueben and onion ring chaser.

When I stepped off the elevator, a receptionist I'd never seen before sat behind the front desk. She was young—couldn't have been more than twenty-five. Her bright-auburn hair sat on top of her head in a confused state. I couldn't figure out if she'd just pinned up the back, not caring about the ends that lay haphazardly, or if it had been a bun and the bobby pins jumped ship. Either way, she needed a mirror and a comb.

Self-consciously, I smoothed the back of my head with my hand, making sure my hair didn't follow suit.

The receptionist looked up to me and gave me a huge smile. "Hello, may I help you?" Her voice was high pitched and lilting, and I definitely heard a Valley Girl twang.

"Hi. I'm Jamie Bond here to see ADA Prince." For some reason I ran a nervous palm down the side of my black pencil skirt.

"Do you have an appointment?" the receptionist asked.

"Uh…" I hadn't expected this to be difficult. I just needed to pop my head into his office to grill him. Our usual routine. Maybe I should've called first.

"Jamie?"

The receptionist and I both looked up toward the voice. Standing a few feet behind her was Aiden. I watched as a slow smile spread across his features, a twinkle catching his eyes that made him look like a kid who'd just spotted a candy bar. He also looked yummy enough to eat, in a charcoal-gray suit with a light-blue button-down beneath.

"Thank you," I whispered to the receptionist and walked to Aiden's side.

He watched my steps, his eyes traveling from my face to my hot-pink and zebra-print pumps to the swing of my hips. He hadn't missed a step, and I may have slowed mine down just so I could watch him watch me. By the time I was at his side, that twinkle had darkened into a deep, stormy blue, and my cheeks were getting warm. Didn't they have AC on in this place?

"What a pleasant surprise. Let's go to my office." He grabbed my elbow and led me down the corridor.

Maybe it was the soft pull of the carpet or the jelly in my legs, but my knees may have buckled once at his warm touch. Definitely not more than twice.

He pushed open his door just enough that my shoulder brushed against his chest as I entered. If I was the suspicious type, the one who didn't believe in coincidences, I'd say that he purposely made me touch him. And I'd have to say that I really didn't mind.

"Take a seat," he said and walked around the large desk to his own leather chair.

I'd been in his office several times, but for some reason it felt smaller today, and the air was heavy with his musky scent.

He leaned back in his chair and crossed his legs. "Is that a new skirt? It fits you like a glove," he said.

My breath hitched. I hadn't been expecting the compliment. And while I'd had a suspicion that he was watching my butt as we'd walked to his office, it was unlike Gentleman Aiden to say so. I felt my cheeks go warm. But I had to admit, I didn't necessarily hate this new bold side.

"Um, thank you. I-I…" I almost forgot why I was there. "About Mrs. Claremont. Did she turn herself in?"

"Yes, she and her lawyer came here this morning." He paused. "And the fact that you know that means you must still be working for her."

"Yes, I am."

He raised an eyebrow. "She has other cheating husbands?"

I cleared my throat, not sure if he was flirting with me or making fun of me. "No, she wants me to look into her husband's death."

"The police are already looking into it."

"The police are looking at *her*."

He nodded, that slow smile spreading over his face again. I noticed his eyes leaving mine and sliding lower, ending somewhere in the region of my silk blouse. "Touché."

I barely resisted the urge to fidget under his hot gaze. "Mrs. Claremont said she had an alibi for the time her husband died. She told me she was at a hair salon on Rodeo."

His eyes moved up to meet mine with deliberate slowness. If I didn't know better, I'd say he wanted me to catch him staring at my breasts. "Did she?" he asked.

"I'm assuming she told you the same story?"

Aiden nodded.

"And did you look into the alibi?"

He crossed his hands in his lap, looking very cool and unaffected—by either my questions or the sudden heat in the room. Seriously, where was the AC?

"We did follow up on her story. However, the timeline didn't fit."

I felt a frown crease my forehead. "So she wasn't at Lucerne's having her hair done?"

"She had been, but according to her stylist, the receptionist, and another patron, Mrs. Claremont left a solid hour and a half before her husband was killed. She could have easily made it home in time."

Perhaps… "But her car wasn't there," I protested.

"If I was going to shoot my spouse, I wouldn't leave my car in the driveway in case someone passed by."

He was right. I guess I'd just hoped she hadn't been lying to me.

"So you're charging her?"

He paused. "We're questioning her. Whether we formally make the arrest depends on what she tells the detectives with her now."

"Which means you don't really have a case yet?" I asked, trying to read between his lines.

He shrugged. "Our theory? She could have been in the house and left through the side or back as you and your associates were entering. As for motive—she killed him for the money instead of going through a messy and possibly less-than-lucrative divorce."

How very interesting. Not only his theory about Mrs. Claremont but also that Aiden was telling me all of this.

"Unless you have other theories…" Aiden trailed off, looking at me expectantly.

And there was the reason. I narrowed my eyes at him and shook my head in the negative.

Aiden leaned toward his desk and gave me a sly smile. "Come on, Bond. I showed you mine. Now you show me yours." The seductive edge in his voice was not lost on me. Why did I have the feeling he wasn't just talking about trading intel on Bristol Claremont?

But I shook my head again. "You know I can't break client confidentiality."

He stood up, nodded, and walked around to the front of his desk. He sat on the edge, his knees a mere inch from mine. "I understand that. And I applaud your professionalism. I respect you, Jamie Bond."

I raised an eyebrow his way. Predictable Aiden was anything but today.

"Now, if you have any other questions about Mrs. Claremont…" he started.

Then he did something even more unpredictable.

Aiden reached down, grabbed my hands, and gently pulled me up to stand directly in front of him. He tugged my body flush with his. Every nerve ending in my body was on full alert. The desire in his eyes was obvious…and infectious.

With our bodies a mere inch apart, he finished in a low, husky tone, "…you can ask me at dinner tonight."

I sucked in a breath. Was he asking me out? It felt like more of a demand, but in all honesty it wasn't one I'd have any problems complying with. I felt myself nodding dumbly.

"I'll pick you up at eight." His eyes trailed down to my chest again.

If I were the swooning type, I would've been a swooning puddle. I nodded dumbly again as his gaze moved up to meet mine. We stayed frozen in that spot, staring into one another's eyes. Neither of us moved or even seemed to breathe. I wished I was able to step into his mind and hear what he was thinking. As for my own thoughts, they were impure and involved chocolate sauce and inappropriate body parts.

The phone on his desk buzzed, and the receptionist's Valley Girl voice interrupted my fantasy. "Mr. Prince, there's an Elliot Chandler here to see you. He says it's urgent."

Aiden's chest rose and fell deeply. Then he gave me a half smile and reached back to the phone. "Tell him I'll be with him shortly." Then to me, he said, "A witness for a case. I'm sorry to cut this short."

I stepped back and cleared my throat. "No, I understand. I'll see you tonight."

I headed for the door. He followed me with his hand on the small of my back. Then he reached for the knob, but instead of opening the door, he just stood there staring at me.

"I'm looking forward to it."

"Me too." I swallowed hard. My body was still in a high-alert state. My pulse raced, butterflies had invaded my stomach, and I was so very hot. I wasn't physically or mentally ready to step out of this office. Mostly because I wasn't sure I could take a step without my knees turning to Jell-O.

"Why don't you wear that red dress? The one you wore the first time I met you."

The first time we'd met I was undercover at a charity benefit. I'd worn a red strapless evening gown.

"Where are we going?" I couldn't imagine any restaurant in the area that was a white-tie event.

"Leave that to me." He opened the door.

* * *

After leaving Aiden, I was pumped and hungry. According to Maya, I had new prospective clients coming in later in the afternoon, so I only had enough time for a quick lunch. I didn't want to eat alone, but mentally going through lunch candidates left me leaving my cell in my purse. Danny and I had just had breakfast together, and Derek was being…well, Derek. That left the girls. Maya was having lunch with her mom, and Sam had a dentist appointment. Caleigh said she was just going to pick up a Hoagie and eat at her desk, but maybe I could catch her before she grabbed a sandwich.

I dialed her phone.

"Hey, Boss, what's up?"

"I was wondering if you've gotten lunch yet. It's gorgeous out, and I'd rather not eat alone."

"Are we talking about Hoagies?" There was excitement in her tone.

I chuckled. "That's fine. There's one not too far from where I am now. I'm at Aiden's office."

"I'll meet you there. I'm on my way."

I parked out front of the Hoagies and waited for Caleigh in my car. My stomach had started to grumble, and I didn't want to stand in the store and salivate. To pass the time, I played a riveting game of Candy Crush on my phone and then let it charge for a bit because that game drained my battery.

Caleigh pulled up beside me, waved, and then drove ahead until she found a vacant spot.

I grabbed my phone and purse and met her on the sidewalk. We walked inside, and I was so glad to see only one customer ahead of us.

"What can I get for you?" asked the Hoagies employee.

We each ordered the Roger special, except I added banana peppers to mine for an extra kick, and Caleigh asked for a squirt of oil and vinegar. This store had a self-serve soda machine, so we took our cups and filled them with soda. Then we sat at one of the tables by the windows.

Caleigh bit into her sub and smiled. "This tastes even better than the one from earlier."

I frowned, not sure what she meant. "Earlier today?"

She nodded.

So I had called her too late. "You already had lunch?"

"Yeah, but that was like a whole hour ago, and I only had coffee for breakfast. So, really it was kinda like brunch."

I sipped my soda and marveled at her logic. It made sense.

We ate in silence. It just tasted better that way. Then while we digested, she asked how it had gone with Heavy Cash. I filled her in and noticed that she hadn't asked about my being at Aiden's office. Maybe she didn't want to pry, or she assumed I'd talk about it if I wanted to. I was grateful because I wasn't sure I could do anything but blush if she brought it up. Plus, I figured there would be so much more to tell tomorrow—after our dinner.

When we got back to the office, Maya handed me a manila folder and informed me that my new clients were waiting in my office.

When I entered, I walked around my desk and stared at an older couple. According to Maya's notes, they were Mr. and Mrs. Henderson. They were in their sixties, both fair complexioned, and the husband had light-brown hair that was graying at the temples. He wore khaki pants with a light-green polo shirt.

Mrs. Henderson had a blue-and-white floral scarf around her head, so I couldn't tell her hair color, but I got the sense that she was either bald or was close to it. Her brown eyes were clear and focused, but her face looked tired and sickly. She wore a white blouse and khaki pants as well.

People said that when couples spent their lives together, they started to resemble one another. Mr. and Mrs. Henderson definitely had that going on.

I shook each of their hands and immediately noted Mrs. Henderson wasn't swift getting up out of her chair, but her smile was bright and infectious.

I sat down. "So how can I help you today?"

The husband cleared his throat but didn't answer. He glanced to his wife with tenderness, but as he looked away, it morphed to something closer to annoyance. I raised an eyebrow, my radar perking. It wasn't common to have both spouses in my office together in the first place, let alone one annoyed one.

I opened the folder and was about to start reading Maya's notes, when Mrs. Henderson said, "This may be an odd request, but we're here to find my husband a wife."

I froze and blinked several times. "Excuse me?"

She pointed to the top of her scarf. "I have stage-four cancer. I'm dying, and my husband, Jeffrey, is too young and too loving to spend the rest of his life alone."

I glanced to Mr. Henderson, who grimaced and was doing his best to keep a semi-smile on his face, but it was obvious he disliked this conversation. I didn't blame him. I was starting to feel a bit uncomfortable myself.

"Linda," he said and patted her hand.

She glanced at him before continuing. "I've spent thirty-five years with this man, and I know he won't be able to get along without a woman to take care of him."

Spots of pink colored Mr. Henderson's cheeks, and he kept his gaze on the carpet.

"I love him tremendously, and I want to make sure he's taken care of before I go."

He turned to her, and this time his expression was just pure love.

My chest tightened, and I glanced at the box of tissues by the desk lamp. I'd never cried in front of a client, but I wasn't sure if I'd be able to continue to say that after today.

I swallowed hard, finally able to find my voice. "And how exactly can I help you?"

She opened her purse and pulled out a sheet of off-white stationary. She handed it over, and a light wave of lilac scent filled the air.

On the top of the page, there were the initials *LHA*, and surrounding them were two small bouquets of pink roses. Written with a deep flourish down the sheet were the names of three women.

Jenny Pepin
Penny Samson
Leonora Toll

Let me guess. The last one was nicknamed Lenny?

"I've discovered three women that seem to fit Jeffrey, but I need to know more about each one to be sure. I'd like you to investigate each one thoroughly so that we can pick the best new wife for him."

I did some more blinking at Mrs. Henderson. I'd never heard of such a thing. I didn't want to deny this poor dying woman her wish, but this was odd and slightly creepy.

"I know how it seems," Mrs. Henderson said, picking up on my vibe. "At the very least, it's morbid."

She was right there.

"I'm sorry—where did you find these women?" I suddenly pictured a dating site for the soon-to-be widowers.

Mrs. Henderson smiled. "I've been keeping my eye out. They're just women I've met here and there. Believe me—I know my husband's type, so I very carefully picked out these three."

Her husband squirmed in his seat again but said nothing.

"I don't know…" I hedged. I looked down at the three names again. It would be simple enough to run background checks on the women and make sure none had criminal records or other red flags in their past. But vetting them out as marriage material? I wasn't sure that was within my field of expertise.

"Please," Mrs. Henderson pleaded. "I don't want to die knowing he'll be alone."

Mr. Henderson sought out her hand again, and this time he held it.

"I want to go forward with as little stress as possible. Will you please help us?"

I searched his face for some clue. I'd say he was more than uncomfortable, but he was here. He must've agreed to this situation to some extent. Even if it was just to make his wife happy.

I felt myself nodding. I couldn't turn this woman down. "Yes, of course."

This was definitely going down in history as the weirdest case to date.

After the Hendersons and I went over particulars of billing and what sort of info she wanted on each woman, they left. I instructed Maya to start digging on the three future Mrs. Hendersons. If Maya had any feelings about how squicky this situation felt, she kept them to herself.

I was just opening the Hendersons' file to read over the preliminary notes, when my cell rang. I looked down at the readout to see Danny's name.

"Hey," I answered, preoccupied with the Hendersons' file. Mrs. Henderson had included candid photos of each candidate.

"Hey, yourself." He gave me his standard greeting. Then he paused. "So…"

Confused and not really paying attention, I said, "So what?"

He sighed lightly. "So, do you have an answer for me yet?"

"Answer?" I asked, flipping to a photo of Future Mrs. Henderson Number 1.

"About dinner. You and me, tonight."

Oh crap. I forgot. How did I forget?

I cringed, thinking of Aiden. When he'd asked me to dinner, I hadn't hesitated. Granted, he hadn't actually asked me so much as told me, but I hadn't minded the shift from Good Old Reliable Aiden to Bad Boy Aiden. Guilt colored my cheeks pink, and I was glad that Danny couldn't see me right now. It wasn't that Danny wasn't on my radar, but that moment in Aiden's office had been so overwhelming that I'd almost forgotten my own name, let alone my awkward conversation with Danny from breakfast.

"Jamie?" Danny asked over the palpable silence on my end.

I squeezed my eyes shut, hating myself for the lie I was about to tell… "I'm sorry. I can't. Work is super busy right now." There was no way I'd admit to Danny that I already accepted a date with another man.

Danny was quiet for a few seconds, and I nervously bit my lower lip. While I wasn't sure what our future was, the last thing I wanted to do was hurt Danny.

Finally, he said, "You can't stall forever, James."

I took a deep breath.

I could certainly try.

CHAPTER SEVEN

———

A couple of hours later, Sam appeared at my door and knocked on the wall beside it. "You got a second?" she asked.

I closed the Henderson file and leaned back in my chair. I needed the eyestrain break anyway. "Of course. What's up?"

She took two steps inside my office. "I was hoping I could leave early."

She had that look on her face again—the distracted one that told me something was up. "Everything okay?" I asked.

She shrugged. "Define 'okay.'"

I gestured to the seat in front of my desk. "Sit. Spill."

She sighed, but she gave me a smile as she sunk into the chair. "I'm taking Julio to his dad's for the weekend, and I plan to give Julio Senior a piece of my mind about not sending the child support."

"As deserved," I agreed.

"Anyway, I wanted to leave a little early to beat some of the traffic down the 405." She paused. "If that's possible."

It had been a slow afternoon, if you didn't count the older couple looking to add a third. Caleigh had been wrapping up some paperwork on past cases, Maya was checking into the three possible Henderson brides, and I was chewing on guilt at leading Danny on and anxiety at whether or not Aiden was leading me on.

"That's fine," I told her. "I hope he comes through for you."

Sam rolled her eyes. "Me too. Thanks."

Between wrestling with my guilt, I did a little catching up on Facebook, updated our website and social media, and checked into some new advertising avenues. You know, in case it turned out that our one semi-celeb client was guilty of killing her husband. After a couple hours I ran out of things to do, and I headed into the lobby to catch up with Maya and Caleigh.

Though I stopped short when I noticed their outfits.

Caleigh had on a red-and-purple tie-dyed halter jumpsuit with bell bottoms. Platform wedges were fastened to her feet, and her hair was teased higher than her hound dog cousin's. Maya had on a short-sleeve, white minidress with white go-go boots. Her hair hung in two loose braids.

"What's going on?" I asked and looked around, half expecting John Travolta to appear and start dancing.

Callie fidgeted with an enormous gold hoop earring. "Maya got into Elaine's cell records. She's going out tonight."

"With the Bee Gees?" I asked.

"Ha-ha," Caleigh shot back. "She's going to the disco bingo. Plus, I've been dying for an excuse to rent a costume from this shop near where I live. The clerk has the most adorable dimple."

I smirked. "What exactly is disco bingo?"

Maya held up her compact and applied an extra-heavy coat of mauve-colored lipstick. "I think there are disco balls that twirl from the ceiling, everyone is dressed as if they stepped out of the '70s, and 'I Will Survive' by Gloria Gaynor plays while we play the game." She snapped her compact shut. "At least that's what the text from Elaine's friend, Janet, said."

That made sense.

The agency door opened, and three older women in disco gear walked in. I immediately recognized them as Charley Alexander, Maya's mom, and Mrs. Alexander's two friends, Ruth and Abigail. I'd gone to lunch at Charley's house one afternoon, where I'd met her and her friends. They were delightful and adventurous women who had a soft spot for detective work. I suddenly had my suspicions about why they were dressed up.

"Mom," Maya said and rushed toward the woman in front of the pack. They hugged, and Maya gave hugs to the other women as well. Then she turned to me and said, "I thought it would be best if Caleigh and I didn't stand out so much, so I invited my mom and her friends."

I smiled at the women. Each of their light-blue, paisley, and brown bell-bottom pants seemed authentic and not from a costume shop. I was impressed. If I could still fit into anything that was in fashion now when I became their age, I'd be a happy camper indeed. Hmm…maybe if I kept up my Hoagies diet…

"It's so good to see you, Jamie," Charley said and wrapped me in a tight hug.

I shut my eyes and breathed in her rose scent. Her and Maya's bond reminded me of my mom. I'd welcomed the chance to get closer to Charley, as she was the closest person I had to a mother.

"This is so exciting." Ruth rubbed her hands together. "I love nabbing the bad guy."

I raised a brow to Maya, feeling my suspicions confirmed. She immediately glanced away.

"There are no bad guys tonight, Ruth," Maya said. "We're just going to keep an eye on a friend and see what she does."

I appreciated Maya's vagueness with them. The last thing we needed was any of them accidentally spilling the beans to Elaine that she was being tailed by her suspicious boyfriend's daughter. And her friends. And her friend's mother. And her friend's mother's friends.

Abigail giggled. "Either way, this is going to be a blast."

Charley turned to them. "That's right, ladies. The Senior Sleuths are on the case."

Oh boy, this was going to end well. Not.

* * *

When I returned home, I had plenty of time to soak in a long, luxurious bubble bath and enjoy a glass of red wine while soaking. I rested my head against my gel pillow and shut my eyes. My thoughts drifted to Derek and Elaine. I hoped they would be okay. One, because I was tired of worrying about him, and two, because I liked her, and she grounded him some. And three, so that he'd have someone else to call next time he got arrested. Wait—that might've been the wine talking.

I pushed those thoughts aside and contemplated the Hendersons. If I were married, happy, and dying, would I want my husband to move on after my death? Of course. Probably. Maybe. But would I want to find him a wife before I passed? No. I didn't think I could think of him with another woman while I was dying. Yes, I'd want him to be happy, but I'd want him to grieve me and move on naturally.

Maybe I was just selfish.

Besides, what did I know? I couldn't even face my best friend's feelings for me. Though to be honest, I wasn't exactly sure what those feelings were, since I was too scared to face him. Scared. Was that it? Was I a coward? I've never thought of myself in a cowardly way in my entire life. I'd always faced every challenge head-on, every hard situation, everything that life had thrown at me. So why was I avoiding Danny?

I thought about that until the water cooled and my second glass miraculously emptied. I flipped the drain to open and stepped out of the tub before grabbing an extra-large yellow towel and wrapping myself in it. After slipping into my pink silk robe, I grabbed the blow-dryer and did some damage to my hair. I decided to leave it down around my shoulders, and then I opened my makeup bag. I didn't usually wear a lot of it, but I had the feeling tonight was a special occasion. With a steady hand, I applied a thin line of black liner to the base of my top lashes and did a smoky eye thing.

I dressed in the red strapless Aiden had suggested and stepped back to inspect the final look in my full-length mirror. Aiden was right. This dress fit me wonderfully and looked great. All I needed was red hair, and I'd definitely feel like Jessica Rabbit. Va-va-voom.

I took my wineglass to the kitchen and set it beside the opened bottle of Merlot. I considered having another, hoping to take the edge off my nerves. But I didn't want to get tipsy before he even arrived. I just needed to take a few calming breaths, and I'd be fine.

I couldn't quite understand my nervousness. This wasn't our first date, but my stomach was full of butterflies. Think of something else, Jamie.

I grabbed the remote from the coffee table and flicked on the television. I didn't have the focus to watch anything, nor did I plan on sitting and wrinkling myself, but a little distraction was a good thing. There was a commercial promo for that sitcom set in the eighties, and my thoughts jumped to disco bingo. I hoped it was all going well. I considered calling Caleigh, but I feared a ringing cell might alert everyone to turn her way, and I didn't want Elaine to know she was being followed. Better to play it safe.

There was a knock at my door, and my pulse jumped.

Calm down, Jamie. This was just Aiden. Gorgeous, newly unpredictable, bad boy Aiden.

I clicked off the TV and returned the remote to its home. As soon as I wrapped my fingers about my doorknob, my pulse returned to almost normal, my stomach calmed mostly, and my excitement grew. See, this was going to be amazing. I put on a smile and opened the door.

He stood there in a black suit, white shirt, and a light blue-slash-silvery tie. Amazing wasn't half of it. His eyes widened upon seeing me. Just as they should have. "Wow, you look more amazing than I remembered."

I felt my smile brighten. Amazing was good. We were definitely on the same wavelength. "Thank you. You don't look half bad yourself."

He grinned as if he knew it and stepped into the room.

"Where are we going this fine evening?" I asked, proud at how calm and even my voice sounded.

"That will be a surprise." He winked at me. The butterflies responded accordingly, flapping their wings with gusto. "How about a drink before we leave?" He eyed the Merlot on the counter.

My apartment had an open plan, so the kitchen, dining, and living rooms were all seen from one another. I leaned on the back of my sofa and watched him eye the bottle of wine on the counter and reach into a cabinet for a glass. I loved how comfortable he felt in my home.

He poured himself a full glass and downed half of it before he reached me. I guessed I'd be driving tonight.

"The wine okay? I'm not a huge connoisseur, so I wasn't sure about the vintage—"

"You are breathtaking," he cut me off.

I shut my mouth with a click.

He set his glass on an end table and wrapped an arm around my waist. Then he pulled me closer. His head lowered to mine, and before I got a second to revel in the anticipation of the kiss, his mouth pressed against mine.

At first my head and heart filled with giggly glee. Without realizing, my leg bent at the knee, and my high-heeled foot rose. It felt like the movies. I was a leading lady, and Aiden was my hero. A giggle rose in my throat, but I pushed it away and focused on his mouth.

He tasted like wine with a hint of cinnamon. He must've had coffee earlier. When he brewed it himself, he added a cinnamon stick to the grounds. His hands roamed my sides, holding me firmly against him. My fingers were laced behind his neck. Despite his firm grip, I felt lightheaded and needed the extra support.

I don't know how long the kiss lasted, but when we came up for air, I was panting.

"That was…" I trailed off, suddenly at a loss for words.

His eyes went dark, his hands moved to the zipper on my dress, and he dove back into my mouth with gusto. His lips hit mine. Hard. Demanding.

Well, part of me was floating on cloud nine at the bad boy nipping at my lower lip, but a tiny voice in the back of my head started waving little red flags. Something was off. And when Aiden reached behind me and grabbed my butt, lifting me onto the couch, I couldn't deny that this wasn't the Aiden Prince I knew. Not that butt grabbing wasn't awesome…but it wasn't him.

I pulled back and turned my head so his lips brushed against my cheek. "What are you doing?"

He lifted his head and frowned. "I think that's obvious."

I put my hand against his chest and pushed myself back away from him out of his embrace. Then I rubbed my butt where his fingers had been. "Maybe we should grab some dinner," I said, angling away from him.

That sly smile I'd seen in his office hit his lips again. "Maybe we should just order in," he murmured, moving closer to my lips again.

I ducked and weaved, doing an almost choreographed pirouette out of his arms. I'll admit I wobbled a little on my heels but quickly summoned balance.

He gave me a hard look and turned back to his wineglass. "I thought we were going to have a good time tonight."

I felt my back straighten, and I involuntarily bristled at the tone in his voice. "Yes, so did I. I thought it involved dinner and possibly dancing. And maybe some making out, and who knows what after. But…"

"But what?" he said, setting his glass back on the table a little harder than necessary. The sound made me flinch.

"I don't know. Look, you've been different lately. At first I just thought maybe it meant you were ready to move on, but…" I trailed off, biting my lip. Mentioning his dead wife right now was so not the right move.

He cocked his head to the side. "I think I just made it pretty clear. I am ready to move on."

I shook my head. "Not like this."

"Like what?"

Honestly? I wasn't sure. All I knew was that this guy was not the Aiden I knew and loved. Wait—did I just say loved? I felt my head swirling with the conflicting emotions of lust and caution mixed with two glasses of non-vintage Merlot. Did I want to move on with Aiden? Yes. But as much as this new Bad Boy Aiden was exciting, it wasn't him. The realization hit me like a ton of bricks falling on those butterfly wings. He wasn't over his wife. He wasn't over the shooting. And whatever was going on right now, it wasn't about me.

"What are you saying, Jamie?" he pressed. All of the lust had been drained from his eyes too, almost as if he'd come to the same realization I had.

"I'm saying that maybe you're trying to work through the shooting and whatever's happened to you lately through me." I hadn't thought of that until the words came out of my mouth, but now that they were in the air, it made perfect sense. This wasn't about me. It was about him and his own guilt.

He scoffed. He drained his glass of wine. And then he turned and headed to my door.

"Are you serious?" I cried after him. "You're just going to walk out like that?"

He stopped and turned but didn't look at me. His gaze was off by my television. "What's there to talk about? You're standing there psychoanalyzing me while I just wanted to have a good night. There's nothing wrong with *me*."

It was such a guy statement. But I kept my composure and said, "If you truly were okay—if I hadn't just hit a nerve—you would've just calmly said I was wrong rather than getting offended and wanting to run off."

He looked down to his shoes and then up into my face. A half smile lifted the right side of his mouth but never quite made it to his eyes. "You look beautiful. Good-night, Jamie." Then he turned and walked out of my apartment.

I just stood there for several seconds with my mouth hanging open.

Great. I kicked off one shoe, but the other I had to bend down and pull off the back of my ankle. I flung it over the sofa. It hit the remote on the coffee table and then tumbled to the floor.

I rolled my eyes and sighed. At one point today I'd had two dates. And now none. Nice one, Jamie.

CHAPTER EIGHT

After ordering Chinese takeout for one and finishing the bottle of Merlot on my own, I spent a long night tossing and turning. Guilt kept invading my dreams—both at the accusations I'd thrown at Aiden and the lack of explanation I'd given Danny. How was it that I'd managed to screw up two relationships in the span of a few hours? It had to be a record. Even for me.

By the time the sun rose, I gave up tossing and turning and gave into showering and dressing. I tossed on a pair of skinny black slacks, extra-high heels to compensate for my extra-guilty mood, and a light, white silk T-shirt to compensate for the heat that I knew would be rising into the hundreds by midday. A blow-dry, a couple of swipes of mascara, and a venti caramel macchiato later, I was ready to actually face the day.

Since I still hadn't heard from my client, Bristol Claremont, I decided to check out the first woman on Mrs. Henderson's list. Jenny Pepin. Maya was still running background checks on the three women, but she'd managed to get me the basics on both Jenny and Penny. And since Jenny's days evolved around a carefully scripted schedule, she was the easiest to track down.

I ran by the agency, snagged Caleigh, and hightailed it to The Aqua Fit—a swanky new gym in Studio City that specializes in aquatic fitness, with an Olympic-sized pool and an organic juice bar. This was according to Caleigh. I assumed the juice served was organic, and not the actual bar.

When we arrived, the receptionist, a bubbly blonde (Studio City standard) greeted us with the pep of a cheerleader. Caleigh, used to being the bubbliest in the land, made a disgruntled sound in her throat, but she kept her vivacious smile in place.

"Hi, we're here to see Je—" I paused. I realized that I hadn't prepared our covers on the ride over. Rookie mistake. I took a deep breath to get my head back in the game and away from any man I might or might not ever be invited on a date with again.

"We heard great things about your pool and bar, and we're wondering if we can have a look-see." I finished with a bright smile.

The receptionist wore a light-blue, one-piece swimsuit with matching shorts and an open track jacket. Not exactly a standard uniform, but maybe they were known for their pool emergencies.

"Oh, we just love visitors, especially when they turn into members." She held out a pamphlet to each of us.

Caleigh and I glanced to one another before taking the glossy advertisements.

"There's an aerobics class currently rejuvenating in our pool."

I widened my eyes and faked uber interest. "Oh, I'd love to see a class in action."

The receptionist nodded. "Okay, well you're more than welcome to have a seat at the bar and watch." She pointed to a door off to the left. "If you have any questions, please don't hesitate to ask me or our juicetender."

Caleigh and I exchanged looks again. A juicetender?

The lobby was small, so I wasn't expecting much, but when we entered the bar area, I sucked back a small gasp. The bar itself was designed as a long wave. It took up the entire side wall and was a pale-blue color. The whole room was varying shades of blue and green, from the floor to the walls to the furnishings. Clamshell-shaped stools dotted the bar. The left wall was all glass, and on the other side sat an enormous pool. A handful of high, bistro-type tables and chairs filled the space between the pool and bar. And there were several doors along the back wall. I imagined they led to lockers and bathrooms.

I scanned the people in the pool for one that looked like the photo I'd seen in the Hendersons' file. Jenny had sandy-brown hair and big blue eyes. As long as she hadn't drastically altered her appearance, she shouldn't be terribly difficult to spot. I scoped out the eleven women in the pool, minus the instructor, and spotted Jenny immediately. Except for the being wet part, she still looked exactly like her photo.

She and the ten other women raised their arms toward the ceiling, and then in perfect synchronization moved them out in front of them and to the sides. It all looked oddly peaceful.

"Can I help you?" asked a tinny voice. The juicetender wore the same uniform as the receptionist. She was brunette, tall, and slender, and had thigh muscles that looked like they could break a walnut.

Caleigh stepped forward. "The woman up front said we could watch the class. We're thinking of joining."

The juicetender clapped her hands together. "That's awesome. Would you like a juicetail? Everything is organic and fresh. I promise you'll love it."

"Absolutely," Caleigh said.

Their personal dictionary was starting to give me a headache, so I just smiled my acceptance.

The juicetender went about filling a blender with fresh-cut pineapple, two giant handfuls of kale, some liquid concoction that came from a plastic container, some freshly squeezed orange juice, and exactly four ice cubes. Several whizzes later, she set two dull pea-green glasses before us. They each received a long, bendy straw and a chunk of skewed pineapple.

I was hesitant to try it, but the juicetender looked like she eagerly awaited our approval, so I sipped. Surprisingly it was delicious. It tasted just like a pineapple-orange smoothie—sweet, thick, and luscious. When Caleigh and I smiled and nodded, the juicetender clapped. She was so proud.

Caleigh and I sat at one of the bistro-style tables and faced the pool. "I may have to join here," Caleigh said. I knew she frequently looked for interesting ways to stay active, but they usually involved a room full of sweaty, muscled men. This place definitely had a more feminine vibe. Maybe it was the lack of weight lifting machines.

We sipped our drinks and watched the women perform in perfect synchronization. I leaned back on my high-backed stool and relaxed, feeling the tension of the night before slowly slip away. What was that mystery ingredient in the container? That juicetender was a magician.

Eventually the women climbed out of the pool and grabbed towels to dry off. That was when I realized that one of the participants was a man with a low ponytail. Oops, my bad for thinking they were all women.

They entered the juice bar, all seemingly eager to get a glass of their daily nutrients and antioxidants.

Jenny received her drink first. When she turned away from the bar, Caleigh waved her over. Right before she reached us, Caleigh whispered, "She's cute."

Caleigh was right. Jenny was short and slightly round around the waist and hip area, but there was something in the way she walked that reminded me of Mrs. Henderson. No wonder the Hendersons had added Jenny to their list.

She wore a lime-green bathing suit with a pink towel wrapped around her waist, and yellow flip-flops. She approached our table with excitement, as if we were long-lost friends meeting for lunch.

As she sat down, she held out her hand. "Hi, I'm Jenny. Did you want to see me?"

Caleigh and I each shook her hand. She came off as so trusting—which struck me as extremely odd. I couldn't imagine that in this world today. Though, there was a possibility that following cheating spouses and nabbing the occasional murderer had helped shape my worldview.

"I'm Jamie, and this is Caleigh. We heard about this place from friends, so we came by to check it out. You looked so natural in the pool. You must've been coming here for ages. We're hoping you can fill us in on this place."

Her baby blues lit up. "Of course. I've only been here for a couple of months, but the routine is so simple that anyone can do it."

I glanced to Caleigh. "That's what Linda and Jeffrey Henderson said too."

Jenny frowned for a moment. "You know the Hendersons? I've never seen them here."

I faked surprise by placing a hand to my chest and clutching my invisible pearls. "You know them too?"

"Yes, I met them at a charity benefit for children with special needs. It was a few weeks ago. Charming event and a lovely couple. They seem quite in love."

"Yes, they are," I said, and I thought, *if only you knew*.

We spent another thirty minutes trying to squeeze personal information out of Jenny without making her suspicious, and by the time she had to leave, we'd discovered she owned a cat named Mr. Rupert, loved gardening, and knitted Christmas gifts for her fourteen nieces and nephews every year. Whether or not that made her wife material for Mr. Henderson, I had no idea. But I would have to report that I'd gotten a good vibe from Jenny. She was warm, kind, and compassionate. Those were things I'd want in a wife for my husband if I were dying.

As soon as Caleigh and I got back to the office, Maya hung up the telephone and waved me over.

I sat on the edge of her immaculate desk. "What's up?"

"I dug up some info on Roger." She poked a pad of paper with her pen. "You were right to check legal records."

I raised an eyebrow at her. "Oh? Do tell."

"Turns out he was being sued by his former boss, the wrapper."

I frowned. "Heavy Cash?" That didn't seem to make a lot of sense. I didn't know of Heavy ever having been Roger's boss. He may have acted "like a boss," aka confident and in control in his videos, but as far as I knew, this was their first time working together.

"No, not the *rapper*." Maya bobbed and weaved her head and chopped the air with her hands in some crazed karate moves that I assumed were supposed to simulate a hip-hop dance.

I bit my lip to keep from laughing.

"The *wrapper*. Ian Jenkins is the owner of Lite Wraps."

Oh! Well that made much more sense.

"What's Lite Wraps?" I asked.

"A restaurant in Gardena. Roger worked there when he was on the Hoagies diet and lost all the weight."

"Ah!" I nodded. "Okay, so why are they suing him?"

"Well, when Roger went public and got all the fame and endorsement money, Lite Wraps sued, claiming that at least some of the weight Roger lost was due to their low calorie wraps that he ate while working there."

This all became very interesting. Another suspect. I loved them like presents on my birthday.

I stood up and smoothed my hands over my skirt. "I guess Mr. Jenkins deserves a visit."

Maya grinned. "I thought you might say that." She handed me a piece of paper with the address of Roger's former employer on it. "They're open until seven. If you want to beat the lunch rush, I'd leave now."

I couldn't help letting out a laugh as I took the paper. "Anything else?"

Maya shrugged. "According to Yelp, their Swiss cheese and ham wrap is their most popular item."

"Duly noted," I promised her as I moved toward the door. I only got a couple of steps, however, before my cell rang. It was Derek. I tried to channel my inner Zen as I hit the *on* button.

"What do you want?"

Clearly my Zen was as DOA as my relationships today.

"Is that any way to greet your old man, James?"

I took a deep breath and tried again. "To what do I owe this honor, Father?"

"Is that sarcasm I'm detecting in your voice?"

"No, it's Zen."

I heard a couple loud huffs on the other end, but thankfully Derek dropped it. "How's it going with Elaine?" he asked.

I closed my eyes and thought a dirty word. With all that had happened in the last 24 hours, I'd completely forgotten to grill Caleigh and Maya for an update on disco bingo. "It's great. Fine. When I have something worthy to report, I'll let you know." Or when I remembered to ask for an update. Whichever came first.

"Did you check her cell records?" Derek asked

"Yes."

"Any men calling her?"

"No." Unless he wanted to count Dr. Steingarden.

"Any suspicious activity?"

"None."

He grunted. You'd think the guy would be a little bit happier to hear that his girlfriend *hadn't* done anything suspicious. Instead he muttered a "Keep digging" and hung up.

I slipped my phone into my purse and turned back to Maya.

"Derek's looking for an update. How did it go with Elaine last night?" I asked.

She glanced up from her monitor and leaned back in her chair. The look on her face told me something was up. Gosh, I hoped I wasn't about to eat my words.

"Well, I'm not sure you're going to like this…"

Uh-oh. "What?"

"Well, Mom was sort of obvious in her spying. Like, she was hovering over Elaine's shoulder all evening."

"And?" I asked, fearing there was more.

"And, Elaine finally asked what was up, and Mom kinda told a small fib."

I narrowed my eyes. "How small?"

"She said she had a single cousin, and Elaine was just his type."

"And what did Elaine answer?"

Maya cleared her throat. "She laughed and said she was already seeing someone."

Well, that was a relief. Of course, Elaine hadn't mentioned whether that someone was Derek or her possible man on the side.

"After that Mom and Elaine got to talking and, well, they kinda got friendly. So friendly that Elaine's going out with Mom and the girls somewhere tonight."

I smiled and let out a relieved breath. That wasn't bad at all. In fact, I didn't mind at all if the Senior Sleuths did my dirty work for me and kept an eye on Elaine.

* * *

Lite Wraps was located in Burbank, in an area that wasn't my favorite, even though I was very familiar with it. It sat across the street from The Spotted Pony, a strip club I'd once worked at as an undercover server. I'd been hired to keep an eye on a seemingly wayward husband who'd been seen going to the club. His wife had thought he was cheating, but it turned out he'd just been trying to track down his long-lost daughter, who it turned out was a dancer at the club. Ah, the titillating days as a private investigator.

I tore my eyes away from The Spotted Pony (whose sign looked like it needed a light bulb change on the *d*) and turned to the strip mall that housed Lite Wraps. It was also home to a dry cleaner, a talent agency, and a 24-hour doughnut shop. I had a feeling the doughnut shop probably did better business when The Spotted Pony let out at night than a healthy wraps place.

I pulled open the door and stepped inside Lite Wraps. The place was larger than I'd assumed from the outside, but its condition was just as bleak. Dark laminate floors with matching tables and counters. The walls were a muted shade of light green. It was set up similar to Hoagies, in that a long counter full of veggies took up a large portion of the store, but it held more tables, and the menu hanging on the wall revealed more than just sandwiches. They also had pasta dishes, salads, and a few desserts. The scent was an odd mix of lemon cleanser, yeasty bread, and cheese.

A man younger than I stood behind the counter. He was wearing a pair of brown pants and a green polo shirt that matched the decor. He grabbed a small container of shredded lettuce and tossed it on top of the browning bits already sitting out. Then he gave it all a stir.

I grimaced and stepped forward. I would definitely not be eating here. "I'm looking for Ian Jenkins," I told him.

"I'm Ian Jenkins," the man said. His voice was high pitched and squeaky. That mixed with the cheese odor made me think of Mickey Mouse.

I narrowed my eyes at him. There was no way someone this young owned this place.

Standing directly across from him, I got an up-close look at a diamond-shaped birthmark on his cheek. It was small enough to appear like a regular beauty mark from far away, although there was nothing beautiful about this man. Sweat covered his round face and thick neck, and I couldn't help wondering if any of it had fallen onto the food. He had reddish-brown hair and murky-colored eyes. A wide nose took over his face, and dotted scars suggested he'd once had a severe case of acne.

"Are you the owner?"

"No, that's my father. Who are you?"

"I'm Jamie Bond. I'm investigating the death of Roger Claremont. Can I speak with your dad, please?"

He gave me a once-over, wiped his hands on the once-white but now-grease-stained apron around his waist, and screamed, "Pop!"

I flinched and looked away. My gaze landed on the array of wrap offerings, from mushy-looking tomatoes to shaved steak with the appearance of leather. Slices of ham had a sheen on them, as if they were slimy and had been sitting under the lights way past expiration, and the small blocks of cheese looked congealed. There was a salad, maybe tuna or chicken, that had dried bits closest to the top.

The whole thing made my stomach flip. How could anyone eat this stuff? How were they still in business? No wonder they wanted to sue. They probably needed the money to stay afloat.

"Can I help you?"

I looked up to the voice and watched an older version of the son, minus the pimply scars, step forward. Same hair, same nose, same brown pants and green polo shirt, and same disgusting apron. It was like looking into the future, or the past, depending on whom you stared at.

"Hi, I'm Jamie Bond," I told him. "I'm looking into the death of Roger Claremont." I didn't bother to offer my hand to shake. I couldn't remember the last time I'd had a tetanus shot, and I was fresh out of hand sanitizer.

"How can I help you?" Senior Jenkins asked, but his pursed lips and shifty glance gave away his disdain in either discussing Roger or his death. Or maybe both.

"I understand that Roger used to be an employee of yours."

"Yeah. So?"

"I also understand that you and he didn't part ways amicably."

The son scoffed. "That's an understatement," he mumbled.

Senior Jenkins shot him a glare.

"Where were you the afternoon Roger was killed?" I asked. There was no sense in beating around the bush. Plus, I really wanted to get out of here and jump into a vat of bleach. I took a step back, closer to the front door and farther away from the assortment of food. My left shoe stuck to the floor for a second, and I prayed I had napkins in the car.

"What's it to you? You a cop?" Jenkins asked.

I shook my head. "Private investigator."

"So who you workin' for?" he challenged.

Normally I didn't like to give out client info, but considering Bristol Claremont's arrest was likely to be front-page news, I didn't see the harm.

"Bristol Claremont hired me."

Jenkins's posture softened some. "That woman's a looker, huh? I ask you—what does a hot number like that see in a guy like Roger?"

If I had to guess, dollar signs. "You weren't Roger's biggest fan, I take it."

Jenkins pursed his thin lips and narrowed his eyes. "That two-faced, disloyal, rat fink of a sandwich pimp can rot in Hades for all I care." He paused. "Not to speak ill of the dead or nothin'."

I tried not to smile. I was liking this guy as a suspect more and more. "When was the last time you saw Roger?" I asked.

Jenkins shrugged, his gaze wandering to the poster of a spinach wrap loaded with veggies about a week fresher than anything in this store. "I dunno. Not recently."

"Not, say, two days ago?"

Jenkins's eyes shot back to mine, their murky depths narrowing into slits. "Hey, I said I didn't love the guy. I didn't say I killed him."

"Where were you when he was killed?" I asked, returning to my original question.

"I was here. All day," he answered.

Of course he was. "Customers can attest to that?" I asked.

"I can," the son quickly jumped in. "He was in the office doing the books and inventory. All day."

Well that didn't mean much. The son could've easily been covering for him.

"It doesn't matter though," Jenkins said. "I don't have a motive."

I raised an eyebrow his way. "What about your lawsuit against Roger?"

Something shifted in Jenkins's eyes, as if he was surprised I knew about the suit. Dude, I was a PI with a crack team of hackers. If the information was out there, we would uncover it.

"Look, if you must know," he said, "my lawyer said they were close to settling. In my favor! So I got no reason to want Roger dead."

I bit my lip, tasting peach-flavored gloss. While these two were slimier than the ham, if he was telling the truth, Roger would be worth more to him alive than dead.

"What happens with the lawsuit now?" I asked.

Jenkins shrugged. "What do I look like, a freakin' lawyer? I dunno." He crossed his arms over his chest and gave me a hard look, signaling that he was done answering questions.

"Thanks very much for your time," I told him, quickly making for the door. I'd have Maya check into the lawsuit as soon as I got to my car and disinfected my shoe.

I took in a clean lungful of air as I left the store and walked to my car. I dug in the glove compartment for something I could use for the bottom of my pump and found two individual wet wipe packets. I had no idea where they'd come from, and I didn't care.

After wiping down my shoe, I pulled my key from my purse and pushed it into the ignition, but instead of turning the car on, I gave my mind a minute to digest the conversation with the Jenkinses. It would be difficult to prove his story about the lawyers being close to a settlement, and I had a feeling that he knew that. Neither side's attorneys would breach confidentiality to the police, let alone a PI. On the other hand, it would be equally difficult to prove his shaky alibi. While it didn't look like Jenkins had any motive beyond simple anger, there was definitely something shifty about both him and his son. Almost like they'd had that alibi rehearsed ahead of time. Something in my gut told me those two were hiding something, and I wasn't just talking about the brown lettuce.

My eyes wandered across the street as the door to The Spotted Pony swung open, and an inebriated guy in a rumpled suit stumbled out. I felt the corners of my mouth lift up into a smile as I suddenly got an idea.

CHAPTER NINE

———

At this time of day, The Spotted Pony wasn't booming with business. But it was open, and there were three men seated by the stage, getting their rocks off on the tantalizing dance moves of Pepper Le Pew. Seriously, that was her name, according to one of the men cheering her on. She even had a long white streak down the center of her black wig. And she was currently using scarves in ways I'd never imagined but made a mental note to add to my own private repertoire.

The place was quite big, but most of the tables were roped off and not used until the nighttime crowd arrived. It had been years since a smoking ban had been set in California, yet this place still smelled of it. It was faint but there. The stage was straight center from the doors, and the bar was to the left. It ran most of the length of that wall, and doors beside it led to the dressing rooms, office, and kitchen. Though, I wouldn't say The Spotted Pony wasn't known for its cuisine. It definitely wasn't the reason customers returned. But the line cooks made some righteous fries and buffalo wings ranging from mild to *caliente*. I'd never fully understand the desire to serve finger foods in a place noted for sticking money in women's clothing. But hey, I wasn't the owner and didn't set the rules.

The bartender—blond, beefy, and middle aged—was new, and I hoped he wouldn't give me a hard time. In a place like this, the staff was usually pretty protective about the dancers. They had to be. There were too many idiots who believed a woman flashing skin was eager and always willing for more, and some took it too far. But while the owner would vouch for me, and most of the nighttime staff remembered me from my server days here, to this guy I was just a stranger.

"Hey," I said and flashed my most dazzling smile. "Are Candy and Apple around?"

He gave me an up-and-down, but unlike with the greaseballs across the street, he didn't make me feel like I needed a shower. "Who's asking?"

"I'm Jamie. I used to work here." He didn't need to know I'd been undercover and not an actual server or a stripper.

He smiled and nodded while his eyes still roamed. I guessed he was imagining me in Pepper's place. "They just got here."

"Great. I'll go say hi." I took two steps toward the back doors before he flew around the bar and grabbed my arm, jerking me back.

"You can't just go back there." His grip was unbearably tight, his voice was gruff, and his breath smelled like one too many cigarettes. Not that I knew how many it took to go from pleasantly smoky to offensive. Maybe he was part of the reason the place still smelled like the stuff.

I wrenched myself free, now thoroughly annoyed, and frowned. "Ow. Don't manhandle me."

Shouldn't this jerk know not to touch women? Look at where he worked. I considered having a little chat with the owner, but I really had no business being here. While the owner had been a great help during my very first murder case a while back, it didn't mean he wouldn't mind my chatting up his employees while they were on his clock.

Just the same, this bartender had pissed me off, and I was about to protest and protest loudly, when I heard giggling. I turned to see Candy and Apple walk from the back of the house into the front. They saw me and waved. They seemed as excited to see me as I was to see them.

"See, I know them, and they know me," I said smugly to the bartender and walked to the girls.

"What are you doing here?" Candy asked. She wore denim capris, a white blouse with ruffles down the front, and the cutest red strappy heels. Her long, black hair was pulled back with the thinnest red headband. She looked more college student than exotic dancer, but maybe that was the style she was going for. Guys couldn't resist the naughty-schoolgirl image.

Apple stood in bright-yellow heels and a matching skintight halter dress. Her dark-auburn hair fell in ringlets around her shoulders. She widened her light-green eyes and smiled. "Do you need our help with something?"

The excitement on her face made me laugh. They knew me well, and their eagerness was catchy. They'd helped me with a past case when I'd needed a distraction in the form of double Ds, short skirts, and long legs. The girls were always up for an adventure, and they never asked questions. They were a private investigator's dream come true. Not that I'd ever put them in harm's way, but they had a way with men that came in handy.

"Actually, I was hoping for some information," I said. "Do either of you know Ian Jenkins? From Lite Wraps across the street?"

They each wrinkled their noses in unison and then glanced to one another. "Senior or junior?" Candy asked.

"Both? But mostly senior."

"He's a regular," Apple said. "He seems pretty skeevy, but I haven't had much interaction with him. Thankfully."

"Me neither," Candy said. "But I've heard the others girls talk about him." She nodded toward the stage. "Pepper's roommate, Sunshine, knows him better, I think."

I glanced to Pepper and her many scarves. "So I should talk to Pepper."

"Nah," said Candy. "She's new. She only started yesterday. And Sunshine's been sick, so I don't know when she'll be in again."

"I think she's preggo," Apple whispered.

Well that couldn't be good for business.

"What is it you wanted to know about him?" Candy asked.

I pursed my lips together. Honestly, I wasn't sure. "Anything you can find out."

Candy nodded. "We can ask around and let you know if any of the other girls know them better."

"That would be great. Also ask about Roger Claremont."

Apple cocked her head to the side. "The sandwich guy?"

I nodded. "Did you know him?"

"Just from his commercials," she answered. "And the news. Didn't his wife kill him?"

That's what I was going to find out.

I hit the sidewalk, and the sun blinded me for a moment. I glanced at Lite Wraps, but from the angle of the sunlight on the windows, I couldn't see inside. For all I knew, one or both of the Jenkins men were watching me. I wasn't usually paranoid, but the hair standing at attention on the back of my neck told me there was something off with those two. Was Jenkins a murderer? I wasn't sure yet. But Apple was right. The men were skeevy.

My cell rang. I cupped my hand over the top of the display to read the caller ID. It was Sam.

"Hey, what's up?" I asked.

A car sped past me, and the passenger leaned out his window and flicked his tongue at me. Clearly he thought I worked at The Spotted Pony.

"Um, I need help," Sam said. Her voice was wavering and laced with uncertainty. It put my radar immediately on high alert.

"What's wrong?" I sprinted across the street to my car.

"Julio wasn't home last night when I went to drop off our son."

I frowned. "So you didn't get the child support payment from him?"

"No, but it's more than that. Julio's never missed his day with Julio Junior. I tried calling, but there was no answer on his cell. None again this morning either."

"And I take it he's not back home?"

"No. I checked on my way to the office. I've been calling all the places where I think he may be, but no one has seen or heard from him. This isn't like him, Jamie. I'm really worried."

I slid onto my driver's seat and shoved my key into the ignition. "Where do you want to start?"

She released a breath, and I could hear the relief take over. "His house." She rattled off the address. "I'm going back there now."

"I'll meet you there."

* * *

I found an empty spot across from the address Sam had given me. Her car was parked two cars ahead of mine. We walked across the narrow street, to the small one-story house, and met on Julio's front lawn. Or what was left of a lawn. It was more a patch of dirt with several small groups of grass poking through. He obviously wasn't into his landscape. We stared at the front of the house. It wasn't anything special to look at as far as architecture. A small utilitarian box mass-produced for the booming fifties economy of Hollywood. But the windows were clear, and the light-blue siding was clean. He'd probably hosed them down recently.

"So what happened exactly?" I asked Sam as we walked to his front door.

She repeated how she'd come by yesterday, with Julio Jr., and Julio Sr. hadn't been home. "He's never missed a scheduled date with his son, and he hasn't been answering his cell," she repeated. "And I can't express just how much he loves that thing. He just bought the latest iPhone, and it's like his baby. He's never without it. It's his lifeline."

I twisted the knob on the front door, but it was locked. Of course. Why wouldn't it be? "I don't suppose you have a key?"

She shook her head, causing her dark curls to bounce around her head. "And I didn't look around last night because I didn't want to alert little Julio that something may have been wrong."

"Let's do that now." I took a left and walked past his garbage can to the back of the house.

Because of the sparsity of the front, I expected the back to be empty as well, but clearly Julio Sr. enjoyed entertaining outside. There was a round frosted plastic-topped table with a hole in the center, but there was no umbrella. Three dark-green chairs and one white plastic one surrounded the table. A light-blue cooler sat by the white chair. I lifted its lid and saw two unopened cans of Coors swimming in warm water.

On the other side of the house stood a gas grill. It was shut. Sam opened it, and other than needing a good cleaning, it was empty. The remains of whatever Julio last cooked were charred. The yard itself wasn't big. A tall wooden fence separated his property from the ones on the other three sides. Nailed onto that fence was a paper bulls-eye. Four darts were stuck to it. One had landed completely out of bounds, and the other three were dead center. Someone had great aim.

A tire hung from a tree by a rope, as evidence of Julio Sr.'s new devotion to fatherhood.

Sam tried the back door, but it was locked too. It wasn't surprising, but it was definitely annoying. Now we needed to find another way in. A way in which we wouldn't get arrested if a neighbor was watching and figured us to be hot burglars.

I thought of Derek and his arrest for peeking in Elaine's windows. This was different though. (A) I was licensed, and (B) Sam and I were concerned for Julio's safety. We weren't paranoid that he was cheating on us.

Sam pushed on a window, and it went up. She glanced at me, and I nodded my approval. Not that she needed it. She knew how to conduct herself in an investigation, even one that wasn't official. I watched her grab one of the plastic chairs and place it under the window. She stepped on it and sat on the windowsill before ducking her head into the open space and swinging her legs in.

Something crashed. Instead of following her, I replaced the chair to its original position and waited by the back door. I glanced at the surrounding houses. They were all one story as well, so I doubted anyone could see what was going on over here. I hadn't noticed any cars in the adjacent driveways. Hopefully no one was home.

The lock clicked, and Sam opened the back door. She was brushing something off the leg of her black pants. On the floor, right above the counter with the window she'd just climbed through, was a broken plate of heavily buttered toast. It looked cold and old, as if it had been sitting there for days.

I didn't comment about it. Sam was worried enough. I stepped into the kitchen and immediately noticed the pungent scent of bacon grease. Normally I'd think *oooh, bacon!* But this was heavy, as if bacon was all he'd cooked for the past month.

I glanced at the mail scattered across the kitchen table. It was mostly addressed To *Resident*, except for an unopened gas bill in Julio's name.

There was about a mug's worth of coffee sitting in the bottom of Julio's coffeepot. A skillet with rubbery-looking scrambled eggs sat on the stove. A black spatula sat beside it. Along with the toast, it all looked as if he'd left before he'd gotten to eat his breakfast.

My stomach tightened at the thought that Julio's departure hadn't been planned. While this wasn't conclusive evidence, why would someone leave home after he cooked but before he ate? It didn't make sense.

Other than these few items, his kitchen was bare. Off-white walls, cheap tile that had chipped by the refrigerator, and mini blinds in lieu of curtains. I glanced to Sam. Her lips were pressed firmly against each other. I wasn't sure what she was thinking, but it didn't take an Einstein to realize that the lines between her brows meant she was worried too.

We hit the living room next, but there wasn't much out of order other than the TV remote being on the floor by the brown leather couch. It was a bare room, much like the kitchen. An oversized armchair sat diagonally beside the couch. The coffee table and a couple of side tables made of oak filled out the room, along with a standing lamp between the armchair and couch and a smaller lamp that sat on the floor in a corner. That made no sense. Why not stick it on one of the tables? But I knew better than to try to understand how men thought. Julio didn't have much in the way of a decorator's flair. He was the typical bachelor with a giant flat-screen TV.

We stepped down a short hallway to the left of the front door. Sam hit the bathroom while I rummaged through a linen closet. Instead of just holding towels, sheets, and washcloths, there was a huge, gray plastic bin on the bottom shelf. I pulled it out and popped the top. It was full of naked-women magazines. Dang, this man loved his centerfolds. I flipped one open and held it up. The blonde model wore brown cowboy boots, a beige Stetson, and a smile. A staple had pierced her navel, and I suddenly knew her as intimately as her gynecologist.

Sam stepped into the hall. "If my son has seen those, I'm gonna kill his father."

I smirked, put the magazine back, and pushed the bin into the closet.

"Anything out of the ordinary in the bathroom?" I asked.

She shook her head. "No, just shaving cream and toothpaste gunk in the sink. He never remembered to rinse."

I paused for a moment. I contemplated squeezing her hand or offering a hug. She wasn't a touchy-feely woman, at least not with her girlfriends, and I didn't want to intrude on her space. But she looked like she wanted to cry or scream and was carefully holding it all inside.

We headed to the bedroom. It was a small room with barely enough space for a full-sized bed, a couple of end tables, and a tall armoire. The navy comforter was half on, half off the bed, and the light-blue sheets beneath were rumpled. The closet door stood open. I stepped over to it while Sam opened the armoire. The closet held a row of hung pants, shirts, and a few jackets. On the floor were a scattering of shoes, from flip-flops to work boots, dress shoes, and sneakers.

"Crap," Sam whispered.

I turned and saw that she stood at the foot of his bed. On the floor, between the bed and the window, sat a cell phone.

My stomach flipped. It was definitely out of place, and coupled with the almost eaten breakfast, my gut was now screaming that something had happened here. Something not good.

"Is that Julio's?" I asked.

She nodded, and her worried expression deepened. "He'd never leave without it."

I stepped over to her and put an arm around her shoulders. "It's okay. It may not be a big deal. Maybe he thought he smelled gas and ran out."

Of course, that didn't explain why he hadn't come back once he realized it was a false alarm.

She gave me an *are you serious?* look. Okay, so maybe it wasn't one of my better pep talks, but I was nervous and didn't always think clearly when concerned.

"Maybe we'll get some insight from his phone. His last call or text."

I waited for her to nod before I let her go and walked to the phone. I bent down to pick it up, and that was when I noticed several drops of blood on the beige carpet beside Julio's lifeline.

CHAPTER TEN

———

Sam and I took Julio's cell and headed to the office, where Sam promptly plugged it into a charger. Julio's phone was dead, but hopefully when it had enough charge to turn on, we would find some information on it that would lead to Julio's whereabouts.

I was about to head to my office, when Mrs. Claremont stepped through the frosted glass doors. While still polished looking in a cream-colored pantsuit, her expression was full of frown lines. I hadn't expected to see her smiling, but she seemed more upset than she had the other night. If that was possible. If she was innocent of Roger's murder, dealing with the police and the media on top of her grief must've been unbearable.

Without a word I led her into my office and motioned to a chair across from my desk. I shut my door and sat in my own chair. "How are you?" I asked.

"A wreck. The police let me go a few hours ago."

"That's good. It means they don't have enough evidence to charge you." Which didn't mean she wasn't guilty, I reminded myself.

She nodded. "Yeah, my lawyer found out that the ballistics report came back. The bullets from Roger's shooting were a match to a previous crime. The same gun had been used in a robbery at a convenience store, so they had to let me go. Too much—what did my attorney call it?" She wrinkled up her nose trying to recall. "'Reasonable doubt.'"

I perked up. Things were looking better for Bristol already. "That's good news. They have a murder weapon with no connection to you."

"I guess." She lowered her head and sniffled. Her body posture was different today. Her shoulders were slumped forward, her hands clasped tightly in her lap, and she leaned slightly forward so her elbows stabbed the middle of her thighs. Despite being released from police custody, she seemed to be caving in on herself.

I pushed a box of tissues to the edge of my desk so she could reach them.

She grabbed one and dabbed the corners of her eyes.

"Do they know who owns the gun?" I asked.

She nodded, her eyes coming up to meet mine. Despite the tears still brimming, I could see a flash of anger. "Heavy Cash."

Whoa. I leaned back in my seat. I guess I shouldn't have been surprised. The man looked like a walking crime scene. "Do you know if they've arrested Heavy Cash yet?"

"No, they haven't. Apparently he's in Las Vegas playing DJ at a private party at one of the big casino hotels. ADA Prince said he would fly there to question him but that ownership of the gun wasn't enough for an arrest."

My body tensed at the mention of Aiden's name. I'd pushed our disastrous date from my mind the best I could. Okay, so that was a bold-faced lie. Memories and anxious thoughts had crept into my mind every few hours, but I had managed to push them aside so I could breathe easier and focus on the numerous other things on my plate. The job came first. It always had, and it always would. Besides, this wasn't just me posing in a bikini on a tropical beach to make a living. I had employees, and they depended on their paychecks.

Bristol cleared her throat, and I figuratively shook my thoughts from my head.

She leaned closer to my desk. "I'm worried they still consider me to be a suspect. The way they kept saying the gun wasn't conclusive…" She trailed off and pursed her lips together, making a small spot of lipstick bleed over her lower lip. "I need you to keep investigating. Find something conclusive that tells them I didn't do it."

I nodded. Even though I wasn't sure that was the outcome I'd find. "Have you spoken with your husband's estate attorney yet?" I asked, watching her reaction.

She wrinkled her nose again. "I only spoke to him briefly."

"Did he mention anything about how Roger's estate would be divided?"

She shook her head. "He hasn't gotten into any details yet."

He was probably waiting to see if she'd be arrested and tried for Roger's death. I couldn't tell if she honestly knew nothing of her finances or if she was lying. With her love of Gucci and pricey hair salons, you'd think she'd want to know about that sort of thing. I would.

And speaking of Lucerne's, I wasn't sure if I should mention her faulty alibi. If she thought I believed her, and if she trusted me, she was far more likely to show her hand and let something incriminating slip. I decided to let it go for now and tried a different tactic. "Where did Roger keep his financial information?"

She blinked at me and gave me a blank look. "Huh?"

"I mean, did he keep paper files or pay bills from his computer or have his accountant take care of it..."

"Oh." She paused for a moment, as if this was the first time she'd thought of any bills. "Um, I know he had an accountant take care of all the Hoagies royalties and stuff. But I saw him pay some bills on his laptop. Like credit cards and things."

I pursed my lips. "His laptop. Which the police probably have," I mused.

But Bristol shook her head. "No, my lawyer got it back. I guess the police already made copies of all his files." She paused. "Would you like to look at it?"

"Yes, please." If the police hadn't found a smoking gun on it, chances were we wouldn't either. But if they'd been focused on mounting evidence against Bristol, there was a chance they might have overlooked some information that pointed in a different suspect's direction.

Bristol nodded and stood up. "I'll have it dropped off. You will be able to help me, won't you, Ms. Bond?"

I got to my feet and opened my office door. "We will do everything in our power." I never made promises—it wasn't wise in this business.

As she walked out, my cell rang. It was Danny.

"Hey," I said as I shut my office door and returned to my seat.

"Hey yourself," he responded. "What are you up to?"

"Now?" I glanced around my empty office. "The usual."

"Saving the world one cheating husband at a time?" he joked.

"Very funny." But I found myself laughing before I could stifle it. "You know, it's not smart to make fun of a girl with a gun."

"Point taken." I could hear the grin in his voice. "Okay, let me make it up to you. Dinner tonight." The tone was light and casual, but there was a rawness to his voice, like he was pinning something on my answer.

"Um…wow, tonight?" I stalled.

"You busy?"

"N-no," I said. "I mean, I have a few cases I'm working—"

"How about eight?" he cut in.

I took a deep breath. "Okay," I finally said. What was I so worried about? It was dinner. I'd had dinner with Danny dozens of times. Probably hundreds in the years we'd known each other. It was no big deal.

"Great. How about we meet at Spinelli's?" he asked, picking one of my favorite Italian places.

"Okay," I squeaked out again. Clearly my voice hadn't gotten the no-big-deal memo.

"See you then, Bond."

"Okay." Apparently it was the only word I knew how to speak.

I hung up and let out a long, exaggerated sigh. Instead of sitting and worrying over what the night would hold, as if I could see the future, I headed up front to Maya.

"Do you have the itinerary on the other two women on the Hendersons' potential bride list?" I asked.

Maya clicked several keys on her computer, and then the printer began to hum. "I've tracked down the second one. Penny Samson. The third, Leonora Toll, I don't have yet."

"That's fine." I could only interview one woman at a time anyway.

As the printer spit out the sheet of paper, I went to Caleigh's office and knocked on the open door.

She looked up from a file she was reading. "Hey, Boss."

"Wanna go on another bride field trip?"

"Where to this time?" She grabbed her purse and stepped around her desk.

I looked down at the printout. According to Maya's intel, at this time of day, Penny Samson was at an address near the airport. "Near LAX," I said.

"What's out there?" Caleigh asked, standing to read over my shoulder.

Maya tapped her computer monitor. "According to Google Maps, it's a bunch of buildings. They look abandoned, but according to Penny's Facebook status, she spends every afternoon there with a small group of friends."

What the heck was this woman up to?

* * *

"Maybe they're a group of real estate agents and designers who purchase and flip buildings," Caleigh said. On the ride over, she'd conjured half a dozen reasons Penny Samson spent her afternoons over in this part of town. This was Caleigh's most logical, but the "maybe she's a spy in training" had been my favorite.

I took a left turn and saw several cars parked up ahead. "I get flipping houses, but buildings? What's the appeal there?"

Caleigh shrugged. "Who knows? Maybe it's a big market. I dated a real estate agent once, and he was loaded. Kinda boring though…we only went out once."

I parked beside a black SUV, unclipped my seat belt, and opened my car door. "Well, let's go check this out."

My heels wobbled on the gravel and small rocks that were scattered in the dirt. Not exactly the place for Jimmy Choos. They weren't new, since I couldn't afford them nowadays. They were left over from my modeling days and still in mint condition. I took exceptional care of my valuables.

There were two buildings before us, with about seven feet of space between them. One was four stories tall and the other three. The exterior of the four-story one seemed still intact, but there wasn't any glass in the windows anymore. The three story was similar except there was a chunk of wall missing on its second and third floors, which allowed a view inside. Considering it was partly exposed to the elements, it was relatively clean, minus some leaves and dirt.

A blond man in black shorts and a bright-blue hoodie stood on the ground several feet away. He had his back to us. He didn't turn at the sound of our footsteps. When I stood beside him, I realized why. He had ear buds in, and his eyes were shut. He stood perfectly still, all six feet of rock hard, sinewy muscles, and he appeared to be meditating rather than jamming to music.

I tapped his arm, and his eyes shot open. I smiled as an apology for how I'd scared him.

He glanced from me to Caleigh and then took out his ear buds.

"Sorry if I startled you," I said.

"No, it's fine. I was concentrating, and I tend to tune the world out." His accent was richly Australian, which made Caleigh stand up a little straighter beside me.

"You're from down under?" she asked with sheer delight in her eyes.

He bowed his head slightly. "Yes, ma'am."

Caleigh's smile turned into a frown. "'Ma'am?' How old do you think I am?"

That was never a safe question. It was like asking a man if he liked her outfit. Some things should never be asked.

I stepped forward. "Um, do you know Penny Samson? I was told I could find her here."

"Oh sure, mate. She's the purple one. Purple for Penny."

I glanced to Caleigh and raised an eyebrow. She looked as confused as I was. "Excuse me?"

He stuffed his ear buds into his pocket and switched off the iPod he had clipped to his jacket. "Some of us have difficulty remembering names, so we decided to nickname ourselves." He tugged at his hoodie. "I'm Blue Ben."

Caleigh and I said "Oh" in unison. Penny must've been wearing purple.

I glanced around but didn't see her or anyone else. "Where is she?"

"Warming up with everyone else." He glanced at his watch. "They'll be starting soon. You'll have to wait until they're done to talk to her. I need to be getting up there myself. Have a good day."

Warming up for what and where?

I didn't get a chance to actually ask though before he jogged off toward the three-story building. He disappeared out of view, and then I heard voices.

"I'm so confused," Caleigh said.

I looked up and caught a spot of yellow on the third floor. "What is that?" I said.

Caleigh and I moved back several feet, and a group of people, in varying colored tops, came into view. That was when I saw Purple Penny. I pointed to her location, but before Caleigh commented, Penny started running. And running. When she got close to the edge of the building, I assumed she'd take a sharp turn and run back the way she came. But instead, she turned onto the outside ledge of the building.

Caleigh gasped.

Whoa, what was Penny doing?

The ledge couldn't have been more than a foot wide. It went around the exterior of the building on all three floors, but parts of it had crumbled away in sections. Penny kept running, and when she reached a spot with no ledge, she jumped over it. Then she turned the corner and disappeared out of sight.

I held my breath, placed a hand on my chest, and prayed we wouldn't be calling 9-1-1.

The rest of her group took off running too—some stayed inside the building and others ran along the ledge as well. When Purple Penny came back into view, she was on the interior of the second floor. Suddenly footsteps sounded behind me.

We spun to see a man who appeared to be in his early thirties, in a red T-shirt and navy shorts, approaching. He had long, light-brown hair tied into a low ponytail. "I'm late," he said with a smile.

I held out my hand. "Hi, I'm Jamie."

He shook mine and Caleigh's hands. "I'm Roy."

Red Roy? Of course he was.

"Are you joining our group?" he asked.

I laughed. "No, we were passing by and saw all of this. What does your group do? Are you training for something?"

"No, this is just for fun."

"Fun?" Caleigh asked. "You think nearly dying is a sport?"

Red Roy chuckled. "It can be dangerous, but that's all the fun. This is called free running, but I also do parkour."

"I've heard that word before, but I don't know what it is," I said.

"It's similar to this, but it's basically getting around as quickly and efficiently as possible. So it involves jumping over a flight of stairs rather than walking down it. Vaulting over a wall rather than climbing. Stuff like that."

"Why?" Caleigh asked.

"It's fun." He smiled again.

If he said so. I preferred my feet firmly on the ground.

"And these others do parkour as well?" I asked.

He nodded. "A few of them."

"What about the one in purple? She seems pretty fast." I pointed even though Penny had disappeared again.

Red Roy squinted, and when Penny came into view back on the third floor, he grinned. "Penny? No, she doesn't. She's a spitfire though. She's in her fifties yet can outrun all of the younger girls and half the guys. She used to be a track star in high school and college, and she runs in every marathon within driving distance." He chuckled.

"What's so funny?" Caleigh asked.

"Penny once told me that everyone thought she was a little old lady who loved to bake and knit but that she hated sitting still."

Well, she'd definitely keep Mr. Henderson on his toes.

CHAPTER ELEVEN

We hung around the abandoned building long enough to catch a few minutes with Penny. She was just like Red Roy had said—a spitfire. I didn't know what Mrs. Henderson saw in Penny Samson when they'd first met, but the woman Caleigh and I spoke with swore like a sailor and didn't stand still. Also like Red Roy had said, she jogged in place the whole three minutes we got her alone. By the time she had to go, I was exhausted. In my humble opinion, I couldn't see her and Mr. Henderson together.

As Caleigh and I drove back to the office, my cell rang. Caleigh turned it on to speakerphone.

"Jamie? It's Apple," said a strong Valley Girl accent.

Excitement rushed through me. She had to have good news. She wouldn't have bothered calling if she had nothing. I tried to not sound like a kid eagerly awaiting Halloween and a night full of candy-induced stomachaches. "Hey, did you find out anything?"

"Yep. Turns out Sunshine knows something about the wrap guy."

I glanced to Caleigh. "Is she at the club now?"

"Yep. She goes on stage in an hour."

I jerked the wheel and made a U-turn right in the middle of midday traffic. Thank goodness there were no cars nor cops in the immediate area. Caleigh giggled, and I wasn't sure if it was due to the excitement of getting a lead or swinging through the street.

"We're on our way," I shouted while nearly missing the curb.

The universe must've been smiling down on us, because we didn't hit traffic the entire way. I parked in The Spotted Pony parking lot, shooting only a cursory glance at Lite Wraps as we hurried inside.

This time the new bartender gave me a nod of recognition. I felt so honored.

The stage was empty, as were all the tables except one. An older man with a potbelly was slumped in his chair, his chin resting on his chest. Maybe he was napping until the next show. A glass of amber-colored liquor sat on the table in front of him. The bartender must not have minded the man being half asleep as long as he was a paying customer, but I didn't doubt that the owner would mind, if he knew.

Candy stood near the entrance to the back of the club and waved us over to the side of the stage.

Apple and another dancer hovered beside Candy. Today, Candy and Apple were dressed in matching pink silk robes—they must've been getting ready to go on stage soon. The other woman looked vaguely familiar. I wasn't accustomed to hanging out in The Spotted Pony, but I'd been by enough times to speak with Candy and Apple that some of the newer dancers' faces had made an impression. And this woman—brunette, five ten, dressed in a white boa, white cowboy boots, and matching white miniskirt and bikini top with sparkling rhinestones—was hard to miss. Especially with the white rhinestone-studded Stetson in her hand. If the rumors were correct and she was pregnant, she definitely wasn't showing. Her belly looked tight enough to bounce a quarter off of it.

"This is Sunshine," Candy said. "She knows the wrap guy."

"Hi, I'm Jamie. What do you know about Mr. Jenkins?"

The woman blinked and looked to Apple. She had a deer-in-headlights expression on her face.

Apple nodded and nudged her with her elbow. "It's okay. Jamie's good people. You can trust her."

Sunshine cleared her throat gently and said, "He was here the day the Hoagies guy was killed."

"Are you sure?" Caleigh asked.

Sunshine smirked. "Absolutely. I was giving him a private lap dance, and he let it slip that he not only knew the famous Hoagies guy, Roger Claremont, but he was going to see him later that day."

Very interesting.

"How do you know it was the day Roger Claremont was killed?" I asked.

"That night, when I got off work, I heard about the murder on the car radio. It stuck with me because the wrap guy had just said his name."

Caleigh looked to me with a *gotcha* smile.

I wasn't ready to take out the Dom Pérignon just yet. While I wanted to believe we'd uncovered the real killer, I wasn't sure what Jenkins's motive would be. He needed Roger alive to get any money he'd be awarded from the court case. But I'd definitely felt like he was hiding something. Maybe the slimeball had another reason to want Roger dead. I wondered if that meant Slimeball Jr. was lying about Senior's alibi.

We started to head back to the agency, and my stomach grumbled. That was definitely a cry for help, so I drove to the nearest Hoagies—the one that Roger used to eat at. Caleigh's eyes lit up as I parked. "I hope you don't mind," I said. "I could use a bite."

"Not at all. Ever since I started eating Hoagies, I feel so much better already."

"Do you? I haven't noticed any difference." I pulled open the heavy glass door.

Caleigh lowered her voice as we stepped inside. "Maybe that's 'cause you're also trying to gain world peace with your attitude at the same time. I firmly believe in making one life change at a time."

She had a point, but it wasn't as if there was much heavy lifting involved in eating sandwiches. You ate them, and if they made you feel better, that was their job.

"So you feel better how?" I asked and looked up to the menu. I didn't know why I bothered reading it though, since I already knew I wanted the Roger sub.

"Like mentally. I just know I'm doing the right thing for my body."

Kinda like Penny Samson but less dangerous.

We each ordered the same as last time we shared a Hoagies lunch, and took the table by the front window. It wasn't long before we were moaning and sighing with our mouths full. When we reached the midway point of our subs, we each took a deep breath and sipped our sodas. Inhaling Hoagies sandwiches for lunch was becoming our thing, for Caleigh and me. Thank goodness they were diet food.

"So what do we think about Jenkins?" Caleigh asked.

"I think I'd like to know why he told Sunshine he was seeing Roger the day he was killed," I said, wiping my mouth with my napkin.

"You think he really was?" she asked. "I mean, he could have just been trying to impress her."

I nodded. Unfortunately, that seemed like exactly the kind of thing he'd do. "Maybe," I agreed. "But he still lied about being at his store all day."

"I hate to point this out," Caleigh said, "but lots of guys lie about being at strip joints."

I sighed. "I know. I know. Just because he's a slimeball doesn't mean he's a murderer."

"Should we go talk to him? Like, maybe we could do a Lite Wraps dinner?"

I shook my head. "I didn't get a very cooperative vibe from him, so I doubt he'll break down and confess." And oh…there was nothing on earth that would make me eat that stuff. "Besides, I've, uh, got plans tonight."

"Oooo…what kind of plans?" Caleigh asked, sitting up straighter in her seat. "Like a date?"

I bit my lip. "Kinda."

"With Aiden?"

I cleared my throat. "No. Danny." A bite of sandwich lodged in my throat. I reached for my soda. When I glanced up, Caleigh was chewing and giving me the stink eye. "What?" I asked.

"You don't look thrilled."

I shrugged, not sure how to put my feelings into words and not sure if I wanted to. "What about you? How's your love life?"

She grinned. "Fine, we'll change the subject, and my love life is currently pitiful. Why is it that every guy either ends up having some weird foot fetish or still living at home, having Mommy make his bed?"

"Maybe they're just saving money. The economy is hard."

She shook her head. "Or maybe they just can't function without a woman taking care of them. That may have sounded great when I was twenty, but now at the ripe old age of"—she paused—"a *little* older than twenty, I want an independent man. Is that too much to ask for?"

I smiled. "Not at all." I rolled up my sandwich wrapper into a ball and sipped on the last of my drink.

Caleigh leaned back in her seat and tugged on the waistband of her black pants. "I don't understand why these feel tighter. I've been eating all this diet food." She pointed to her own empty wrapper.

"Maybe they just shrunk in the dryer," I said.

"Yeah, that's probably it."

We threw away our trash and went out to the car.

When we walked into the agency, Maya was tapping away on the keyboard of a laptop I didn't recognize.

"Is that Roger's?" I asked.

Maya nodded. "A messenger just delivered it," she said without looking up. Whatever she was working on, she was in the zone, and I knew better than to interrupt.

Sam sat on one of the reception-area chairs and fiddled with Julio's phone. The charger was still stuck into the end of the phone in one direction and in the wall in the other, which suggested Sam had gotten tired of waiting for a full charge before taking a peek.

Caleigh filled the others in on our findings. "We found out that the wrap guy, Jenkins, probably lied about his alibi. And that he said he was going to meet Roger the day he was killed."

"At least according to Sunshine at The Spotted Pony," I added.

Maya and Sam didn't respond. They didn't even twitch. It was as if they hadn't heard us, too preoccupied with their toys.

Caleigh shrugged and headed to the restroom. "I have to tinkle."

"So how about those Dodgers?" I asked, seeing what it would take to get a reaction from Sam and Maya. Anyone who knew me knew I had zero interest in sports. Neither of them budged.

I tried again. "I saw a UFO on the drive over. The aircraft landed right in the middle of the street, and six miniature aliens hopped out."

Nothing.

"They said they want to drain our planet of water, and considering California's been in a drought since the beginning of time, I thought it was kinda funny they'd land here."

Not a blip.

"And then after making the earth a dry oasis, they want to have sex with us."

Sam glanced up. "Huh?"

I grinned. She, evidently, needed to get some.

"Yes!" Maya shouted and beamed an *I'm amazing and you'll want to give me a raise* smile.

"Whatcha got?" I stepped closer to her desk.

This made her smile even more. "Roger loaned a lot of money to Heavy Cash."

"Really?" My palms grew itchy, and my Charlie's Angels radar beeped. "How much?"

"Fifty grand."

Whoa. That was a hefty loan. That must've been some friendship. "Any idea what Heavy needed that kind of money for?"

"According to this, it looks like it was to finance his latest single and music video," Maya said. "The loan is past due and not repaid."

I walked around her desk and stared at the laptop's monitor. "Where are you getting this from? Are all of Roger's financials on there?"

"No. I didn't find anything about his insurance or bank statements, and I haven't figured out how to hack into his bank account. I'm sure Caleigh can."

Caleigh could hack into the Pentagon. I felt an overwhelming surge of pride for my girls.

Maya tapped the screen. "I got the loan details from Roger's email. See?" She pointed to the middle of her screen. "It refers to the loan, 'Money Fo' My Hos.'"

From the corner of my eye, I saw Sam's head snap up. "Wait. What did you say?"

Maya repeated the ridiculous and offensive title.

Sam rushed over and shoved Julio's phone in our faces. "There's a reference to 'Money Fo' My Hos' on his phone." A slight blush crawled up her neck. "I skimmed over it, thinking Julio was just lonely and paying for it these days."

I smiled on the inside but kept my professional expression on. "Show me."

Sam flipped through the phone until she found it and handed the cell over.

The restroom door squeaked open, and Caleigh walked out.

On the cell, there was a text sent to Julio's phone. But there was no caller information other than a number. "Where is the 702 area code?" I asked.

Caleigh stepped over to us. "That's Las Vegas."

That Charlie's Angels radar was beeping loudly again.

"That's interesting, considering Heavy Cash is in Vegas right now," I said.

The girls stared at me.

"What does this mean?" Maya asked.

I smiled. "It means we're going on a Vegas road trip."

* * *

The four of us agreed to go home, pack, and meet back at the office in an hour. We were going to carpool in the agency's largest SUV. I wasn't crazy about driving the beast, since it felt like steering Derek's houseboat compared to my Roadster, but we wouldn't all fit comfortably in any of our cars.

I was lucky enough to miss traffic on the way home, though as soon as I got there, I stared at my empty luggage, not certain what to pack. I expected we'd only be there for the night, two at the most, but I wasn't sure what we'd get into. So I decided to go with something casual—white capris, a light-blue tank, and sandals—and something business casual—a black skirt and blouse—and a black cocktail dress and heels 'cause a little black dress worked for any occasion. I added in a pair of jeans, shorts, and T-shirt to sleep in, undergarments, and a white cardigan in case it got chilly at night. At the last second, I reached for something slinky too—a royal blue, midthigh halter dress with a V-neckline so deep I had to tape my boobs in place, and a side slit just high enough to not look hoochie. Oh, who was I kidding? It was 100 percent hoochville. But we *were* going to Vegas.

I tossed an extra pair of strappy sandals into my luggage, just in case, and headed to the bathroom to gather my toiletries. The last time I'd been in Vegas was years ago. It was before I'd taken over the Bond Agency. Way before I'd met Aiden and before Derek had become a permanent part of my daily landscape.

Sam and I had snuck away from the modeling for a weekend of sin. While it was supposed to have been two days of gambling and dancing, it ended up being two days of us getting drunk and whining about our careers. Deline Modeling Agency had been weaning Sam out of jobs because she had a kid and five extra pounds of post-pregnancy weight. And it had been evident I was getting older. If the calendar and the number of candles on my birthday cakes hadn't told me, Deline certainly had by passing me over for jobs in favor of their younger girls.

I zipped shut my cosmetic case and placed it beside the sandals. This time would be different though. There would be no need for whining. We had secure jobs. And there'd be no headaches or hangovers. We were going to find a killer.

* * *

I got back to the office, snagged the keys to the SUV, and locked up before walking to the back of the parking lot. I opened the hatch and pushed my luggage inside as Sam and Caleigh pulled in. Sam grabbed an oversized purple camo tote bag from her backseat, and Caleigh lifted a large rectangular piece of luggage with wheels out of her trunk.

"You know we won't be gone for a week, right, Caleigh?" I asked as she trotted over, dragging her luggage behind her.

She batted her baby blues. "You never know what kind of situation you'll be in and what you may need. Better to be prepared than not."

I couldn't argue with her logic.

After piling their things in and leaving space for Maya's bag, which hopefully wouldn't be as big as Caleigh's, I asked Sam about Julio.

"He's fine. A neighbor's watching him. He loves staying with Craig—the boy who lives next door to us. They are fast friends, and Craig's mother is strict. Not as bad as my military father but enough that I have peace of mind when Julio's over there." She smiled, but it didn't reach her eyes.

"But you're worried."

She shook her head and swallowed. "Not about him. About Julio Senior. What's going on with him? He's never acted this way before. Yeah, he sucked as a boyfriend, but he's been a good father lately."

Caleigh laid her head on Sam's shoulder and gave her a quick squeeze. "It'll work out. You'll see. And if you need someone to hold him down while you kick the crap out of him, I'm your girl."

That made Sam smile. A genuine one this time.

Caleigh widened her eyes. "I even have handcuffs, if we need them."

Sam and I exchanged glances. I didn't bother asking if they were lined in pink fur.

Maya's car pulled into the lot, and she parked on the other side of my Roadster.

My stomach knotted when three car doors opened simultaneously. Maya had either suddenly become a magician or she wasn't alone. That's when I saw her passengers. Her mother, Charley, and Elaine.

Seriously?

Maya tugged her large backpack from her backseat and sprinted over. "I'm so sorry. I couldn't say no."

"What happened?" Caleigh asked.

Maya glanced over her shoulder before continuing, probably making sure they weren't in earshot. "When I got home, Mom and Elaine were there. I tried rushing them out, but they lingered and kept talking."

Elaine and Charley slammed their doors shut and walked toward us.

Maya sped up her words, making it almost impossible to understand the line of gibberish. "They pushed me for info. They knew I was hiding something, and I finally caved in and told them your plans. Then they insisted on coming. I had to stop at Mom's and then Elaine's so they could pack. The most surprising part is they each did it in ten minutes flat."

Caleigh gasped.

That was impressive.

Maya frowned. "I'm so sorry."

I shook my head. "It's okay. It's not a big deal. The more the merrier."

Elaine and Charley heard that last part and smiled and "ooohed" in relief.

I wasn't sure I believed my words. This could put a major crimp in our plans. On the plus side, however, at least I'd be able to keep my eye on Elaine.

CHAPTER TWELVE

————

It was dark out by the time we arrived in Sin City. Even though I'd been there before, I smiled in awe at the bright lights and general feeling of excitement in the air. There were people and cars everywhere. Cheers echoed from a car beside us, and a few others honked their horns in rhythmic fashion. People on the sidewalks turned and waved—it was like one giant block party.

Charley "oohed" from the third row of seats. "This is so exciting. I've never been here before."

Elaine gasped. "Why on earth not? We live so close."

She shrugged. "My husband and I weren't the gambling type. What other reason is there to come here?" Charley asked.

She was definitely a Vegas virgin. Gambling may have been the highlight, but there was more than just that to this town. There were shows and plenty to see, like the Shark Tank at Golden Nugget and the Mob Museum, one of my personal faves. And there were tons of great places to eat and sightsee. Vegas had so much more than the casinos and quickie weddings of the past.

We headed straight for our hotel, The Elite, one of the new mega high-rises just off the strip, and checked in. Caleigh had managed to reserve us a suite while we'd traveled. She'd also managed to make sure it was in the same hotel where Heavy Cash happened to be staying. How she'd gotten that info, I wasn't sure. And I wasn't sure I wanted to know. There was the teeny-tiniest chance it wasn't 100 percent legal.

A bellhop secured our luggage on a cart and showed us to the fifth floor. He swiped a key card, and the red light turned green. Then he opened the door and waited for us to enter. We stepped into a living area with a minibar, television, seating for at least seven, and a desk. There were open doors on each side of the space, and they led to the bedrooms, which each held two double beds.

Charley was totally starstruck. She stepped out onto the balcony with Elaine at her heels. The rest of us acted as if we'd never left the job. We tossed our luggage into our rooms—Caleigh and Maya took the one to the left, and Sam and I the one to the right. Sam and Maya used the glass coffee table to set up Roger's laptop alongside mine as a mini command center. Caleigh put on her Bluetooth headset and began calling around for Heavy Cash's current whereabouts. By the time Charley and Elaine stepped back into the room, it looked like PI headquarters.

"What do the two of you plan on doing tonight?" I asked. "It's probably too late to get tickets to a show, but…"

They both shook their heads. "No. We didn't tag along to take in the sights," Charley said.

I raised my eyebrows, suddenly feeling nervous about their expectations. "You didn't? But this is your first time here."

Charley waved away my words. "I can come back."

"No. We came here to be a part of the investigation," Elaine said.

My nervousness rose. "You did?"

They nodded in unison.

"You know you can't actually go out and do much. I can't allow you to do anything risky or illegal."

They smiled to one another with big grins. "We don't want danger," Elaine said.

"Just excitement," Charley added.

I chuckled at their jovial expressions. How could I deny them a little adventure? We'd find some way for them to help out without putting them at risk.

"Got it," Caleigh shouted and removed her headset. "The party Heavy Cash is DJ-ing at? It's a private event being held downstairs at the hotel's Palm Bay pool. And it's just gotten started."

"Perfect," I told her.

She beamed.

"Wait, did you say it's a private party?" Charley said.

Since I'd never met a party I couldn't crash, that would be a piece of cake. "No problem. We just have to look stunning enough to be VIP arm-candy material."

Charley widened her eyes. "All of us?"

Everyone stared at me, waiting for my answer. It was obvious Charley and Elaine wanted to tag along. This could be the one chance to include them. How dangerous could a party be?

"Any chance either of you brought something slinky to wear?"

Elaine cackled and ran to her luggage. I had no doubts she'd pull out something…interesting. Charley, on the other hand, looked a bit troubled. She went to her bag and began rummaging. The rest of us split up, and somehow the six of us managed to get ready in two bathrooms in record time.

I chose the black cocktail dress for this occasion. It was sexy yet still tasteful. When I emerged from the bedroom, Caleigh and Sam were ready and waiting. Caleigh wore a red strapless minidress, and Sam had on camo short shorts and a midriff black halter top. Each rocked three-inch heels. They looked to me and shook their heads.

"What?"

"We're not going to have a martini at the bar," Sam said.

"Or appetizers served on silver trays with white doilies," said Caleigh. "This is a private pool party, and Heavy Cash will be there. I imagine there will be Jell-O shots, club music, and a lot of exposed skin."

The others joined us at that moment. Maya wore a shimmery gold tank top and a black miniskirt with fringe. Elaine had changed into a silver sleeveless tunic with white shorts, and even Charley had the right vibe in a light-blue slip dress.

I glanced back down at my outfit and suddenly felt like I was going to a funeral compared to them, so I turned and headed back to my room. "Fine, but I'm gonna need some tape."

* * *

We took the elevator down to the Palm Bay pool, which had been closed off to the regular guests for the evening. Someone had dished out big money to do this. A couple of tall, big men, dressed all in black, stood guard at the curtained double doors.

Caleigh, Sam, and I stood side by side and strode over in true Charlie's Angels style. Maya, Charley, and Elaine brought up the rear.

Caleigh started to step forward, probably to greet them with her effervescent nature. I laid a hand on her arm and silenced her. If the girls had been right about the party— and I wasn't standing here about to flash two strangers for nothing—then bubbly was not going to get us in the door.

I looked to Sam and gave a soft nod.

She stepped forward and laid out her best street-tough attitude. "Yo, we're here fo' the party. You gonna move or what?"

The guy to the right said, "I need to see your invitation."

Of course he did.

I stepped to Sam's side. "We don't have one. Heavy Cash told us to come along if we were in town, and look at that—we're in town."

The big guys seemed less than impressed.

"No invitation? No entry," the first guy said.

Sam narrowed her eyes at him. "You mean to tell me you goin' against Heavy's wishes?"

"Call Heavy. Have him put you on the list, and I will obey his wishes." I swear I saw the guy smirk as he said the last word.

I was about to give up and see if there was a wall we could scale somewhere, when Caleigh cleared her throat beside me.

"Um, excuse me, boys," she said, her southern accent coming out in full sugary force.

Both beefy heads turned her way.

"Hi." She gave them a little one-finger wave. "Surely you recognize me, right?"

Both gave her blank stares, and the first guy shook his head. "No, ma'am."

Caleigh gasped. "Oh, I am insulted. It's me...Caleigh Presley!"

More blank stares.

She rolled her eyes and giggled. "Well, I guess I don't bear *that* much resemblance to my cousin, but I would have thought ya'll would recognize Elvis's kin."

It was as if she'd said the secret Vegas password. Both men stood up a bit straighter, and the chatty one's voice took on an apologetic tone. "Uh, I'm sorry, Miss Presley. Of course."

"That's all right, sugar," Caleigh crooned, running one finger down his lapel. "We all make mistakes from time to time. I won't tell Priscilla." She gave him a wink, and he moved aside, easily letting her saunter into the party.

If I were a cartoon, I'm pretty sure my jaw would have dropped to the floor.

Caleigh paused, turned her baby blues over her shoulder, and flicked a finger toward us. "Oh, they're with me, boys."

"Yes, Miss Presley," the guy said, nodding us through the curtain.

I made a mental note to give Caleigh a raise as we quickly skittered through the doorway before they changed their minds.

As soon as we stepped through, I stopped for a moment and took a deep breath. Finding Heavy Cash wasn't going to be as easy as I thought. The poolside was mobbed. Scantily clad bodies lay both in and out of the clean blue water, gyrating to music loud enough to shatter eardrums.

There were two rectangular-shaped pools side by side, with a strip of concrete separating them. Along that strip were six squares of concrete that were set into the sides of the pools, three to each one. And on each square was a double-size canopy bed for people who wanted to rest, and possibly nap, poolside. Now there were young bodies lying, talking, dancing, and one couple heavily making out on them.

To the opposite sides of the pools were rows and rows of dark-brown lounge chairs. Most of them were empty. The sun had already gone down, and those who were near the chairs were dancing and drinking, not sitting. At the far back, behind the pools, stood a microphone stand, musical equipment, and a DJ bobbing his head to the beats of the music.

To our left was a large wraparound wooden bar— also mobbed. And set into the side of the hotel itself was a lounge area with sofas and cushioned chairs. When a few people parted, I noticed doors, which must've led to restrooms.

This reminded me of so many parties I'd been to during my modeling days, back when a pounding bass worked its way through my bones and made me move my body. Now, it just left me wanting to leave and enjoy a drink in a quiet bar, or better yet, a nice soak in a quiet bathtub.

When the heck did I become old?

It didn't matter. Tonight wasn't social, and I could pretend with the best of them. I turned to the girls. "Everyone mingle, and keep your eyes out for Heavy. If you spot him, call me. I want to talk to him myself."

Five heads nodded. I smiled at Charley and Elaine, then walked up the center strip between the pools, gazing at each face I passed. They laughed and talked, bodies rubbed against one another, and by the time I reached the top or end, depending how you looked at it, of the pools, I felt like a voyeur. I worked my way around the sofas and then to the lounge chairs along the sides.

A lot of heads turned my way. Some men and women smiled in that flirty way that suggested I stop and chat with them. I just nodded and kept going.

Was it possible Caleigh had gotten Heavy's whereabouts wrong? Maybe he was at a different poolside party at a different hotel. There were, after all, many in town.

On my way to the alcove a man in swim trunks grabbed my hand, shook his hips to the music, and twirled me into a spin. Then he gyrated more, and if I wasn't on a mission, I would've found it funny. He had long, curly hair, tanned skin, small round vintage sunglasses that reminded me of John Lennon, and his Speedo was neon lime green. The guy was runway model slender, and all the components together were an odd combination.

I twirled again, giggled, and went on my way. When I glanced back, he had grabbed another woman's hand, but she wasn't nearly as accommodating. She yanked away with a scowl on her face and returned to her group of scoffing girlfriends. The dude barely seemed to notice. He just kept on swinging his hips and dancing.

As I stepped into the alcove, I immediately noticed a guy in a sleek navy suit with a sheen that caught the strobing lights like a wearable disco ball. Heavy Cash's manager, Johnson. Yes! This meant Caleigh hadn't gotten it wrong, and Heavy was definitely close by. Before I could approach Johnson though, my cell buzzed in my hand. That was what happened when your dress was too tight and short and you forgot to pack a small evening purse. You had to hold your phone.

I glanced down. It was a text from Derek.
How's Elaine?

I looked up and to my right. Elaine was just outside the alcove toward the bar, twerking with some hot, young guy. At least I believed that was her idea of twerking. The guy seemed somewhat respectful considering how close their bodies were, but at least he wasn't groping her. There was a look of pure joy on her face, and she looked relaxed and like she was having a great time. Something was so mesmerizing in the way she threw her hair around, so youthful. Shoot, Elaine acted younger than I did.

I looked back to my phone and typed in: *Elaine's having a quiet night in.*

Derek didn't need to know the truth.

Heavy Cash's manager headed toward me, and I realized Heavy was right behind him. This was perfect. But before they got to my exact spot, they veered off and headed out to the pool.

I followed as quickly as I could, but there were so many people. I pushed past a couple of bodies. With my head titled up, looking over heads to keep my gaze on Heavy, I didn't notice the little person until I nearly mowed him down.

"Watch it, honey. Not everyone is a giraffe." He came up to my navel and was dressed in bright-blue swimming trunks.

"Oh my God. I'm so sorry."

He pushed a lock of black hair behind his ear. "Eh, I get it all the time in crowds. Nice tatas." He pointed to my chest and walked off.

I raised a hand to my cleavage, suddenly feeling more exposed.

"Thank y'all for coming tonight," Heavy's voice echoed over the speakers. I spotted him at the mic. His manager stood nearby. "How's everyone doing?" Heavy asked.

The crowd cheered. I caught Charley and Maya on the other side of the pools. Charley clapped enthusiastically. She even softly jumped on the balls of her feet a couple of times.

"Are you ready to hear a special sneak peek of my new song?"

Screams and cheers surrounded me. So this was why he was here tonight? It was a singing gig.

The music returned, but the beat changed from electronica to heavy bass. He began rapping, and the crowd went nuts. Everyone cheered and clapped for a few seconds, and then some began dancing while others rocked to the beat.

I wasn't going to get a chance to speak to him anytime soon, so I moved my gaze back to the guy in the shiny suit beside him. His manager was free.

I managed to catch up with Johnson, doing only minimal damage to partiers' toes. "Hey," I screamed. "This is great."

He turned and gave me a long stare, probably trying to figure out where he'd seen me before, and then he nodded and turned his attention back to his client.

I was a bit offended. Despite living a life undercover half the time, no one usually forgot my face.

"What? You don't remember me?" I asked.

He glanced at me again. This time he checked out my cleavage before turning his eyes back to me again. "Now's not a good time."

Ah-ha. So he did recognize me. Good.

"I can wait if you want. Wait until Heavy's done and all of his adoring fans circle him. And then I can bring up his relationship with a dead man and ask him about the fifty-thousand-dollar loan."

Johnson glared at me from the corner of his eye.

I raised a challenging eyebrow his way. A glare wasn't going to deter me. He'd have to do better than that.

"Okay, fine. It wasn't that big a deal," Johnson said, finally turning to face me. His voice was raised above the music, but he leaned in, his eyes shifting to both sides as if trying to keep the conversation as private as possible. "The loan was between two friends. And Roger knew Heavy was good for the money. Look at him."

I did, watching Heavy bob and weave to his lyrics. His moves were small and limited, possibly due to his size, and his stamina didn't seem to be too great either.

"Sure, he hasn't had a number one hit in a while, but with what great shape he was getting into thanks to Roger's diet, he's poised for a comeback."

Heavy did a spin, and the crowd went nuts. Johnson cheered. But I could see sweat cover Heavy's forehead, and he looked tired. It didn't seem like there were many number one singles left in him. It looked like he needed a nap.

"What about Julio Gonzalez?" I asked.

Johnson shrugged and genuinely looked unaffected. "Never heard of him."

"Someone in Vegas called his cell."

"Goody for him."

"And he's missing now."

Johnson didn't move. No shrug. No comeback. Not even a blink. Either he really had no idea who I was talking about, or he was playing his poker face hard core.

"Does Heavy know Julio?"

"No," Johnson answered quickly. Almost too quickly.

"Maybe I'll just wait around and ask him," I threatened.

Johnson moved his shiny shoulders up and down again. "Suit yourself. But Heavy's got three more songs to do. And he might be kinda outta breath by then."

I looked up. Heavy looked like he was out of breath now. I hoped whoever had hired him for this party had paid by the minute.

I stepped away, none the wiser for our conversation but grateful that Johnson at least hadn't called on the door goons to make me leave. Spotting Caleigh chatting up some guy who was all teeth, I pointed toward the exit, hoping she'd get my drift that I wanted to get the heck out of here. While Johnson hadn't given me much to go on, I had a feeling that Heavy would follow his manager's lead. There was little point in sticking around to question him, especially with Johnson in tow.

Caleigh nodded and walked away from the guy while he was still talking. She obviously wasn't having the time of her life either. As she wrangled Maya and Charley, who then headed over to Sam and Elaine, I stepped farther back toward the exit. The quicker I was out of here, the better.

Someone stepped up behind me, and my super Spidey senses kicked in. Ten years ago I would've been dirty dancing with the rest of the crowd, but this was no longer my scene, and if some jerkwad thought he'd get a cheap thrill by putting his hands on me, I'd…

I spun around, ready to punch the dude in his throat. One quick jab usually did the trick. But when I got millimeters from his larynx, I froze.

I recognized the jerkwad copping the feel.

ADA Aiden Prince.

CHAPTER THIRTEEN

———

"Wow," he shouted. "Weapons down."

I blinked several times. My heart rate raced up and down from the shock of seeing him and almost injuring him. I lowered my arm, thinking of the last time I'd decked him. It was back when we'd first met and he and the state of California had believed I murdered a judge. "What are you doing here?" I asked.

"What are *you* doing here?" he countered, his tone flat, eyes assessing. He was in full-on prosecutor mode tonight.

"I asked you first." Yeah, it was a childish thing to say, but I didn't care. My head was starting to pound, I hadn't eaten anything since that delicious Hoagie earlier, and my feet hurt from these shoes. Plus, I think the tape was drying out, and soon enough I'd have to hold the front of my dress together with both hands.

"I'm here on official business." His voice held an edge to it.

I hated to point out that I was too. Technically, the district attorney's office had more pull than a private investigator, but my work here was just as important. At least to me. And Bristol Claremont.

"And you?" he asked.

I shrugged. "I'm here with Elvis's cousin."

Aiden's eyes narrowed. "Jamie…"

"What?" I blinked innocently at him.

His jaw clenched, his eyes going from me to Heavy up on the makeshift stage.

"You talk to Heavy?" he asked.

I shook my head. "Nope. Not a word." Which was the total truth. "Scout's honor." I held up three fingers.

He took in a deep breath and looked as though he was mentally counting to ten to find some semblance of Zen. I could have told him that didn't work.

"This isn't a game, Jamie," he finally ground out.

"Nope. It's a party." I flashed him a big cheesy grin. One he did not return. "You need to leave."

Clearly he was pissed that I was butting my head into his "official" investigation. I wanted to understand, and I might have even felt the same way if our roles had been reversed. But that didn't mean I was going to roll over and let him push me out of my own investigation.

I took as wide of a stance as I could in my tight dress. "Or what?" I challenged.

Aiden made a sound that was half sigh and half growl. Then he grabbed me by the wrist and yanked me toward him. "Come on," he ground out.

I started to resist, but before I knew it, he'd pulled me toward the alcove, placing a hand at my hip and pressing my body against his.

"W-what are you doing?" I asked, but while the words were audibly clear in my mind, they came out all breathy. I really needed to have a stern talk with my libido. It was taking on a mind of its own lately.

Aiden wore navy trousers and a white button-down shirt, all very ADA-like. But he'd removed his jacket and tie, and the top two buttons of his shirt were undone, revealing a small section of his tanned chest. The scent of his musky cologne circled around my head, intoxicating me.

He swayed his hips, and my body followed. We moved to the beat of the music in perfect rhythm. Anyone looking on might've thought we danced like this all the time, with how in sync we moved. It all happened on some gut level. I tried to not pay attention to it, in fear that I'd accidentally step out of beat and ruin the whole magical moment.

As if we weren't already close enough to hear one another's heartbeats, he pulled me tighter.

A breath hitched in my throat, and my pulse rose. Las Vegas suddenly felt like a hundred degrees.

He laid his cheek against mine and said, "Nice dress. It definitely beats the red one."

And here I thought he hadn't noticed. I gulped, feeling myself sway out of rhythm. I tried to pull away, but he didn't let me go fully.

As Caleigh's face appeared in my peripheral vision, I turned my head and noticed Maya, Sam, Elaine, and Charley right behind her. Damn. I tried to take a step back, but Aiden's hold remained strong. "I need to go," I said.

A wicked grin replaced the stern look from moments ago. "Or what?" he said, his vice low and husky enough to make my knees weak.

I licked my lips, praying my libido kept her big mouth shut. "I, uh, the girls…" I trailed off, cocking my head toward the women hovering near the exit now.

He glanced toward the women and nodded his understanding. But instead of letting me go, he said, "I need to talk to you. Alone."

I swallowed hard. My head already spun from our close contact, and I wasn't sure how much more I could tolerate before I was a puddle at his feet.

"Okay, give me a moment." I stepped out of his embrace and caught up to Caleigh. "Why don't you guys go up, and I'll be there in a bit."

Caleigh's eyes flashed behind me to Aiden. His answering grin was as wide as it was mischievous. "Anything you say, Boss."

Elaine leaned in to Charley but stared at Aiden. "He's hot," she told her new BFF.

Charley hummed her approval.

As they turned to walk off, Caleigh tossed a wink over her shoulder.

I felt Aiden grab my elbow, and he pulled me farther into the noisy alcove. If he truly wanted to talk, I had no idea how he expected to do it among the music and crowd. When we reached the far wall, he kept going and pulled me into the men's room. My pulse hijacked my body. Yuck. Couldn't we have at least gone into the women's, where there may have been an air freshener?

There was no way I'd dance or snuggle beside a urinal. On the upside, my libido was suddenly nowhere to be found.

"What are you doing in Vegas?" he asked, his voice back to professional interrogation mode.

I stared at him in disbelief for a second. His Goldilocks routine was starting to get to me. One minute he was angry, the next sexy, and now professional. I wondered when he'd find the personality that was just right.

Definitely tired of playing games, I sighed and said, "Fine. I'm here because we think Roger loaned Heavy some money. Heavy hasn't paid it back, and we wanted to talk to him." I left out the part about Julio and the possible link with Heavy's video. I didn't know how much Aiden already knew, and the last thing I wanted to do was drag Sam into the mess any further than her baby's daddy might already be.

"So you think Heavy killed Roger?" His eyes were assessing me like he would a witness, watching for any little nonverbal clue.

I shrugged. "I think it's just as likely as the wife. Maybe more so."

"Why is that?" he probed.

"Well, at first I just assumed Bristol was a trophy wife. But now, I'm not so sure."

He tapped his chin. "Why?"

I shrugged and stared at the white porcelain triple sinks. "It's mostly a feeling. She seemed sincerely distraught over Roger's death. I think she really loved him."

He sat on the very edge of the sinks. "It's possible. But she has no alibi, and that troubles me."

"You know what troubles me?" I asked, feeling like this info-fishing expedition was just a little one sided.

He shook his head.

"Why you're still talking about Bristol when I know you're here because of Heavy's gun."

He raised one eyebrow. "You know about the ballistics?"

I nodded. "Bristol told me."

"Ah." He stared down at the tile floor thoughtfully. "Is that also where you heard about the loan?"

"More or less."

"Okay." He took a step forward. "So, would this loan be for *more* or less?"

"More," I settled on. "A friendly fifty-thousand-dollar loan."

He paused and ran his hand over his chin. I'd bet my own money this was news to him. Clearly his pals in forensics had been so intent on proving Bristol's guilt that they'd overlooked the emails on Roger's computer.

"You're sure?" he asked.

I nodded. "His manager confirmed it."

"The same manager who is providing his alibi?"

He had a point. There was a chance Johnson might not be the most honest source in town. But on this score, what reason would he have to lie?

Aiden took a step toward me. "Well, I have to admit it, Bond. You've been busy."

I couldn't help but smile, taking it as a compliment.

Then he reached up and brushed a strand of my hair off my cheek, his fingers lingering on my skin. Oh boy. There was my traitorous libido again.

He grinned and leaned his head toward mine. I felt his hand snake around my neck and his lips brush against mine. He was going to kiss me…right here in a public bathroom? Part of me didn't even care, and part of me was a little squicked out, but when his lips made contact, both parts melted into a pool of goo. I was just about to lose all conscious thought, when my cell buzzed in my hand.

I flinched. I didn't want to answer it, but in case it was one of the girls, I needed to. Darn.

I raised it to my ear, and without looking or thinking, I said, "Hello?" There I went sounding all breathy again—this time with very good reason though.

"James?" Danny's voice came on the other end.

I froze.

"Danny?"

"Are you okay?" His voice sounded urgent. Worried even.

"Uh, yeah." I quickly took two steps away from Aiden, ducking my head down as if Danny could magically see through the phone to what he'd just interrupted. "Why? What's going on?"

"Well, when you didn't show at Spinelli's, I thought maybe something had happened."

I shut my eyes and thought a really bad word. My date with Danny. In everything that had happened that day, I'd totally forgotten about it.

"No, I just…uh, something came up."

"Where are you?" he asked. I was certain he could hear the music thumping in the background, even though it wasn't nearly as loud in here.

"Vegas," I said before I could think better of it.

There was silence on the other end for a moment, and then Danny repeated, "Vegas."

Wow. When he said it, it sounded like a dirty word.

"Uh, yeah. Look, it just sort of happened—"

"Is Aiden with you?" he cut in.

I bit my lip and looked up at gorgeous Aiden. His lips were still slightly red where my lipstick had stained them. "Um…well, kinda…"

Danny was quiet for another second. I expected him to yell or curse or something. But instead all I heard was a click.

Oh crap, crap, crap.

I felt my cheeks flushing and guilty tears well behind my eyes. I really screwed this one up. I quickly dialed him back, but it rang once then went to voice mail. I hung up and dialed again, but this time it went straight to voice mail. He'd turned off his phone.

"Is everything okay?" Aiden asked.

I looked into his beautiful blue-green eyes. "Um, yeah. It will be." I hoped. As much as I'd had mixed feelings about going out with Danny, the last thing I'd wanted to do was hurt him. I was such a jerk. I was scum. He'd hung up on me. He'd never done that before, not in all of the times I'd been a crappy friend. Though, I guess now I was sort of more than a friend. Or, maybe less after this. The math was making my head hurt.

Aiden looked toward the door. "I need to go. It sounds like Heavy Cash is almost done with his set."

I listened. Sure enough, the song was winding down.

"I have a few questions I need to ask him," Aiden said.

"So do I. Mind if I tag along?"

"Yes, I most certainly do mind."

Well darn, and here I thought we were getting along so swimmingly.

"Look," he continued, "in no way are you to go near Heavy. Got it?"

I sucked in my cheek. If he thought he had me on a leash just because he kissed me, he had another think coming.

"You are to go back to L.A. immediately. Is that clear?"

He spoke as if I were five and didn't know how to follow directions.

"And if I don't?" I asked, pulling out my defiant tone again.

"Heavy Cash has a record, and if things get dangerous, I don't want you near the situation."

I paused. Okay, that was actually kinda touching. But I couldn't help feel like he was giving me the brush-off. "Okay. No problem. I need to get back to the girls anyway."

I slipped out of the restroom and pool area and hurried up to my suite. Aiden may have been interrogating Heavy, but I had another angle to work.

I needed to find Julio.

When I stepped inside our room, Sam and Maya nearly pounced on me.

"We've reconstructed Julio's texts, Boss," Maya said with sheer glee in her voice. "We've cross referenced most of the numbers with phone company records to put names to them."

I glanced at her computer screen to see a neatly outlined spreadsheet. One of the texts on the day he disappeared was from Edwin Johnson. "Heavy's manager?" So he had lied to me.

Maya pointed to my laptop on the coffee table. "He and Heavy are staying in the penthouse."

"Julio may be up there too," Sam said. The tight edge to her voice gave away her worry.

I pursed my lips. "Johnson already lied about knowing Julio. I doubt he's going to be more forthcoming if we just knock on the door and ask."

"We need to get a good look around the place ourselves," Maya agreed.

I nodded. "But Heavy and his manager know Sam and me. They're not likely to let us in to snoop around."

"And he might have seen me with you at the mall," Caleigh chimed in.

"Which means there's only one of us he wouldn't recognize…"

I turned my gaze to Maya. Sam and Caleigh followed suit in unison.

Maya looked to Sam and then me. She sighed heavily. "Oh, this is when you ask me to go undercover again, isn't it?"

I imitated Caleigh's earlier mischievous grin.

CHAPTER FOURTEEN

———

Walking along the strip at night among the people and lights was exhilarating. Dragging Maya in and out of stores looking for an appropriate outfit was not. Partly because she was reluctant about going undercover again and partly because of the outfits Caleigh kept holding up against her body. Also, I hadn't thought about changing before we left the hotel, and the tape was definitely slipping now.

We stopped in front of a small boutique whose mannequins in the window display looked like hookers.

"Oooh, let's go in here," Caleigh said and practically ran the couple of feet to the door.

Maya groaned.

Charley and I followed. Sam and Elaine had gone to check out surveillance equipment. I thought for sure Elaine would've preferred to shop for clothes and Charley would've been interested in spy gear. I suspected Charley tagged along with us as support for her daughter and to make sure we didn't dress Maya in anything too risqué. So far, however, Charley had approved of every item Caleigh had picked out. It had been Maya refusing to wear the pieces. Now here we were at the fourth shop, and I hoped we could finally convince Maya to agree to something. The night wasn't getting any younger.

The bell above the door jingled, and the store clerk behind the register nodded to us as we entered. She wore her long, blonde hair slicked up into an alarmingly high ponytail. The tip of her winged eyeliner met the edge of her thick brows, giving her large eyes a slightly slanted look. Or maybe that was just the way her skin was pulled back so tightly from the ponytail.

"If you need help with anything, let me know," she said.

"Thank you, dear," Charley said and lifted up a red bustier to inspect.

The radio played a hip-hop beat through the small wall-mounted speakers. There was less than a handful of other customers looking for something inappropriate to wear. Two of the four women were tall, broad, and had long, shiny brown hair. One even had bulging muscles and a tat on her arm of a heart with the word *Mom* beneath it. The tatted woman faced me, and I did a double take at her five o'clock shadow. Oh, oops, my bad. They weren't women but men in drag.

By the time I turned around, Caleigh was already deep in the store. "Look." She grabbed a purple leather miniskirt and raced back to us. She held it up to Maya's body. "This is adorable. I might have to borrow it later."

Maya glanced down at it. Her arms were crossed over her chest, and her expression was defiant. This wasn't working. I didn't want to force her into doing something she hated.

I stepped to her and gripped her shoulders. "If you are dead set against this, say so. I think you'd be great at it. I have total confidence, but if you hate it, you don't have to do it."

She unfolded her arms and let them drop to her sides. "Then how will we get inside the penthouse and see if Julio's in there?"

I thought about this for a moment. "We can buy a wig and some heavy disguises, and I can go up. Or, if that doesn't work, I'll ask Elaine." Although that idea sent chills through me. It wasn't that I didn't trust Elaine, but she wasn't experienced enough to know what not to say. And Derek would kill me if he found out.

Maya shook her head. "No, this is for Sam and the agency. I'll do it."

"That's my girl," Charley said and kissed Maya's cheek.

I dropped my hands and smiled. "Thank you."

"So…" Caleigh held up the purple leather mini. "Yay or nay?"

Maya grinned. "I like it. It's cute. Do I get to keep the outfit when we're done?"

I chuckled. "It's all yours."

Maya's eyes lit up. "All right then. Let's get shopping."

Things sped up at this point. We ransacked the store, having Maya try on at least eight different tops and shoes with the skirt before settling on a skintight, purple-and-black, cropped halter top and black thigh-high boots.

While she tried outfits on, I took the moment to try calling Danny again. Again it went straight to voice mail. I didn't have the heart to leave a message. Mostly because I wasn't sure what to say. Everything he was suspecting was true. Okay, maybe not *everything*, but my lips still tingled with Aiden's kiss, and instead of feeling as sweet as it had in the moment, it just made my insides twist with guilt.

At the register, I handed my credit card to the clerk and overheard Charley whisper, "I still think the black bustier was a more hoochie choice."

"Mom, I'm your daughter. You should be mortified, not encouraging it," Maya said.

Caleigh giggled.

Charley playfully smacked Maya's butt. "Getting the bad guy trumps showing some skin."

When we got back to our hotel room, Sam and Elaine were already there. I changed into my denim shorts and a light-pink tank top. Super casual and super comfy. It was a far cry from the outfits I wore to work, but this was Vegas. And other than the girls and possibly hotel staff, no one was going to see me. Plus the tape was totally unstuck at that point.

Maya stepped out from her room, and Sam and Elaine whistled in approval. Maya spun around. "I do kinda like it."

I smiled, glad she was no longer kicking and dragging her heels.

"Is anyone else famished?" Charley asked. "I'm calling room service, and it's my treat."

The five of us nodded and mumbled our desire to stuff our faces. Maya opted out. She wouldn't have time to wait, and I assumed her stomach wasn't calm enough for food anyway.

While Charley ordered, Sam pinned a tiny microphone to the inside of Maya's halter.

"It's so amazing how those things work, and they're so small," Elaine said.

Sam glanced over her shoulder and widened her eyes at me. She was trying to tell me something, but I could only frown. I didn't read bulging eye language. She lifted a black choker from the coffee table and turned back to Maya. Then she stood behind Maya, fastening it to her neck, and I noticed a white, iridescent stone on the center.

"Look," Elaine shouted and pointed to my laptop.

Suddenly I was on the computer screen. I lifted my arm, and the me on the monitor did the same. Very cool. The opal-looking stone was a camera.

Charley hung up the phone and joined Elaine on the sofa beside me. "They said thirty minutes. I hope they hurry."

I smirked at the conversation. "Okay, so you know what to do, right, Maya?"

She nodded and swallowed hard. Her nervousness was clearly returning. "Yes, I need to get inside, look around, and see if I find any sign of Julio." To Sam, she said, "I got this."

Sam squeezed her hand and looked very grateful. Then she pulled out her phone, swiping the screen. "I'm sending you a recent photo of Julio. You can use that photo to show around, in case someone up there has seen him."

Maya nodded, waiting until the text came through on her own phone before slipping it into her little black purse.

"Just play it cool," I said.

"But how do I get in again?" Maya asked, her confidence bubble popping. "The elevator isn't going to just take anyone up to the penthouse. Won't I need special access?"

Caleigh and I had already thought about this. I nodded to my associate, and she stepped forward. "Yes, that's why you'll have to hitch a ride."

Maya raised her brows, and I felt the panic simmering inside her just from her expression. "Excuse me?"

Caleigh wiggled her phone in her hand. "According to social media, the party is still going. It was a birthday bash for someone. Heavy was just performing, and he's invited some people up to his suite. Do you remember the guy in the Speedo?"

Maya snapped her fingers. "With the John Lennon glasses?"

I grinned, so proud at how observant they'd been.

"Yes. He and several others are heading up. Now. Just find one of them and tag along. They should be pretty drunk and hopefully won't notice so much. Here, I took pictures. These are the others who I found out were going up. But some may have left already, so you'll need to hurry."

I gave Caleigh and Maya half a minute to run through the photos on her phone, and then I got to my feet. "Okay, let's do this."

Maya gave a weak smile to her mother.

"You're gonna be fine, baby," Charley said.

Elaine cheered. "This is so exciting."

Maya and I stepped into the hall and over to the elevator. Then I gripped her by the shoulders again and gave her the best "go get 'em speech" I could muster up, filled with encouragement and words like *confident, trust,* and *exceptional.* It was basically the speech from the boutique, just ramped up.

When I could no longer think of encouraging words, I finished with, "I really appreciate this."

She took in a deep, boob-lifting breath and exhaled slowly. "I know. What if I can't get in though?"

Obviously my little speech hadn't been as successful as I anticipated. I cupped her face with my hands and stared into her eyes. "You are one of the most capable women I know. You're smart, beautiful, and brave. You can do anything you set your mind to. Don't forget that."

She smiled as the elevator dinged.

I let go, and she stepped on. And as the doors closed around her, I felt like a proud mama.

When I walked back into the hotel room, her real proud mama stepped forward and wrapped me in her arms. "Thank you," Charley whispered in my ear.

I'd momentarily forgotten they were able to see and hear us. "I meant it."

Charley moved over to the sofa, and I waved Sam over.

"What were you trying to tell me before with your eyes?" I asked.

She chuckled. "When we were in the store, Elaine was very interested in the small spy cameras. Under her breath, she said they would be great for catching cheating boyfriends." Sam pursed her lips. "I thought you'd want to know."

I inhaled deeply. Derek and Elaine were going to be the death of me if they didn't stop suspecting one another of being unfaithful. As far as I could tell, they loved each other and needed to stop acting like they were in high school. Then again, if she planted a camera, maybe we could put all of this to rest finally. "Did she buy anything?"

"No."

"Okay—thanks." There was nothing I could do about any of that right now, even if I wanted. And I didn't want to, but I had half a thought to sit them both down when we got back to L.A. and give them a stern talking-to.

Sam walked to the sofas and sat beside Caleigh. Charley and Elaine sat together on the other one. They all intently stared at the laptop, while I stood behind the sofa and paced. I couldn't sit still when one of my girls was undercover. It didn't matter that Maya had limited experience. I would've felt the same way if it had been Sam or Caleigh in an elevator headed to the penthouse. Okay, so maybe I paced a drop faster because it was our sweet, innocent, scared-of-earthquakes Maya.

Where was a burger when you needed it? Didn't Charley order room service?

Maya stepped off the elevator at the pool party. The guards either recognized her from earlier or really approved of her new outfit and let her through without a hassle. The party was still going strong. If people had left, it hadn't been many. Maya immediately zeroed in on Speedo guy. This was going to be interesting.

The volume of the music and the chatter of partygoers distorted the mic some, but we could see Maya coming on to the guy. Like Caleigh had suspected, Speedo was too drunk to suddenly wonder why this beautiful woman was giving him any attention. After ten minutes of whispering and giggling, she managed to get him over to the elevators. He pulled a key card out of his trunks, and there was a chorus of "ewws" in my hotel suite. I couldn't see Maya's expression, but I was certain she was grimacing as they rode up to the penthouse.

"You must be super important if you have your own key," Maya said.

Speedo wiggled his brows up and down. "Heavy and I go way back."

"What if she gets hurt?" Charley asked.

"We won't let that happen," Sam said and placed her Taser on the table.

Charley and Elaine inhaled sharply, but Charley leaned closer to look at the weapon. There was a gleam in her eyes that had me making a mental note to not leave Charley alone with it.

"I need to get one of those," she said.

My point exactly.

Speedo inched closer to Maya, and the camera jumped.

"What was that?" Elaine asked.

"He probably pinched her butt," Caleigh said then shot an apologetic look toward Charley. Maya's mom had to have known this could get sticky, but knowing that and seeing it, or in this case assuming it, were two different things.

The elevator dinged and then opened to a small hallway. There were two sets of double doors across from one another.

I stopped pacing and sat on the edge of the sofa, beside Caleigh.

Speedo stepped forward, and suddenly the camera was teetering. Charley softly gasped. Elaine squeezed her hand. The camera shifted to Speedo on one knee on the elevator floor.

"I'm so sorry," Maya said. "I didn't mean to make you fall. I must've had too many shots." She giggled.

Speedo stood up and wobbled. "It's okay. It's a party, right? Come on, sugar."

He waved her forward and stepped off the elevator.

Maya stood several steps behind. Then she raised her hand and showed us Speedo's key card.

Sam and Caleigh squealed. "Way to go, Maya."

I chuckled. That was my girl.

Maya slipped the card into her purse as Speedo turned right and pushed open the double doors.

We all sighed at the breathtaking view of luxury, from the dazzling chandelier to the skyline past the floor-to-ceiling windows behind the long mahogany dining table and eight upholstered chairs.

Maya tentatively stepped into the penthouse and turned around counter clockwise, giving us a visual of the surroundings. She knew more than she gave herself credit for. I was going to have to sit down and talk to her when we returned. But she'd receive a praising. After this, she may need a raise too.

To her right were two archways. One led to a couple of doors and the other led to what looked like a kitchen. Along the wall to the kitchen was an elaborate and well-stocked glass bar. Several women and men in bathing suits and towels sat on the stools. Maya showed us the dining room table next, and up close I saw that it was set with the most brilliant white and gold-trimmed dishes. Several vases of fresh flowers—purple, yellow, and white—sat in the center.

To the left was the living room, with white and beige ultramodern sleek sofas, a large flat-screen TV, and various other tables and chairs that were hard to make out with all the bodies on them. These people didn't seem to have come from the pool party though. The men were fully dressed in low-hung pants, jerseys, sneakers, and a lot of gold jewelry. A few women in outfits as skimpy as Maya's were draped over the sides of the sofas.

Maya stepped closer, and a coffee table full of money, a few guns, pills, and beer cans came into view. One of the guys walked over to her. "Hey, *chica*. What's your name?"

Bass throbbed in the background, but the music wasn't as loud as at the pool, so his voice came across loud and clear.

"Maria," she said. "I'm looking for my boyfriend. He's up here. Julio. Have you seen him?"

The guy sucked in the corner of his mouth and checked Maya out from head to toe, lingering suggestively on all of the important parts. "No, *mija*, but if you can't find him, I can be your daddy."

Elaine snorted. Charley didn't make a sound. I imagined she wasn't too thrilled.

But Maya giggled in character. "Sure thing." When she turned toward the bar, she whispered, "Never gonna happen."

Charley's turn to snort.

Maya approached a girl in a bright-yellow bikini at the bar. She grabbed her phone her from her purse and pulled up the photo of Julio. "Hey, any chance you've seen this guy here?"

The girl squinted, shook her head, and went back to sprinkling salt on the side of her hand.

Sam sighed. I'd doubted this would be easy, but I hoped we wouldn't leave here with nothing.

Maya moved on down the bar, asking each of partygoers. No one recognized Julio. Which, with the currently average level of inebriation, didn't necessarily mean they hadn't seen him. She turned toward the living room, and her steps were slow, as if she was nervous about venturing inside. I understood how she felt.

"She shouldn't be in there," Charley whispered.

There was a knock on the door, and the Senior Sleuths flinched.

Oooh, room service.

Charley rose and answered the door. It was just as well she was distracted at this part of Maya's assignment. As the hotel staff rolled a cart of tantalizing scents into the room, I leaned forward and kept my eyes on the screen.

Maya entered the living room, and the TV showed one of Heavy's music videos. It looked like an old one 'cause Heavy was thinner and younger. Maya sat on the edge of a sofa. I assumed she was trying to blend in.

The guy who wanted to be her daddy jutted out his chin and made a kissy face.

The server pulled the cart out of our room, and Charley thanked him. Then she went about opening the dishes of food, and the aromas attacked me. Sam, Caleigh, and I looked behind us, taking our eyes off the computer for a moment.

Charley must've noticed us drooling, because she said, "I ordered a bunch of items, so we can all share. Take whatever you want."

She didn't have to tell us twice. I jumped up and grabbed a plate.

I served myself some salmon, risotto, Caesar salad, and green beans almandine and then quickly returned to my seat. Leave it to a mom to order healthy choices. We were all lucky. If it had been up to me, I may have ordered burgers and fries.

"Can you grab me a bottle of water?" I asked and kept my gaze on Maya.

She shoved the photo of Julio in the face of some guy with dreadlocks. "Have you seen him? It's my boyfriend, and I'm trying to find him before the cops do."

The guy shook his head. "Nah. What'd he do?"

"Held up a liquor store."

The guy looked unimpressed. A girl with cornrows and a lip ring glanced over briefly before turning her attention back to the television.

Sam handed me a bottle of water and sat beside me. "Do you think she'll find him?" she whispered.

"I hope so." I wished I could've been more certain.

Maya started to step back into the dining room, and suddenly Heavy's manager appeared at her side.

He looked her up and down, eyes narrowing. "Who are you?"

"Maria. I'm with him." She pointed to Speedo, who was dancing by the bar.

The manager rolled his eyes and went into the living room. I heard Maya let out a sigh of relief as she headed to the bar. But before getting up close to Speedo, she changed course and walked toward the kitchen. She peeked inside. It was long and narrow with granite counters and stainless steel appliances. It was also empty.

"Go on, Maya. Look around," I whispered to myself and stuffed a forkful of fish into my mouth. Oh my God, it was so succulent.

Maya stepped back and glanced around her, but it was so quick that everything was a blur. Then she stepped into the second archway, which was a small hallway. She opened the first door and entered a bedroom. A bedside table light was on, and the room was empty. She shut the door behind her and walked farther in.

"That's my girl," I whispered low enough that no one heard.

Caleigh, Charley, and Elaine returned to their seats with full plates.

Maya showed us the black jacket lying across the brown comforter of the bed. Peeking out from under the jacket was a black wallet. She flipped it open. Edwin Johnson. This was the manger's room. She headed around the bed, opened the closet to reveal several suits on hangers, and then peeked into the empty bathroom. Nothing of interest.

She went back into the hall, took a deep breath, and then went to the other door.

Elaine opened a tiny bottle of vodka and sipped it. "This is so exciting."

The second bedroom was enormous compared to the first. This was the master bedroom. The long burgundy drapes were open, and the fabulous view from the dining room was present in here as well.

"This is making me so nervous," Caleigh said. "She needs to move faster. What if Heavy Cash walks in?"

Charley made a moaning sound.

"She'll tell him she's looking for a bathroom," I said. That's what I would do.

Maya did the same inspection as the last room, starting with the closet and ending with the other door in the room. She placed her hand on the doorknob and hesitated.

I leaned closer. "Do you hear that?"

Muffled sounds came through the microphone, but we were too far away to make it out clearly. Maya pressed her ear to the door. "It sounds like a couple is going at it," she whispered.

"Well, open the door and go on in, honey," Caleigh said as if interrupting hot sex was an everyday occurrence for her.

Maya started to walk away but then stopped and listened again. "Actually, I'm not sure it's ecstasy I'm hearing. It almost sounds like someone is hurt."

The hairs went up on my arms.

Sam glanced to me, and in her eyes I read the fear that maybe Julio was in there.

Maya softly rapped on the door. If it was a love nest, someone would tell her to go away. Instead, the muffled sound grew louder, and I could clearly hear it this time. It sounded as if someone had their mouth covered.

"Go in," I mumbled and wished I'd been able to go up there myself.

Maya turned the knob, but of course, it was locked. She looked around the room quickly. I doubted Heavy had bobby pins lying around. She jerked open the end table drawers and then the dresser. Nothing. She went back to the closet and opened the luggage on the floor. As luck would have it, 'cause sometimes the universe was on our side, a switchblade was in a side pocket. She unfolded it and went back to the bathroom door. She jammed the tip of the knife into the lock, and I mentally crossed my fingers while shoving the rest of my green beans into my mouth.

She tried over and over again, and then finally with a sharp twist of her wrist, we heard a distinct click.

"She needs to teach me how to do that," Elaine said.

It was probably a really good thing that Elaine didn't become a private investigator.

Maya pushed the door open. Instead of finding a half-naked couple, we stared at a man. He sat on the tiled floor, and sure enough, a strip of duct tape was pressed to his mouth. He wore a short-sleeve T-shirt, and his very pale skin allowed Sam to take a breath of relief. Or maybe it was disappointment, because if it had been Julio, at least he would've been found.

But when Maya knelt beside the man and peeled the tape off his mouth, I got a better look at him. I almost choked on my green beans as I realized I was staring into the face of Ian Jenkins, aka Wrap Guy.

CHAPTER FIFTEEN

───────

Maya used the switchblade to cut through a piece of rope that held Jenkins's arms behind his back, and then she helped him get to his feet.

"We've got to get out of here. These guys are dangerous," he said. He wore the same brown pants and green polo shirt from Lite Wraps.

"What happened? How did you get here?" she whispered.

But he shook his head. "Later. We need to leave. Now!"

Okay," she answered. I had to agree. The interrogation could wait. However Jenkins had ended up tied up in the bathroom, I didn't want Maya around when the tier-upper returned. She helped Jenkins to his feet and accompanied him through the bedroom. Then she tossed the blade onto the bed as they walked past it. Normally I'd leave a room the way I found it when investigating, so that the occupant didn't know anyone had been there. But in this case, that would be obvious as soon as Heavy checked his bathroom.

I set down my plate with a clatter and stood up, ready to start pacing again.

Maya peeked her head into the hall, and a man headed in their direction. She shut the door and slapped Jenkins on the arm. "Back in the bathroom. Hurry."

Crap. This was not good.

Jenkins and Maya ran into the master bath. She shut the door and locked it. "Shoot. We can't just walk out. They'll see you."

A low whining filled the mic. Maya turned, and we saw Jenkins pinching the bridge of his nose. The sound was coming from him.

After shushing him, she glanced around the bathroom.

"She needs help," Charley said.

Caleigh stood, clearly feeling the nervous pacing energy I was.

"Wait," Maya said.

"What?" Jenkins asked.

She faced the mirror and looked to be talking to herself, but I knew she was talking to us. She had to know we'd be there in a heartbeat if she ran into trouble. "Give me a minute to think."

We heard a knock at the door.

Jenkins gasped and covered his mouth with his hand.

Maya shushed him again and turned to the door. "I'll be out in a few. I don't feel so good."

The man heading toward the master bedroom must've wanted to use the bathroom. Good thing it hadn't been Heavy. Where was he?

"Hurry up," the guy on the other side of the door said.

Back in the mirror, Maya bit her bottom lip. "Hey, can you get me a plunger," she shouted.

Caleigh let out a laugh. "No guy wants to hear that."

Caleigh was right, and Maya was brilliant. She faced the back of the door, and her eyes settled on a plush white robe hanging up on a hook. "I have an idea."

She pulled the robe off its hook and wrapped it around Jenkins. "Here, put this on."

"Are you crazy?" he asked. "This isn't a disguise."

He was right, and Maya must've known it too, because she started looking around the room again. But there wasn't much to find in a hotel master bath with a shower the size of my entire bathroom at home. From her reflection in the mirror, we saw Maya pressing her ear to the door. She opened it, looked out, and said, "Come on."

The bedroom was empty again. She ran to the closet and tossed a black jacket at Jenkins. "Put this on. And don't give me any lip, or I'll leave you here."

Charley and Elaine cackled. Caleigh eased back into her seat, but I remained standing. As soon as Maya hit the elevator, I planned to be waiting for her.

Maya found a baseball cap and a pair of sunglasses and tossed them at Jenkins. "Here."

It was a decent plan as long as Heavy wasn't out there to notice Jenkins was wearing his clothes.

At the door, Maya turned and stared at Jenkins. "Slump your shoulders and walk with swagger. Got it?"

He nodded and cocked his torso to his right. Not exactly what Maya had in mind, I was sure.

Maya opened the door.

I held my breath. The hallway was empty, but there were a couple more yards before she hit the elevator.

Each step forward was like being in a torture device. Part of me wished she'd run for it, but that would only attract attention.

Maya looked to the right, and all the same people were at the bar, including Speedo. He was still dancing, a Corona in one hand. He kept trying to remove the cap with the palm of his hand, but it wasn't working. Then he resorted to his teeth, swayed a bit too far to the side, and fell into the shelf behind the bar. The sound of glass breaking made everyone look his way.

Good going, Speedo.

Maya took advantage of the distraction and quickly reached the double doors, pulled them open, and stepped into the hall. They were just a few inches from the elevator. Yes! Maya pushed the button.

I tapped my foot. Come on. Come on. Don't take long. I could still hear the bass booming from the penthouse suite. Did one of them not shut the double doors behind them?

"Hey," said a voice close by.

Oh crap. Who was that?

Maya turned and stared into the face of the girl with the cornrows. And sure enough, the penthouse double doors were wide open. Anyone in there could clearly see them leaving.

"What?" Maya asked.

The girl looked over her shoulder and then back to Maya. "I saw that guy on your phone."

Sam sat a bit straighter.

"Oh yeah? Where? When?" Maya asked.

"He was here yesterday. I heard him say something about going to the Gold Bar."

The elevator door opened, and before Maya had time to react, Jenkins moved forward. He started to get onto the elevator but changed his mind and rushed toward a singular door almost opposite the elevator. One marked *Exit.* He was taking the stairs.

Shoot! Jenkins was making a run for it.

I grabbed my Glock and shoved it into the back of my shorts, and then I slipped my phone into my bra. "That's it. Let's go."

Sam and Caleigh jumped to their feet and ran into the hall. I followed closely behind and remembered to turn and point to Elaine and Charley. "You two, stay here. If Maya doesn't get on that elevator in the next two minutes, call me."

The women nodded, and they both had fear in their eyes. Okay, so Elaine had some excitement too but mostly fear.

We ran into the hall. I hit the elevator button, and even though my mind raced, I knew exactly what to do. "Sam, come with me. Caleigh, get to the lobby and make sure he doesn't go down there. I don't care what you have to do, but don't let him leave this building."

"Got it." Caleigh jumped onto the elevator, and Sam and I hit the stairwell. As we entered it, we heard the pounding footsteps heading our way. Jenkins. Our luck was on fire today.

Sam and I took off. We reached him two flights up. Damn, he'd been running fast. He must've been scared of whoever had him in that bathroom. My money was on Heavy, and I couldn't wait to find out why. There was no way I was letting Jenkins get past us. I didn't care if I had to throw both of us down the steps.

Sam and I reached the landing, and he was four steps above us. He didn't pay us much attention. He didn't seem to recognize me at all. It was just as well because it gave me the advantage. When he stepped on the landing, I lunged and threw myself at him.

"What the…" he shouted with a groan as his head hit the wall.

"Did you really think you could get away so easily?" I asked through clenched teeth.

"Get off me," he snarled. He pressed his hands to my shoulders and tried to push me away. He hadn't counted on me being a very annoyed woman. I held my ground, but at this rate he'd get the upper hand eventually.

Sam came up behind me. She put a hand on his forehead and pushed it back against the wall.

His black beady eyes widened with recognition as he stared into mine. "You."

I smiled. "Surprise. Now, let's go. You're coming with us."

I grabbed his wrist and started to jerk him forward, but he wasn't having it. He remained stuck to the spot.

"What do you want?" he asked.

"You, of course," Sam said in a syrupy-sweet tone. She even batted her eyes. If she wanted to flirt to get him to return to our room, that was up to her. I barely wanted to touch his wrist. I was already thinking of the scalding shower I'd take when all of this was over.

"I'm not going with you. You're both crazy." He yanked free of my grip and took off. He managed to get down the next few steps before my legs moved.

"Sonofa…" I ran down one step and noticed he was two away from the next landing. Once he turned, it would be harder to reach him again, so I did what I said I would.

I rose onto the balls of my feet and leapt. If I'd taken a moment to think about it, I never would've done it. Gravity instantly pulled at me, and my heart nestled in my stomach somewhere. I quickly prayed I'd come out of this conscious and not maimed.

"Jamie," Sam shouted. There was panic in her voice. I knew how she felt.

Jenkins turned and widened his eyes as he saw me flying toward him. His expression was comical enough that had I been sitting on the sidelines, watching this crazy woman behaving like a bat, I'd be in stitches laughing. But all I felt in the moment was fear that I'd end up in the hospital.

He missed the last step, and his right leg went down two, throwing his balance off, which really sucked because I ended up landing with my face at his stomach. I fell against him, and we both crashed onto the concrete landing. I was going to need a giant tube of Bengay cream when this day ended.

Fortunately, I was okay, other than his belt buckle digging into my neck. Unfortunately, he seemed to be okay too. Not that I wanted him injured, but a little less squirrely would've been awesome.

"This is ridiculous," Sam shouted, and her footsteps sounded behind us.

Jenkins squirmed and twisted to get to his feet.

That wasn't happening, not after almost killing myself. I dug my hands into his upper arms. The term *biceps* would have suggested there were muscles involved, and that was far from Jenkins's fleshy reality. As he turned to get to his knees, I hung on and moved with him. We rolled twice, until I was back on top, but now we were dangerously near the next set of stairs.

Before I knew what was happening, Sam was beside us. She shouted "Clear" as if she was a doctor on a medical drama TV show. I didn't fully anticipate what was happening, but I trusted her. I sprung off Jenkins and landed on my butt on one of the steps.

Sam flung her arm forward and tased him.

His body jerked several times and then flopped still. I took the opportunity to grab his right arm and pin it behind his back, incapacitating him.

With my other hand, I touched my throbbing lip and pulled back to see blood on my fingertips. I must've hit it against his belt. "Nice work."

"Thanks." She blew the end of the Taser and frowned at me. "Are you okay?"

I nodded. "I will be."

Sam nodded toward Jenkins, who looked dazed.

"Wha…what happened?" he mumbled.

We both ignored him.

"What are we gonna do with him?" Sam asked.

"Let's get him back to the hotel room. I want to know why he was tied up in Heavy's bathroom."

Sam nodded. "That makes two of us."

I pushed him ahead of me, with Sam at his side, threateningly brandishing the Taser in case he had any further thoughts of bolting. He seemed to get the point, as he willingly shuffled his feet down the next flight of stairs and out into the hallway.

As we entered the carpeted hall, the elevator dinged across from us, and I expected to see Maya or Caleigh get off, but it was a formally dressed older couple. Great. Witnesses.

The man held the woman's hand. It was sweet. They were probably in their late sixties. She wore a royal-blue, short-sleeve gown with silver glittery leaves trailing down the length of the dress from the shoulder to the hem at her ankle. The man wore a black tuxedo, white shirt, and a royal-blue tie. They frowned at us as they neared.

I smiled and said, "He never knows how to handle his liquor."

They hurried past, and we continued on. Once inside our room, we brought him to the sofa and let him go. He crashed onto the cushions.

"Oh my gosh, what's wrong with him?" Charley asked and then looked at me. "Are you okay?"

Sam held up her Taser and grinned. "He's just a little dazed."

Jenkins blinked at her and recoiled into the cushions further. "Keep that chick away from me. She's nuts!"

Elaine clapped and cackled.

"We're fine." Nothing a handful of ibuprofen wouldn't cure. I grabbed a bottle of water and wished for something stronger, but I needed to keep a clear head. Plus, the minibar was outrageously expensive. If Elaine hadn't cleaned it out.

The door opened, and Maya walked in. Relief washed away the frown lines along Charley's forehead, but she didn't rush to her daughter and smother her in hugs and kisses. Instead, she patted her on the shoulder and said, "I am so proud of you."

I grinned. "Someone call Caleigh and tell her to come up. Here." I tossed my phone at Elaine, who caught it with one hand.

Maya headed to her room. "I'm going to change. Be right back."

Jenkins squirmed on the sofa, his eyes darting toward the door.

"Don't even think about it," Sam said, tightening her grip on her Taser.

I think we'd created a monster.

Jenkins blinked in mock innocence. "Think of what?"

Sam narrowed her eyes.

Jenkins yipped like a little dog.

"Spill it, Jenkins," I told him. "Why were you tied up in Heavy Cash's bathroom?"

His bushy eyebrows burrowed down into a frown. "How do you know I was in there?"

I curled my toes away from the edge of my strappy sandals and kicked him lightly in the shins.

"Ow, why are you so violent?" He rubbed his leg.

"And why are you such a slimeball? Answer the question."

"What was it again?"

Charley groaned. Sam flicked on her Taser and aimed it at him.

He held up his hands. "All right, all right. A couple of thugs grabbed me outside The Spotted Pony this afternoon and stuck me in a trunk."

"Who were they?" I asked.

He shook his head. "I don't know."

"Well, was it Heavy Cash?" My patience was getting thinner by the moment.

"I don't know. One of them knocked me over the head before I got a good look at them."

I wasn't sure if he was telling the truth, but I had a feeling he was. Why hide his kidnappers' identities? That wouldn't gain him anything.

Maya's bedroom door opened, and she walked out to join us. She wore denim shorts and a tank top like I did, except her top was a soft yellow, and she looked refreshed and clean, while I was sure I looked like I'd fallen down a flight of stairs.

"Wow," Jenkins said. "Hot stuff."

"Flattery will not set you free," I told him. "Especially since you lied to me."

He widened his eyes. "No, I really didn't see their faces."

I placed a hand on my hip. "Not about that. About Roger. You had plans to see him the day he was murdered."

Those eyebrows hunkered downward again. "How didja know *that*?"

"Face it, Jenkins. Jamie knows everything," Sam said.

While I wasn't sure that was totally accurate, I liked the sound of it. And it seemed to have the desired effect on Jenkins. He turned a wary gaze my way.

"So did you see Roger the day he died?" I prodded.

Before he got a chance to lie again, Sam turned on her Taser. That was becoming one of my best investments. I would have to look into getting one for each of the girls. I hoped they made pink ones.

"Okay, so I saw him," Jenkins admitted, putting his palms up in a surrender motion. "So what?"

The door opened, and Caleigh walked in. Jenkins did a double take. "Dang, hotties comin' out of the woodwork."

"Focus," I told him. "You were saying you saw Roger?"

He turned his gaze back to me with some difficulty. "Yeah, I saw him, but he was alive when I left."

"Make me believe that," I pushed.

Jenkins's gaze flipped from me to Sam's Taser again. "Look, Roger contacted me a couple of days before his death. He said he would pay out the full settlement on the lawsuit. I asked him why, but all Roger said was that he needed to get his affairs in order. He seemed scared."

Sam and I glanced at one another. Was Roger afraid of Heavy?

"And he had a gun," Jenkins said.

"Roger did? What kind?" I asked.

"Do I look like I know guns?"

I raised a single eyebrow. "Get real."

"Okay, okay, it was a .45. But that's all I know."

That was the same kind of gun that was used to kill Roger. The same kind Heavy owned.

I rushed forward and grabbed his arm. "Come on."

He stood but hesitated to walk. "Where are we going?"

"In the bedroom."

His eyes lit up. "Oh yeah?"

"Ew. Don't even think about it. You're going in there alone."

"I don't wanna."

Sam stepped forward with her Taser aimed at him.

He held up his hands in surrender again. "Okay, take it easy. I'm going." I showed him to my room. Once inside, he took in the surroundings. "Nice digs."

"Glad you like it. Stay here. Don't even think of trying to step out there, or you'll get another shot of voltage," I said.

He nodded and sat on the edge of the bed.

I did a quick inventory of my personal items to decide if there was anything I'd regret locking him up with. My gun and wallet were on me, so other than my hoochie dress and some high heels, it was all good.

I shut the door and turned to face my girls. Caleigh was pacing, Maya was nibbling on her bottom lip, Charley looked deep in concerned thought, and Elaine was going for another mini vodka.

Sam stepped forward. "Now what?" she asked. Her voice wavered with emotion. If I had to guess, the story about being shoved into a trunk wasn't helping her anxiety about Julio any.

"Now we look for Julio," I said decisively.

She smiled her gratitude.

"But I want to keep Jenkins under wraps until we sort this whole thing out."

Charley raised her hand. "I'll stay and keep an eye on him."

"Me too," said Elaine.

That would work, as long as he didn't give them a problem. They didn't have weapons, and I wasn't leaving any with them. Then again, Jenkins wasn't armed either. And he wasn't exactly a heavyweight. The absolute worse he'd do is push one of them out of his way. He wasn't a fighter.

Just to be sure though, I grabbed a chair from the table and propped it beneath the door handle. He wouldn't be able to get through that.

I grabbed my phone, "Okay, let's start with the Gold Bar. What is it, a strip club maybe?"

"No." Maya shook her head. She was staring at her phone. "It's a pawnshop not that far away."

Perfect. "Let's go check it out."

CHAPTER SIXTEEN

———

The phrase *What happens in Vegas, stays in Vegas* and all of the flashy advertisements for the family-friendly amusement park-like strip fail to give an accurate picture of the rest of Vegas. A town where prostitution is overlooked and gambling is the source of income is bound to have one or two seedier neighborhoods. The type where a single gal would think twice about roaming alone at night. The kind where drug dealers conduct business on each corner. The kind where the Gold Bar was located.

"Are you sure about this?" Caleigh whispered as we turned down a street with two broken streetlamps and three hookers in fur coats and cheap platform heels.

No, I wasn't. But it was the best lead we'd had so far.

It was dark but definitely not quiet. A woman in a cheetah miniskirt, fishnets, and a tube top—those things still existed?—was yelling at someone in an old beige car. She smacked the passenger side door with her purse several times while shouting expletives.

"I am so glad Mom and Elaine stayed at the hotel," Maya whispered loudly enough for me to hear.

I nodded agreement.

We walked in pairs, arms looped together. Sam and I were just a shoe's width ahead of Caleigh and Maya. If Maya and I had stayed in our previous outfits, we could've blended much better with the "working girls."

The stench of rotting garbage crept up on me. There was a Dumpster up ahead, near one of the many bars. The neighborhood was congested with bars, tattoo parlors, pawnshops, and strip clubs. I'd never seen so many in one area before.

We crossed past the angry prostitute, who continued yelling at the guy and beating his car. A pink door opened a few feet up, and loud music boomed from inside. Two men wobbled out. They were dressed similarly in black pants and vests. One had a white T-shirt beneath, and the other was just muscles and tanned skin.

I heard Caleigh suck in an appreciative breath behind me.

But then the men leaned into one another and kissed.

We stepped around them, and Caleigh sighed. "The cute ones are always gay."

Sam pointed to the yellow lighted sign across the next street. The Gold Bar. We looked both ways and jaywalked over.

There were iron bars on the windows and doors, and hanging on the inside were lit neon signs.

Pawn Buy Sell
Turn in your gold for cash
Instant Cash

Sam quickly yanked the door open and entered first.

Caleigh leaned into me. "She's wound tighter than a two-dollar watch."

I nodded and followed her inside. Though, I didn't blame Sam a bit. Just being in this neighborhood had me on alert.

The store wasn't as big as I thought it would be. A narrow pathway sat between huge glass display cases that ran the length of the room. Then there was a few inches of space on each side before another long display case ran along the back wall. Behind this display case was an archway with a ratty red drape covering it, probably leading to a storage room or back office.

"Welcome to the Gold Bar," boomed a voice to my side.

I flinched and looked to my right. Unless the voice was over a speaker or made by an invisible man, I didn't see a person standing there.

Suddenly a man's head appeared at the top of the display case by an array of gold necklaces. The man jumped to his feet, and I flinched again.

He had a headful of thick, wavy brown hair, and the kind of mustaches that you see on villains in comics—the kind they twirl. It covered his top lip and curled at the ends. I would've bet that if he grabbed the tips and pulled it straight and back, it would almost reach the nape of his neck.

"Hi," he said, still in a booming voice. He widened his icy-blue eyes and smiled so bright that the entire expression looked creepy or crazy. He wore blue trousers, a short-sleeve button-down, green suspenders, and a red-and-white polka-dot bowtie. He reminded me of a clown, minus the red nose and makeup.

"Hi," Caleigh said with her natural bubbliness.

"Are you here to pawn, buy, or sell something?" He pointed to his neon sign as he said the words. There was something very over the top with the way he spoke, as if he was on stage and had to project his voice so his audience could hear him.

"Are you the owner?" I asked.

"Yes, ma'am." He flashed a brilliant smile.

"We're looking for someone," I said.

Sam showed him the picture of Julio.

He squinted, looking like he needed a pair of glasses. She handed the phone to him, but holding it close to his face didn't help. He walked to the end of the display case, toward the back of the store. "Sorry, but the lighting over there is terrible."

There had to be four fluorescents in the ceiling.

We followed him to the back, to the horizontal display case, where he turned on a small desk lamp. He bent over and examined the screen under this extra-special light.

"Oh, yes, he was in here yesterday. He pawned a watch."

Sam sighed in relief. I let out a deep breath myself. I imagined we had all been tense, fearing the worst. The fact that Julio had been alive, well, and pawning just yesterday was a positive sign.

"Can I see the watch?" Sam asked.

"Sure." He walked to the end of a display unit and slid open the back. Then he reached inside, pulled something out, brought it over to us, and set it on top of the glass case. It had a gold band with a white mother-of-pearl face and small diamonds along the rim.

Sam nodded. "That's Julio's. I gave it to him back when we were dating." Fury clouded her face. "The jerk."

Well, at least she wasn't sad and scared anymore.

"He didn't get cash," the guy told us. "He traded it for something in the shop."

I glanced at the displays, searching for what he might have wanted. Like a weapon? But I couldn't see anything other than jewelry and collectibles. That might've been a knife at the far end, but obviously it was still here.

"What did he trade it for?" I asked. "A gun?"

"No. Three life-sized department store mannequins."

I blinked at him.

"Three what-now?" Sam asked, obviously as taken aback at that revelation as I was.

"You know, the kind they dress up in store windows?" the guy said.

"Did he say what he wanted them for?" I asked.

He shook his head. "Sorry. Didn't ask." He paused. "It's best not to know sometimes."

I was thoroughly confused. Unless Julio had a secret plastic fetish, I was stumped.

"Was he with anyone?" I asked.

"No. He was alone. And on foot. I remember that because he looked hilarious hauling the three ladies out of here." He chuckled robustly.

I smiled, not sure what to do with this information. Sam, unfortunately, looked as tense as earlier.

"Thank you for your help," I said.

He nodded and picked up the watch. "Have a great night, ladies."

Sam stared at the watch as the guy carried it back to its new home.

"Wait," I said. "How much are you looking for that?"

He paused and glanced from the watch to Sam. "Three hundred."

I lifted one eyebrow. "Let's be realistic now."

He chuckled. "Okay. Two-twenty. Just because I like you gals."

I shot Sam a look. She shrugged.

"Call it two even, and you have a deal."

The guy beamed, and I had a bad feeling he would have let it go for lower.

Sam touched my arm. "You don't have to do that. This is Julio's responsibility."

"Like child support?" I whispered. "Look, this isn't for him. It's for you. I can see how much this watch means to you." I handed my credit card to the guy.

Sam swallowed hard. "I don't know when I can pay you back."

I smiled and gently elbowed her in the ribs. "You don't have to. Think of it as an early Christmas present, and one day you can give it to your little man, if you want."

Sam smiled, and I grinned even wider. I'd almost forgotten what that looked like on her.

The guy finished the transaction and put the watch in a small bag.

We stepped outside and just stood there for a moment, not sure where to go.

"Do the mannequins mean anything to you?" I asked Sam.

She shook her head. Her curls bounced around her face. "Not a darn thing."

"Maybe he's getting into fashion," Maya said.

Sam curled the right corner of her top lip. "I can't imagine that. He was never a snazzy dresser. He'd wear the same jeans for a week, if I let him."

That didn't mean he hadn't changed over these years, but I tended to agree with Sam. New fashion designer didn't seem like an option.

"If he was on foot, he couldn't have gotten far with three awkward mannequins," Caleigh said.

She was right. I walked to the edge of the sidewalk and looked up and down the street.

"Maybe the strip club?" Maya suggested, pointing to a red awning over a dark door.

Sam pursed her lips. "I don't know. He's honestly more of a dive bar kind of guy."

"We've got plenty of those," Caleigh said, pointing to three bars within sight.

Maya wrinkled her nose. "He'd bring the mannequins in with him for a drink?"

Sam shrugged. "Maybe?"

"Okay, let's split up then," I said. "Caleigh and Maya, you go into The Tavern and ask around. Sam and I will go into The Pit, and we'll meet back here in fifteen."

Caleigh and Maya nodded, then headed toward the neon-lit place on the right.

Sam and I turned left and pushed through the doors of The Pit. Which was very aptly named. Dim lighting was all that was needed to reveal the sand-ridden floor, dingy bar top, worn stools, and peeling wallpaper. The only customers were a scattering of men slumped over their beers, in varying degrees of age, width, and colored plaid shirts.

Sam and I walked to the bar, where a woman was pouring a beer on tap into a mug. It didn't look chilled, though it looked plenty watered down. She had a pouf of short, curly white-blonde hair on the top of her head. Wrinkles around her eyes and mouth were deeply creased, but she didn't look to be more than forty otherwise. As I stepped closer though, I noticed how tanned and leathery her skin was.

She slid the beer to a pudgy guy at the end of the bar before turning our way. When she did, her eyes narrowed. "You lost?" she asked, suspicion lacing a voice that had seen at least a pack a day for many years.

"Not exactly," I answered. "We're looking for someone."

"What kinda someone?" she asked as she took the pudgy guy's money, rang it into an old-fashioned cash register, and set the change beside his mug.

"His name's Julio," Sam said, pulling out her phone. She swiped on a photo of Julio and their son.

The woman wiped her hands on a rag and stepped over to us, squinting at the picture. She stared at it for several seconds, then shook her head. "Cute kid, but I haven't seen the guy. We don't get many people through here other than regulars, and I'd recognize *him*." The corner of her mouth lifted quickly, suggesting she found Julio Sr. to be cute too. "You can ask around, but as you can see, none of these guys are all that observant."

I glanced around. She was right. No one had even looked up at our entrance.

"Wake up," she shouted and slapped the bar.

The guy at the end flinched. So did Sam and I. One at a table glanced up and then looked away again, as if his drink was the most fascinating thing in his life. Another guy grunted and mumbled something about her being a witch.

The bartender chuckled. "Didn't mean to startle ya. I do that every once in a while to make sure I don't need to haul anyone out on their butts."

"Okay, well, thanks anyway," I said, and we quickly left.

Back on the sidewalk, I took a deep breath before sneaking a quick peek at my phone, checking for any missed calls from Danny. Nothing.

Unfortunately, my peek wasn't so quick that Sam didn't catch it. "Expecting a call from someone?" she asked.

I sighed. "No." Which was sadly true. I was starting to wonder if I'd ever be expecting a call from him again.

Caleigh and Maya emerged from the The Tavern. They spied us and shook their heads. I pointed to the third bar on the street, O'Malley's. We crossed the street, and Caleigh and Maya ran over to meet us.

This bar was similar to the last, with the dim lighting and the gritty floor, but otherwise it looked cleaner. The paint was clean and a crisp white. The bar's wood and the stools shone. Plus the few customers seemed alert and not in some drunken haze, despite the time of the night.

I walked up to the bar and waited for the bartender to finish pouring a scotch on the rocks.

"Excuse me," I said to get his attention.

The bartender was a beefy guy. Bald, thicker around the chest than his middle, he wore what I was quickly beginning to think of as standard dive-bar attire—jeans, a white T-shirt, and an unbuttoned red-and-white plaid shirt.

"Any chance you've seen this guy in here lately?" I asked. Sam held up her phone for his inspection.

He stared at the picture. "Yeah, I've seen him." He chuckled. "He was hard to miss with those dummies."

Excitement buzzed through me. Finally.

Sam smiled. The second time in less than fifteen minutes. Maybe her universe was righting itself again. She deserved it.

"This was yesterday?" I clarified.

He nodded.

"Any chance you know where he was heading when he left?"

He grinned. "Sure do."

I felt that excitement kick up a notch. "Where?"

"Out back. He's renting a room from me."

I exchanged a glance with Sam. Renting a room for his mannequins? Inappropriate and gross images came to mind. "Like a hotel room?" I asked.

"No. Hang on." He poured a beer on tap into a frosty, chilled mug, then set it and the scotch on the bar for a couple of guys. They paid, he made change, and we waited.

The two guys were staring at us, smiling and whispering to one another. A quick look around told me that everyone had noticed us. This was definitely a different bar than the last.

When the bartender was done, he cocked his head to the side. "Follow me."

I hesitated for half a second and contemplated trusting this stranger. There were four of us, but he looked like he could hold us down if he really wanted. The fact we were armed was a point in our favor though.

I stepped forward, and the girls followed.

We passed through a small kitchen that was dimly lit. He must've closed that down already. There wasn't much more than a grill, couple of fryers, and a dishwashing station anyway.

He opened a back door, and we stepped into an alley. A dingy privacy fence sat straight across from us, and a blue Dumpster was a few feet away to the right. Farther down from that was a side street. He turned to the left. "This way."

"Where are we going?" I asked, but he must not have heard me over the shuffle of our footsteps on the asphalt. Or maybe he was ignoring me on purpose.

The hairs on my arms rose. My radar wasn't beeping, but this still felt off.

The corner of the privacy fence turned to show a converted warehouse up ahead. Its chipping white paint was dingy, and a black plastic garbage can stood by the door. Its lid was upturned, and the can was full, but I couldn't see with what. Hopefully it wasn't body parts.

As we reached the warehouse, I glanced back at the girls. Sam looked intense again. Her brow was furrowed, and the corners of her mouth were down turned. She firmly held the Taser in her hand. She must've had her own concerns about where the bartender was leading us.

Caleigh clenched her teeth together in a forced smile and gave me two thumbs up, but I could tell she was nervous too. Her eyes darted around, and after she put her hands down, she stuck her right one into her purse. I knew her gun was in there.

I wasn't sure if Maya had a weapon on her. She usually didn't carry one, even though she was licensed to. At least in California. She tugged on her bottom lip with her teeth. She was feeling the uncertainty vibe too.

The bartender opened a door and waved his hand for us to step through. I paused. What if he slammed the door shut and locked us in? I'd seen episodes of *Criminal Minds*. What if this had nothing to do with Julio, and this guy simply needed four hot women to complete his murder spree?

So, did I keep my guard up and possibly risk myself and my friends, or did I listen to my gut and trust that we're four badass women who know how to handle ourselves?

I took a deep breath and went for option number two.

Only when I walked over the threshold, I stopped short.

Standing in the center of the room was Julio.

CHAPTER SEVENTEEN

———

Sam leapt at Julio, with her arms outstretched and her fingers curled. She reminded me of an animal, although I knew of none with her curly mane or fashion sense. She screamed at him about his disappearing and child support. Then she slapped him on the cheek. Hard. The sound echoed, and he yelped. "Ow, *mija*. What's wrong with you?"

Sam's hand had to sting, but the pain didn't register on her face. "Me? I was going out of my mind with worry. I thought you were dead or kidnapped or worse."

"What's worse than death?" Caleigh whispered to me.

I looked around and watched the bartender shake his head before making a hasty exit back to the bar.

The warehouse wasn't very big, and most of it was empty. But right in the center was a hanging green screen—the kind used in movies and on television. In front of it were the three mannequins. Each had on a wig—black, red, and blonde—and they were dressed in booty shorts and halter tops. There was some equipment farther away from the screen. A large speaker and a giant fan, like the ones we used to stand in front of when I'd modeled in order to achieve the sexy windblown look. There were a few other items I couldn't make out, as well as a couple of folding chairs. And there were two tall standing lights on each side, facing the mannequins. It looked like something was being filmed here.

When I turned back to Sam and Julio, he had his arm up, covering his face, while she continued to beat him with her open palm. Caleigh and Maya had joined in the fray, trying to peel Sam off of him. Though, they didn't seem to be trying all *that* hard. I didn't blame them. I had half a mind to smack him a couple of times myself for the worry he'd put us all through.

I stepped forward, wrapped my arms around Sam's waist, and pulled her back. Her heels scraped on the concrete floor. I let her go and hoped I wouldn't need to intervene again.

Julio stood straight and yanked down the hem of his blue-and-white jersey. I hadn't seen him in a long time. He'd put on a little weight but not much, and his hair was longer. It came to about an inch past his shoulders, in waves. He was also sporting a full but short beard. He looked good. Not *that* kind of good. I didn't look at my girls' men in that way. He simply looked healthy and not how I'd feared—tortured or dead.

Julio said, "Calm down, *mija*. I've never seen you so angry. Well, except for that time I sold your…"

Sam charged toward him again, but I jumped in front of her before she could do real damage. "Julio, what's going on here?" I asked.

He blinked at me. "What do you mean?"

"She means why did you leave town," Sam jumped in, "and worry us all half to death?!"

He looked away and shook his head. "I'm sorry, Sam."

"I'm sorry? I'm sorry! Oh, you're gonna be sorry…" She trailed off, making a move for his jugular.

I held her back. "What's going on here?" I asked, gesturing to the mannequins.

Julio's eyes shifted left then right. "I can't say."

Fury seized Sam's face and tensed her body. "You can't say?" Sam shouted. "You miss your visit with Julio. You miss a child support payment. Your precious phone is left behind at your place, and there's *blood* beside it. You disappear. You don't call or check in, and you can't say? Are you flippin' kidding me?"

We all stared at him because she was right. While I wasn't feeling quite as homicidal as she looked, his answer irked me to no end. I was tired, and we needed to get to some truth.

"Look," I said. "Roger Claremont is dead, and Heavy may have been involved. We know he kidnapped another man, someone else associated with Roger. And then you go missing. Sam has been terrified. You owe it to her to tell us what's going on."

Julio looked to his ex. He stared at her for a minute and then said, "Fine. Heavy Cash and I were shooting a secret music video with Roger."

Of all the weird things in this world that people have told me, reasons as to why they were caught with their pants down usually, this had to have been the strangest.

"Excuse me?" Sam asked.

"It was supposed to be top secret. But, man, it was awesome." He waved a hand in front of the mannequins and green screen.

"You already finished the video?" Caleigh asked.

He nodded. "Yeah."

My head started to pound. I rubbed my left temple. "So, what was with the disappearing act?" I pushed.

He sighed. "We had to keep the music video secret because a clause in Roger's contract with Hoagies said he wasn't allowed to appear on film for anything but their commercials until a certain date. That date was coming up, but Heavy needed to keep this all on the down low until then."

"Roger was supposed to be in the video?" I asked.

Julio nodded.

"But didn't you film it here?" Maya asked, piecing the events together. "Roger was killed in L.A."

"Right," he said. "No, we filmed some of it last month in L.A., at Roger's house. His master bathroom is sweet. It's got marble counters, gold faucets, and a shower the size of my entire bathroom. And there's this bathtub with fuel jets. Awesome."

He hesitated for a second, as if he'd forgotten what he was talking about. Listening to how wonderful a bath in that tub would be, I'd momentarily forgotten the topic as well.

"Anyway, we used the hot tub in there to shoot all the parts with Roger. But when he died...well, obviously we couldn't film there anymore, so we finished the rest here. I know a guy here in Vegas who had a green screen. They aren't cheap," he added.

"Could Roger really sing?" Caleigh asked. "I never would've guessed that."

Now that she said that, neither could I. "Yeah, his speaking voice was kinda tinny."

Maya and Sam nodded in agreement.

Julio stared at us blankly. "Who cares if he could sing? He was a celebrity. That's all that mattered. You think half of the musicians have good voices? That's what Auto-Tune is for."

I wasn't well versed in music, but I figured he was at least partly correct. Some musicians definitely had more talent than others. No judgments though.

"Look, Heavy thought that kind of unique cameo was just the sort of thing that would make the music video go viral and kick-start his stalled career again," Julio said.

"I thought Heavy and Roger weren't speaking because of the unpaid loan," Maya said.

Julio shook his head. "No, Roger didn't loan Heavy money that wasn't paid back. That was just his cover story to keep the video secret. He was actually financing the single and music video with Heavy."

"So what happened to Roger?" Sam asked.

Julio shook his head. "I don't know. Heavy burst into my house the other night saying that Roger was dead and the cops were going to come after Heavy for it. He had some blood on him, and I assumed it was Roger's. Heavy grabbed me and shoved me in a car. Like, literally grabbed me and shoved me. Didn't give me a chance to pack or nothing. He was kinda frantic."

Which explained why the cell was left behind. "What did he do then?"

"We drove to Vegas. Heavy said we needed to finish the video ASAP."

"Before Heavy got arrested?" Caleigh asked.

Julio gave us another blank stare. "You chicks really don't know a thing about the music business. We had to finish it before the news broke. You can't buy that kind of publicity! Heavy getting arrested would just add to his street cred, and he wanted to have the video ready to release as soon as that news broke."

"Did Heavy kill Roger?" I asked, getting to the point.

But Julio just shrugged. "I honestly don't know. I've learned to keep my mouth shut and not ask too many questions when working with these kinds of dudes."

"What kind would that be?" Caleigh clarified.

"Dangerous ones."

Word.

Sam shook her head at Julio, but she didn't look like she wanted to kill him anymore. "Of all the stupid schemes. You better just hope that our son has inherited my brains."

I heard Caleigh stifle a laugh.

"Last question," I said, still puzzled about one specific aspect. "Why the mannequins?"

Julio grinned from ear to ear. He had a charming smile. I understood what had attracted Sam to him. "The song starts off about the rich life. Roger's bathroom showed what money could buy, and we put famous places up on the green screen, like New York, Paris, and London. But the song was about how fake the entertainment business could be. The ladies represent that. You know, they're plastic." He chuckled.

I smirked. Nice touch.

Julio got closer to Sam and took her hands in his. "I'm sorry I worried you, *mija*. Tell my little man I'll make it up to him."

I turned away to give them a private moment but not before I saw Sam's hard edge soften enough to give him a tight hug. For all of her smacking him, I could tell she was relieved to find him in one piece.

"So, do we think Heavy did it?" Caleigh asked me as we made our way toward the door.

"I don't know," I hedged. The truth was even though all signs pointed to Heavy as a kidnapper and possible murderer, I wasn't sure what his motive might be. If Roger really was bankrolling Heavy's video and starring in it, it seemed like he might be more useful to Heavy alive. Unless, of course, the whole thing had been to generate more press prior to Heavy's release. Julio had said you couldn't buy that kind of publicity, but would someone really kill for it? "I think it's time we chatted with Heavy Cash," I told her.

We left Julio at the warehouse. He said he was just putting the finishing touches on the music video files, and he planned to return to L.A. tomorrow. He promised to send child support and to call Sam as soon as he was back in town. On the walk back, Sam said she had no intention of waiting for him to call her. She was going to show up at his house, with Julio Jr. tomorrow. I told her I'd happily give her the day off.

Once we got back to the hotel, we wasted no time in taking the elevator up to the penthouse, courtesy of Speedo's key that Maya had swiped. This time we didn't care about disguises. I closed my fist and pounded on Heavy's door.

It opened, and Heavy's manager, Johnson, stood there. He wore a white tank top and his pants from earlier. He held a glass of amber liquid, probably scotch or bourbon, in his hand, and the whites of his eyes were bloodshot. "You're too late," he said before I could even speak. "The detective already took Heavy away."

Detective?

"You mean the assistant district attorney? Aiden Prince?" I asked, remembering our little moment from earlier that night.

But Johnson shook his head, took a swig of his drink, and swallowed hard. "No. He said 'detective.' He had some sort of badge."

I held my hand above my head several inches. "About this tall, blonde, green eyes."

Johnson shook his head again, swaying slightly. "No, this guy was shorter. Dark, greasy hair."

My Spidey senses tingled. That was definitely not Aiden. Were the Vegas cops looking for Heavy too?

"Did he have on a uniform?" I asked.

"No. Brown pants and a green polo shirt."

The uniform of Lite Wraps.

Adrenaline rushed into my body at the prospect that Jenkins was on the loose. Had he busted out of the hotel room? Were Elaine and Charley okay? And why on earth would he pose as a detective to take Heavy away? He'd seemed in a hurry to get away from Heavy earlier when Maya had found him. Was he bent on some sort of revenge?

"Look, you got it all wrong about Heavy," Johnson said, breaking into my wild train of thought. "He may put on a hard exterior," he slurred, "but that's for the public. The fans. I mean, you ever heard of a geeky rapper?"

"Geeky?" Maya asked.

"Yeah. The guy's like read all the *Harry Potter* books and lives for that *Star Wars* stuff."

"Like light sabers and that furry guy?" Caleigh asked.

I didn't know much about *Star Wars*, but I knew the name of Chewbacca. I made a mental note to sit Caleigh down for a movie night in the near future.

The manager rolled his eyes. "Yeah. I don't get it either, doll. It's not my thing. But Heavy's like obsessed with all things nerdy. But I tell you, he's smart enough to know that his fans won't go for it. He wants everyone to think he's a thug so that he can sell records. But in truth, he's just a big, cuddly bear who loves his mama and Jedis and couldn't hurt a fly." He paused, a flash of sobriety flitting across his features for a second. "But don't tell him I said that."

Suddenly pieces started to fall into place. Heavy was the perfect murder suspect. Heck, he practically encouraged the police to think so. What easier person to frame for a murder? This had all been a setup. And I had a suspicion just which greasy, wrap-loving guy had been doing the framing.

Just then my cell rang. I glanced at the display before answering it this time. It was Elaine. Something was wrong. There was no other reason for her to call, and I knew it had to do with brown pants and a green polo shirt. "Hello?" I asked, my voice more breathless than I'd intended.

"Jamie! I'm so sorry. I don't know how it happened, but…Jenkins escaped."

CHAPTER EIGHTEEN

———

We met Charley and Elaine in the lobby near the casino entrance, next to a row of noisy slot machines.

"He couldn't have gotten far," Charley said. "He hasn't been gone more than five minutes."

I wanted to grill them as to how that had happened, considering the chair I'd set up, but now wasn't the time. "Let's spread out and find that weasel. We'll meet back here."

Sam and I went left into the casino, while Caleigh and Maya headed straight ahead, and Charley and Elaine took a right.

We entered the casino. There weren't as many people here at this hour as there had been earlier, but there were still enough to get lost in small crowds. We circled the slot machines first. A middle-aged man in plaid pants and a white shirt pushed in one coin after another. A couple of animated guys about my age sat a few seats over. Each time they pulled the lever and didn't win a grand prize, they moaned and then cheered to egg one another on to try again.

We walked past the blackjack table. No one could hide there. I didn't see Jenkins as a hider. He was more of a runner. But if he knew we were looking for him, he might hide to get away.

Sam shrugged her shoulders at me, as if to say she didn't know where he could be.

The more we walked through the casino, the more defeated I felt. What if he'd already skipped out? Chances were he'd head back to L.A. But what would happen to Heavy in the meantime?

And of course, there were still unanswered questions. Like how did Jenkins convince Heavy Cash he was a cop, and how did he even have time to get out of my hotel room, up to the penthouse, and escape with Heavy before Elaine called me? It wasn't adding up. Not unless Jenkins had an accomplice.

I stopped walking and stared down at my pink painted toenails. That was it. Of course. No, not my choice of polish, although it was exceptional, but Wrap Guy hadn't pulled all of this off by himself. He'd had help. His son, Wrap Guy Jr.

"Keep an eye out for a younger version of Jenkins," I said to Sam. "He may be working with his son."

She nodded and didn't question why. She was good like that.

We circled through the casino, but it was becoming abundantly clear that Jenkins wasn't there.

I snapped my fingers. "Bathrooms."

Sam nodded, and we took off in the direction of the nearest restrooms. Sam hit the women's room, just in case, and I took the men's. I pushed open the door with my left index finger, afraid of what I'd see or smell. The room had a faint scent of urine, which was to be expected, and a stronger aroma of a lemony artificial air freshener. Combined...well, I wanted to get out of there as quickly as possible. Brown tiles covered the floor in a checkered sort of pattern alternating between light and dark shades as they crawled up the walls. Every few inches there was a gold-colored tile, which gave it all a sparkle. The top portions of the walls were covered with a brown speckled wallpaper. The sink and urinal area was, thankfully, empty. There were two stalls, and both doors were shut, so I couldn't tell if they were occupied or not.

I walked over to the first one and pushed it with the same index finger that had opened the door. Better to keep it at one so I could decontaminate it properly. The stall was empty. One down, one more to go. I pushed on it as well, but it didn't budge, and no one called out.

I knocked, and no one answered. If Jenkins was in there and thought I'd just go away, he was kidding himself. "Hello?"

Nothing.

I knocked again. I really didn't want to get on my hands and knees and look under. God only knew what was on this floor. Some men didn't exactly have good aim.

I considered stepping on the toilet seat of the empty stall and looking over. If it was some drunk or someone mute, that would be really embarrassing. But what other options did I have? I went into the empty stall, placed one foot on the toilet seat, and both hands on the dividing wall. I lifted myself up, said a quick, silent prayer I wouldn't see anything I couldn't erase from my memory with a good night's sleep, and peeked over.

The stall was empty. Someone thought it would be funny to lock the door and shut it. I sighed and stepped down. What a waste of time. I walked out of the men's room as fast as possible. Sam was waiting for me.

"Any luck?" she asked.

"No. Let's go back to the lobby and see if the others are around."

I walked to the front desk and approached the pimply young man.

"Excuse me. Can you please tell me which room Ian Jenkins is in, please?"

He put on what was probably the standard hotel smile and said, "We can't give out guests' rooms, ma'am."

Of course he couldn't. That would be too easy.

"Would you care to leave him a message?"

"Can you call him and tell him that…Bristol Claremont is waiting for him?" I wasn't sure if her name would get his attention, but I knew mine would not.

"Yes." He looked up the room number on his tablet. "Did you say Ian Jenkins? J-E-N-K-I-N-S?"

He couldn't find him? That would mean he hadn't registered a room. Or hadn't registered one under his own name. "Yes."

He swiped at his screen and shook his head. "I'm sorry, but he's not a guest here."

Now, was that so hard to begin with?

"Perhaps he hasn't checked in yet? Or he could be at one of the neighboring hotels."

"Thank you," I said and walked away. If Jenkins wasn't registered here, did it mean he was staying elsewhere?

Or had he not even bothered with a room? This place didn't seem to be in his price range anyway.

"Now what?" Sam asked.

We walked around some more until we were back at the slot machines. The others hadn't returned yet. Maybe that was a good sign.

Movement in my peripheral vision had me turning toward it. I didn't know what made me turn. It was a feeling, not about Jenkins, but more…personal. That was when I saw him. Dressed in an old, ratty fly-fishing hat, a pair of sunglasses, and a fake-looking bushy mustache. Dark jeans, a burgundy jacket, and loafers covered his stocky build. Okay, so yeah, the hideous disguise made him more noticeable than not, but it was the gray-and-black boat shoes that gave him away. I'd recognize them anywhere since I'd bought them for him last Christmas.

Derek.

I closed my eyes, thought a whole string of really dirty words, and then I marched toward him.

He had his back toward me and didn't see me coming. In fact, he seemed entirely engrossed in something happening at the bar in the center of the casino floor. As I got closer, I saw exactly what it was. Elaine and Charley were sitting at a pair of stools in the corner with a pair of wineglasses in hand.

Seriously? He'd come to Vegas to spy on his girlfriend?

I reached him and slapped him on the shoulder. I took small satisfaction in the fact that he jumped about a mile.

"What are you doing here?" I hissed at him.

He jerked around, his brows up over the glasses, and his mustache falling lopsided. "Jesus, James, you about scared the crap out of me."

I placed my hands on my hips and scowled. "Answer the question, Derek."

He glanced behind him. Charley and Elaine were showing a photo on Elaine's cell to the bartender. Presumably of our missing Jenkins. I couldn't help watching the bartender's face for any sign of recognition. None. Darn.

"I, uh…" Derek stammered, drawing my attention back to my dad. "Well, can't a guy take a vacation now and then?"

"Nice try, old man. You are here spying on her, and in this silly getup. Did you really think she wouldn't recognize you?"

Derek did an over-the-shoulder toward Elaine before ducking behind the potted palm to his right. "It's not that bad, is it?"

"You look like a porn star going fishing. Yeah, it's that bad. How did you find us?"

He puffed out his chest. "How do you think? I am a private investigator, after all."

"*Retired* private investigator."

"Po-tate-o, po-tot-o." He waved me off.

"More like *stalker*, *restraining order*," I said, not letting him off that easy.

He grinned. "Okay, fine. If you must know, I went by Elaine's place earlier, but it was all dark. I happened to chat with one of her neighbors, who said Elaine was talking earlier about taking a road trip to Vegas with some guy named Charlie. So I booked a flight. Now I'm just waitin' for this Charlie guy to show up so I can give him a piece of my mind."

I rolled my eyes so far I saw blonde roots. Then I slapped him again but this time with less force. My hand was still tingly from the first time. "There is no Charlie guy! *That's* Charley," I said, pointing toward the bar where the Senior Sleuths were now showing the photo to the other bar patrons. "She's Maya's mom."

Derek blinked at me. "What's Elaine doing here with Maya's mom?"

"When Maya went home to pack for the trip, they insisted on tagging along."

More blinking.

"We're here on a case," I hissed at him. I really didn't have time for this. I had a wrapper and a rapper on the loose.

I watched as recognition registered on his face…followed closely by an unexpected frown. "Wait, are you telling me that you brought Elaine to Vegas on a *case*?"

"Well, 'brought' isn't exactly the word I'd use. More like I was bamboozled into letting her tag along might be more accurate—"

"Is this the murder case?"

"Uh, well, sort of—"

"The dangerous murder case? You dragged my girlfriend into the dessert into the middle of a dangerous murder investigation, possibly putting her in harm's way?"

I gave him my best *get real* look. "You're trying to turn the guilt tables on me, aren't you?"

He paused. "Is it working?"

"Kinda," I said honestly. "Look, Elaine's not cheating on you. God only knows why, but she actually likes you."

"You think?"

"I know. Now go home."

Derek shrugged, and for a moment I could have sworn he was actually thinking about doing what I'd asked.

For a moment.

"You know, you lied to me, kid. You said she was having a quiet night in," he said.

Oh yeah. I'd forgotten all about that.

"But you didn't believe me if you went to her house and talked to her neighbors." I was hoping he wouldn't harp on my lying. I knew he had lied to me before—many times—but there was something about lying to my father that left an extra-bitter taste in my mouth. Well, at least when caught.

"Jamie," Sam said, coming up behind us. Saved by the brunette.

She paused when she saw Derek. "Hello, Mr. Bond."

"Hi." He removed the glasses and gave a half smile. I doubted he remembered her name. He usually referred to Sam and Caleigh as Legs Number 1 and Legs Number 2.

"So, are you going to tell Elaine you're here?" I asked.

Derek frowned. "Are you crazy?"

Sometimes I had to wonder.

"If I tell her, she'll think I don't trust her."

I quirked an eyebrow at him. "You don't."

"But I want to."

I laughed. Really, it was all I could do. If I ever wrote my memoirs, this week would definitely be highlighted in the book. They could write a TV show about the Bond Agency, and Charlize Theron could play me. Harrison Ford could play Derek. Or maybe even Pierce Brosnan, if I was in a good mood.

My fame-and-fortune fantasies were cut short as I spotted a flash of pale green out of the corner of my eye. I whipped my head around, feeling adrenaline spike as I instantly locked eyes with Jenkins.

We held eye contact just long enough for me to see his eyes go wide with recognition.

Then he bolted.

I didn't think. I bolted too. In a second I was on his heels.

We ran through the lobby, and Pimply the Front Desk Clerk shouted at us to slow down. Sorry, kid. They'd have to arrest me before I'd let Jenkins get away this time. He ran in a U-turn and headed toward the front doors, but Sam and Derek got there first and blocked him. Way to go, Dad.

Jenkins took a left and turned back into the casino, and we took off. People became blurs, and I was surprised no one had stopped us. Yet. A woman at the upcoming table scooted her seat in, but she left her ginormous purse on the floor, just behind her chair. She reached back to get it just as I was racing past. I ended up jumping and leaping over her arm and nearly kicked her in the face.

"Sorry," I shouted and kept going. There was nothing like an assault charge to add to my disturbing the peace.

I was panting by the time we reached the back of the casino. I felt perspiration run down my back and my sandals pinch my feet. They were adorable, but they were not made for chasing bad guys. Nevertheless, I kept going, even as my breath started coming out in ragged huffs. I mentally reminded myself to hit the gym when I got home.

Before I realized it, we'd left the casino and entered the buffet dining room. Long rows of food covered one end of the room, where people in a line were busy filling plates with shrimp cocktail and crab legs.

Jenkins darted between the tables, surprising the early-morning diners. The little weasel wove between them like navigating a maze. He was outnumbered though. He had to have known that. He was panting too, and I could see a sheen of perspiration on his face. He paused as he rounded the breakfast buffet displays, his eyes darting between me and the exit behind me. I felt Derek and Sam come up just to my left, blocking the path Jenkins had taken into the dining room. A quick glance at Derek had me struggling to hold back laughter. His mustache had loosened and tilted. One half covered a portion of his mouth.

When I looked back, Jenkins had stolen a biscuit and several slices of bacon. How rude.

"Sam," I shouted and moved closer to the breakfast display.

"We got him," she said and went in the opposite direction.

Jenkins just stood there frozen with a slice of bacon sticking out of his mouth. Sam went around one end, and I was making my way toward the other. He was cornered, and the wide-eyed fear on his face stated he knew it.

But instead of coming with us peacefully, he reached into a serving dish and pulled back a handful of scrambled eggs. Gosh, was he that hungry?

Suddenly the eggs were flying through the air and hit me in the forehead.

I yelped. "Sonofa…" They were hot. I stared at him, watched a small blob of egg fall from my eyebrow, and did the first thing that came to mind. I grabbed an apple and flung it at him. It missed by a mile, but there were plenty of others. I refused to acknowledge that my actions were childish. Flying breakfast items were better than flying bullets, right?

Jenkins flung some eggs at Sam and then started tossing around slabs of ham like Frisbees. A slice hit me in the neck. I grabbed a kiwi, but it was hard aiming well with grapes hitting me in the face.

"Hey, that hurt!" I shouted. I tossed a handful of hash browns at him, hoping they were as hot as the eggs.

"Jamie, look out," I heard Sam yell, and I ducked just in time to avoid being hit by a cantaloupe slice being thrown like a boomerang.

"What's going on here?" I heard someone screaming. Out of my peripheral vision, I spotted Charley and Elaine. At first they were fully focused on the food fight...until Elaine's eyes wandered to my right and widened in shock. Or maybe outrage.

"Derek Bond!" she yelled. "What on earth..." She trailed off, taking in his disguise.

"Hey, babe," he said, giving her a little one-finger wave.

"Are you spying on me?!"

"Uh..." Derek didn't get a chance to answer before a glob of cottage cheese whacked him in the side of the head.

"Take that, you suspicious old coot!"

"But, Elaine—"

He was cut short by a handful of pineapple joining the cottage cheese.

Normally I would have been doubled over with laughter, but I was preoccupied by fending off my own incoming fruit salad as Jenkins picked up a grapefruit half and lobbed it at me.

I retaliated with a ladle full of sticky oatmeal that I hoped landed in his greasy hair.

"Gross!" he yelled. Bingo. He grabbed a large serving spoon, dipped it into the eggs Benedict and hollandaise sauce, and shot it at me. The bastard.

I held up an arm to shield my face from the scalding sauce. Luckily, most of it missed me, but a good chunk of my hair now smelled like butter and lemons.

Someone shouted for us to stop, but none of us obeyed. It wouldn't be long until hotel security arrived. And Jenkins knew it, if the panicked look in his eyes was any indication. As biscuits flew through the air, his eyes shifted toward the exit as if contemplating a break for it.

I rushed forward, stepped on a pineapple chunk, and slipped. By holding on to the end of a dessert table so I wouldn't go down completely, I managed to stay off my butt, but my arm leaned into something sticky. Maple syrup. I hoped. This cleanup would take a giant-sized bottle of hand sanitizer.

"Stop," Derek shouted.

Elaine was rubbing orange slices on his head. His hat and glasses were on the floor by his feet. That darn mustache was still hanging on for dear life.

Charley stood back in the archway, with her mouth hung open. She was smart to stay out of it.

I turned my attention back to Jenkins, who was being pelleted by granola. Sam's aim was spot-on whether she held a semiautomatic or oats and nuts.

Jenkins reached for the bacon. Oh no, he couldn't waste the bacon.

I lunged forward and threw myself at him for the second time in less than 24 hours. This time there was no dangerous concrete, and I wouldn't tumble down a flight of stairs, so I didn't have to be as careful. Which was just as well because all of the fallen food made the floor slippery.

I landed on his back, like a giant bug. Since my shirt was covered with various food remains, I started to slip off him, so I dug my elbows into his shoulders and my knees at his hips. Between my weight and the thick Belgian waffle that hit him in the face, we went down.

CHAPTER NINETEEN

———

I'm not sure how long I clung to a cursing and squirming Jenkins, but it wasn't until I saw security swarm the buffet that I contemplated letting him go. I felt someone grab my forearm and start to lift me up and off of the sticky little weasel's back. "Easy there, Bond," a familiar voice said close to my ear.

I didn't need to turn my head to realize it was Aiden. Where he had come from, I had no idea. Of course he showed up *after* I had to single handedly tackle his bad guy to the ground. I rested one open palm on Jenkins's back and pushed against him while I found my footing, which wasn't easy, considering I still had a chunk of pineapple stuck to the bottom of my shoe. Those suckers were slipperier than they looked. As soon as I was off of him, a security guard quickly cuffed the weasel.

When I was finally on my feet, I brushed the fruit off onto the carpet, pushed a chunk of hollandaise-sauce drenched hair behind my ear, and faced Aiden. "Nice to see you," I said, trying my best at a professional voice.

He grinned. "Likewise." He gave me a slow up and down, and I could see laughter threatening to overtake his expression.

Yeah, yeah, chuckle it up, buddy. I probably would've too if the pungent aroma of eggs and maple syrup wasn't starting to make me gag.

"I am so sorry I missed this," he said.

"I'm sure security has it on tape," I said, feeling a bit cheeky.

His face lit up. Then he turned to a security guard holding Jenkins. "I'll need a copy of that, Bob."

They were already on a first-name basis?

Bob didn't look all that happy at the state of the dining room or at being ordered around by an out-of-state ADA. I couldn't blame him. We'd basically destroyed the place. And by this point, we had a small audience watching and filming us on their cell phones. Maya and Caleigh had joined Charley, and luckily Elaine had stopped squishing strawberries on Derek's chest.

The security guard helped Jenkins to his feet. "The police are on their way."

Aiden turned his attention to Jenkins. "Where is Heavy Cash?"

So Aiden had figured out that Jenkins was involved in Heavy's abduction too. I wondered how much he knew about Jenkins Jr.

But Jenkins kept his mouth shut. I glanced at Sam and wished she could threaten him to talk with her Taser, but Aiden and the security guard didn't need to see that. It also didn't need to be filmed and posted on YouTube by all the spectators either. When this night—or day or whatever time it was now—was over, I planned to order the largest alcoholic drink I could find and enjoy it in the bubbliest bath I could find. I was all out of Zen and needed a super recharge.

"If you want to play games, we can," Aiden told Jenkins, putting on his seriously intimidating ADA face. "I'm getting paid to spend time with you. Can you say the same? How is business doing?"

I inwardly smiled at professional Aiden being a shark. It was kinda hot.

Jenkins grimaced and made some sound in his throat.

"Move, move," said a voice in the distance.

I turned to see Heavy's manager, Johnson, trying to elbow his way through the small crowd.

"Mr. Prince?" one of the security guards called.

Aiden gave me an apologetic smile. "Duty calls," he said. Then he moved toward the guard's side, listening intently to something.

While part of me was dying to eavesdrop on the conversation, I didn't get the chance, as Johnson finally made his way through the crowd.

"Jamie!" he hailed me.

I spun to find him still in his rumpled slacks, though he'd thrown a button-down shirt on over the undershirt from earlier. Even though it was horribly misbuttoned. "Jamie," he said breathlessly, like he'd been running. He looked over at Aiden and lowered his voice. "I just heard from Heavy."

That perked me right up. "When? Where is he?"

"He called my cell from a number I didn't recognize. His voice was low, and he only got out a couple of words before it cut out."

"What did he say?" I asked, steering him away from the crowd.

"Parking garage."

That was all I needed to hear.

I signaled to Sam and Caleigh, then booked out of the dining room. I felt my girls hot on my heels, with Johnson huffing a few paces behind. Derek must have seen me bolt, as he turned and joined our chase as well.

The parking garage was located just behind the casino and was almost as tall as the casino itself. If Heavy was being held there, he could be almost anywhere. I paused at the garage elevator for a moment, giving the girls, Johnson, and Derek a second to catch up as I contemplated my options. On instinct, I went with the top floor. If I were trying to hide, that would be the least traveled level. We waited an agonizing minute and a half as the elevator traveled upward. When it opened, I scanned the nearly deserted level and quickly spotted a dark late-model sedan sitting alone near the back corner.

I made a beeline toward it and was rewarded when the driver's side door opened and Wrap Guy Jr. stepped out. He too still wore his Lite Wrap's uniform. When he spotted me, his brows shot up his face.

"That's the man who said he was a detective," Johnson yelled.

I no longer had doubts, but it was nice to get confirmation.

Junior started to get back into the car, probably to drive off, but Sam pulled out her Taser. "Stop right there, or you're barbeque!" she shouted.

Junior's eyebrows went even higher, this time accompanied by his hands as they rose into a surrender motion. "T-take it easy, lady."

Banging and muffled sounds came from the trunk. It had to be Heavy.

"Pop the trunk," I said as Sam pointed the Taser at Junior.

He was a lot smarter than he looked and quickly complied, leaning into the front seat to click the trunk open.

Derek lifted it, and we all peeked inside. Sure enough, Heavy Cash was squished into it like a sardine. How he fit was beyond me. There was duct tape across his mouth and his wrists. His eyes were wide with fear, and I thought of Johnson calling him a cuddly bear.

Derek and Johnson helped Heavy out of the trunk, while Caleigh found a knife in the glove box, which she used to cut the duct tape at his wrists.

When both of Heavy's feet were on the ground, he peeled the tape off of his mouth and stared at me. "Thank you for rescuing me from that crazy dude. I thought he was going to kill me." And then he did a double take. "Whoa, why do you look like you just rolled around in the buffet?"

There was a desperation and softness to his voice that tugged at my heartstrings, despite the food comment. It didn't matter that Heavy was bigger than Junior. The man had genuinely been frightened. "What happened?"

"This idiot turns up at my hotel room with a fake badge and says he's the police. Says I need to go with him to answer some questions."

"And you did?" I asked.

Heavy nodded. "Sure I did. I'm an upstanding citizen, yo. But then this weasel pulls a gun and tells me to get in this lame crap-mobile's trunk, or he's gonna shoot me. Jerk." He punctuated that last barb by kicking Junior in the shins.

"Ow!"

"How did you call me?" Johnson asked Heavy.

"Idiot boy here left his phone charging in the backseat. I reached through the trunk hatch to the backseat and was able to get a couple words out before he caught me." He shot Junior a look. "Of course, then he taped my mouth and hands. Jerk." He moved to kick Junior again, but this time Junior sidestepped him.

"Why did he grab you in the first place?" Caleigh asked.

Junior pursed his lips together like he wasn't talking.

Heavy took a deep breath. "Man, this whole thing's been like a mess. I don't even know where to begin."

"Begin with why Roger had your gun," Sam offered. I had to admit, I wanted to know the answer to that too.

"Okay, look," Heavy said. "Here's how it went down. Roger was terrified of Ian Jenkins. The lawsuit Jenkins had brought against him was being settled, but Roger didn't have the money to pay the settlement."

"Claremont was a bastard," Junior shouted.

This time *I* kicked him in the shins.

"Ow!"

"Roger was planning to file bankruptcy. Turns out his wife had spent most of his sandwich-fame fortune. The last of it was invested into our music video."

Poor Bristol. She hadn't wanted to know about their finances, and she wasn't even aware of her predicament. At least there was the insurance money. I hoped.

"If Roger filed bankruptcy, he said Jenkins wouldn't get a single dime out of the lawsuit after all. Jenkins knew it and had been threatening Roger to get his money, which is why I gave him a gun for protection."

"Why didn't you just tell this to the police?"

"Like they'd believe me. Man, I got a record!"

I bit back a reply that I knew his record was mostly manufactured and any "street fighting" experience he had was likely all with light sabers.

"Anyway, after I found out Roger was killed with my gun, I knew that Jenkins had done the dude in."

"That's a lie," Weasel Jr. shouted.

All of us, except for Heavy, said, "Shut up."

Junior actually looked mildly offended.

Heavy continued his story. "I figured the cops were going to arrest me too, so I went to my friend, Julio's, grabbed him, and we drove to Vegas as quickly as possible to finish the music video."

This part I knew, but I didn't bother to interrupt.

"Only things went south when Jenkins arrived in Vegas too. He came to my hotel room and tried to blackmail me. He said he'd go to the police with a fake witness testimony saying how he saw me shoot Roger. He wanted me to pay up the money that Jenkins was entitled to under the lawsuit settlement. As if I had that kind of cash on me."

Heavy pointed to Junior, who glared at all of us. "But while his son is crazy as a mofo, Jenkins was no match for a group of rappers. We tied him up and shoved him into my bathroom."

He chuckled, and Johnson joined in.

"What were you planning to do with Jenkins?"

Heavy and his manager stopped laughing and gave each other a long look. Then they turned blank stares my way.

I held up one hand. "Never mind. I don't want to know." Sometimes it was better to be ignorant of intended crimes.

I was just about to ask how Jenkins had known where to find Heavy, when I spotted the elevator doors open and a familiar face walk through them.

Aiden. I had to admit, this was one time I was happy to see him crashing my party. My grip on Junior was getting tedious. And the hollandaise smell was making me nauseous.

Minutes later the parking garage was swarming with security guards and local PD, Junior was in custody, and his car had been cordoned off as a crime scene. Heavy told his tale a second time to Aiden, though I noticed Johnson carefully censoring some of the parts this time.

Aiden listened carefully, peppering him with appropriate questions throughout. When he got to the end, Aiden waited a beat to take it all in, staring thoughtfully at Heavy.

Finally he said, "We'll need to get an official statement from you, but from what it sounds, there won't be any formal charges brought against you."

I let out a sigh of relief. Despite what they may have done with Jenkins, they weren't involved with Roger's death, and that's what mattered to me. Plus, Jenkins kinda deserved it.

But Heavy jumped up. A deep frown furrowed his brow. "What? No, dude, I just confessed to giving Roger that gun. And we tied up Jenkins!"

"I am not going to press charges for kidnapping, Mr. Cash. Be grateful." Aiden walked off to join a group of police looking through Junior's car.

"But..." Heavy trailed off, looking defeated.

I thought of Julio's words and how Heavy getting arrested would've been great, free publicity. "Uh, Heavy?" I said.

He turned to me with the saddest pair of puppy dog eyes I'd ever seen. "Yeah?"

"There were some people filming the food fight. The press will probably be here soon, if they aren't already," I said.

Heavy's eyes lit up. He nudged Johnson in the ribs. "You hear that, yo?"

Johnson sighed. "Oh yeah, I heard."

He raced toward the elevators with his manager reluctantly in tow. But before he was out of sight, he turned and pointed at me. "Thank you, little lady."

I smiled and then looked to Sam and Caleigh. Caleigh still looked clean and mostly fresh. Sam, however, had a few grapes stuck in her curls, and her halter top was stained with breakfast. And Derek was a fruit salad mess. I reached over and yanked off his mustache.

"Ow," he said and rubbed his lip.

"What do you say to showers and then breakfast?" I asked. I tossed Derek his fake 'stache.

Sam wrinkled her nose. "I don't think I can stomach anything that involves an egg."

Caleigh linked her arms around mine and Sam's, and we headed to the elevator. Derek followed behind.

"I am hungry though," Caleigh said.

I smiled. "How about some Hoagies? They are diet food, after all."

CHAPTER TWENTY

———

The next day, I arrived at the agency in tip-top shape. In fact, I'd slept so well, it was late morning by the time I got there.

We had all arrived home from Vegas late the previous morning, and after another shower I spent most of the day napping. The shower at the hotel hadn't felt like enough to get the scent of sauce out. When I'd woken up, I'd had a quiet night in front of my television with another Niçoise salad with seared tuna and sparkling water. Followed by wine and ice cream. They really helped me get my Zen back.

Now, the sun shone, the birds sang, and as I pushed open the agency doors, I was greeted by the clicking of Maya's keyboard.

I'd given Sam the day off as promised. I would've offered the same for Maya and Caleigh, but we still had work to do. And I could give each of them a day at another time. On the drive home yesterday, Charley had commented how she hadn't realized how strenuous our jobs were, and then she'd taken a nap with her head on Elaine's shoulder. I didn't know what happened between Elaine and Derek, but she came back with us and remained very quiet on the ride home. That couldn't have meant anything good for her and Dad. Elaine usually loved to talk.

I immediately spotted Mr. and Mrs. Henderson seated in the lobby chairs. I gave the couple a brief wave before stopping at Maya's desk.

"Morning," I said.

"Good morning, Boss." She handed me my caramel macchiato. "It's probably cold. I thought you'd be in earlier, so I bought it at my usual time. I could run out and get another."

I smiled my thanks. I loved that woman. "No, this is fine." I glanced at her desk and saw a Diet Coke in place of her own usually decadent coffee order. I raised an eyebrow. "Diet soda?"

She cleared her throat and looked down. "It's the weirdest thing. When I stepped on the scale this morning, it said I'd gained five pounds since last week. I mean, even with all of the diet subs I've been eating."

I stifled a grin. "Maybe we should all switch to salads for a while, huh?"

She nodded her agreement.

"I see the Hendersons are here," I said, switching gears. "What else is happening today?"

She picked up her tablet and tapped it several times. "You have no other appointments today."

Sweet. Maybe we could all leave early today then.

Maya glanced to the Hendersons. "Their file is on your desk, and Bristol Claremont left a very grateful message along with an IOU for payment of our fee."

I'd never found out about Roger's insurance policy. I hoped he had a substantial one, but with him preparing to file bankruptcy, I wasn't going to hold my breath that Bristol would inherit anything. So much for celebrity clients!

I walked over to the Hendersons. "Good morning. Why don't you come into my office?"

They wore similar outfits again. This time navy pants and a white short-sleeve, button-down shirt for him, and a navy shirt with a white short-sleeve, button-down blouse under a beige vest for her.

They followed me in and sat across from my desk. "We didn't mean to come back so soon, Ms. Bond, but time is very sensitive here," Mrs. Henderson said.

"I understand." I sat in my chair and set my coffee down. Then I flipped open their file, which was center on my desk, and pulled out the sheets Maya had printed for them.

"Were you able to find out much?" Mrs. Henderson asked.

I handed over the printouts. "We've only been able to investigate the first two women on the list so far. Jenny Pepin and Penny Samson. They both seemed to be awesome women. Ms. Samson leads a very active life. I'd say, even to the point of being a bit dangerous."

I didn't want to scare them off of her, but I also wanted to be honest.

"And Ms. Pepin is a lovely woman whose most dangerous activity is water aerobics." I smiled and tried to put Mr. Henderson at ease, but his face didn't relax.

He sat straight, hands in his lap, shoulders tense. He looked slightly more stressed than our first meeting, so I couldn't tell if this was usual or not, but he definitely seemed more uncomfortable.

"If you'd like us to continue investigating and to find out about Ms. Toll…"

Mrs. Henderson shook her head and stared at the pages. "No, thank you. This is fine. We really appreciate it. How much do we owe you?"

"You can settle your bill with Maya up front."

"Okay." She turned to her husband. "I'm going to run to the restroom for a minute."

He nodded and looked at her with sad eyes.

I rose to my feet. "It's up front. I can show you."

They both stood. Mrs. Henderson squeezed the arm of the chair and stayed still for a moment, as if she was trying to steady herself. "No, I can find it."

When she walked out of my office, Mr. Henderson stayed behind. He kept his gaze on where she had just sat. "She likes to be independent."

"Yes, I can see that."

He softly sighed. It was small, and if I hadn't been watching him, I may not have noticed. "She's been more nauseous lately. It's the medication."

"I'm so sorry."

Now his shoulders were slumped, and the wrinkles around his mouth seemed to bring down its corners, although I was sure part of that was Mr. Henderson's grief.

"Do you mind if I ask you a question?"

He looked at me. "No, go ahead."

"Do you want this? Do you want your current, dying wife to pick out your new wife? Are you going through with this?" I hoped the disapproval wasn't evident in my voice.

He shook his head. "Absolutely not. My wife is the love of my life, and once she's gone, I'll be spending the rest of my days alone. I have no intention of being with anyone else."

I felt relief in that. Finding a new wife without the new wife's knowledge was bizarre, to say the least. "But you're here."

His smile was gentle, and I had no doubts it was aimed at his wife and not me. "I want her to go in peace, believing that I'll be taken care of. So I'm going through with this charade for her sake."

My heart swelled, and the feelings of love and sympathy, as well as joy, must've combined on my face, because he said, "She's my best friend, Ms. Bond."

My throat tightened, and I couldn't speak, so I nodded.

Mrs. Henderson returned, and her husband quickly joined her at my door. "Are you okay, Linda?"

She cupped his hand with her own. "I am, Jeffrey. Let's go home."

He kissed her hand. "Yes, dear."

They walked out holding hands.

Their love was honest—well, except for his tiny fib—and real. True and unconditional. I thought of Derek and Elaine and me, Aiden, and Danny. Love wasn't supposed to be complicated.

I caught movement in my doorway and refocused my gaze. Aiden stood there, as if on cue. He looked downright delicious in a navy suit and tie. I walked around to the front of my desk and sat on its edge. "Hey, what are you doing here?"

He strode inside and sat in a chair directly in front of me. "I wanted to let you know how everything turned out, especially since you were the one who brought Ian Jenkins down."

I smirked. I did like the way he gave me credit. "Great, I'm dying to know."

He leaned back in the seat and extended his legs. His black, polished shoe gently touched my zebra pumps. "As soon as they were locked up, Jenkins sang like a canary in order to get a plea bargain."

I frowned. "The father was trying to pin it on his son?"

"And the son on the father. It was a ping-pong match. But it looks like it was Jenkins Senior who pulled the trigger. He went to Claremont's house to threaten him and tell him he was going to get his money out of Roger one way or another. Claremont freaked and pulled out the gun Heavy Cash had given him for protection. There was a struggle."

"And Roger was shot," I finished for him.

Aiden nodded. "Precisely."

"But why didn't we see any of this? Sam, Caleigh, and I were parked outside of the Claremont estate and never saw Jenkins come or go. There wasn't even a car."

"Except there was. Jenkins had parked on the road, like you did. Remember that black SUV you saw?"

I nodded, thinking back, wishing I'd paid more attention to it now.

"That belonged to Jenkins Junior, who was waiting for Dad. He parked there so Claremont wouldn't see him driving in and deny him access. After Jenkins shot Claremont, he started to run out, and he saw the three of you coming in. So he went out the back and escaped without you seeing him."

He really was a weasel. "So now what?"

"Instead of murder one, he's being charged with manslaughter. He'll still be spending a good deal of time in prison."

"And his son?"

Aiden rose, leaned toward me, and rested his palms on each side of me on my desk. "Kidnapping."

I couldn't help a smile. "I hope this isn't how you got your confessions."

Instead of using words to reply, he lightly pressed his lips against mine. It didn't stay light very long though. He placed his hands on my hips, pulling me up and toward him so we were both standing. I wrapped my arms around his neck and pressed my body against his. We simultaneously moaned, and the kiss deepened.

Despite becoming weak in the knees, my thoughts wandered to Mr. and Mrs. Henderson. Yes, not who I wanted to think of in a moment like this, but my brain had a mind of its own. It wasn't just of them, but of their connection. Of them leaving here hand in hand. Of their unconditional love. I wanted that.

I pulled my head back, breaking our kiss.

Aiden opened his eyes and stared at me. "What's wrong?"

"Nothing. I, uh, I…" I panted, suddenly breathless as I searched for the right words. "I just need a little time." I must have startled us both with that line, because his eyebrows went north.

I dropped my arms and stepped out of his embrace. The back of my legs knocked into my desk.

"If this is about the other night at your apartment, I apologize. I…well, I came on a little strong," Aiden said.

While I appreciated the apology, something kept me from stepping back into his arms.

He ran his hand through his hair. "Look, I know I've been going through some stuff, and…well, now I have it all worked out."

I gave a half smile. While I would have been jumping for joy over this news last week, something was still holding me back from stepping into his embrace. "I'm so glad."

He stared deep into my eyes. "This is about Danny, isn't it?"

"No." The lie tumbled out of my mouth, and part of me wished it had been the truth, but deep down I knew otherwise. It wasn't that I didn't want to be with Aiden. But it also wasn't that I didn't want to be with Danny. It was that I just didn't know what I wanted.

Aiden stepped back, went around the chair, and walked to the door. He gave me a long, hard look that I'd swear was daring me to follow him. But instead he just said, "Call me." Then he was gone.

My heart sank. I didn't want him to walk away like that. Like how I'd felt when *he'd* said he needed time a while back. But I knew I needed to let him go, at least for now.

"I will," I said even though I knew he couldn't hear me. I stood there for a good five minutes before I grabbed my purse and went up front.

Caleigh stood by Maya's desk. The usually bubbly blonde pouted. "Aiden didn't look happy."

I didn't know how to reply. I didn't want to talk about this just yet. "He'll be fine. I'm heading out, and I probably won't be back for the rest of the day."

If I knew Danny, he'd be doing lunch soon. Maybe I could catch him, turn it into lunch and a beer? A beer and an afternoon of shooting pool? An afternoon of shooting pool and maybe dinner, and then who knew what after…

"You guys should take the rest of the day off. Maya, can you lock up?"

Caleigh's pout turned into a smile. Maya shared her expression. "Absolutely, Boss. Have a great day."

"You too." I went out to my car. I took a moment to calm my nerves, and then I flipped down the visor and checked out my hair and face in the mirror. I retouched my lipstick, adding a light coating of Passion Red, which was really a soft red color, so someone screwed up that name, and then I headed to Danny's.

On the drive over, I prepared what I would say. I didn't memorize it. I wanted it to be natural, but I didn't want to ramble either. I planned to let him know that I wasn't stringing him along anymore. I wouldn't play any more games, and I was woman enough to admit I wanted to explore whatever this was between us and see where it could go.

My stomach flipped a thousand times, but the closer I got to his apartment, the better I began to feel. I kept hearing Mr. Henderson's words replay in my head. *She's my best friend.* This was the right move. Right? To be honest, I wasn't exactly sure, but I needed to find out.

I parked up the street from Danny's building and turned off my Roadster. I grabbed my purse and practically sprinted up the stairs to Danny's apartment. I paused outside the door, feeling butterflies multiply in my stomach. Why, I wasn't sure. I'd knocked on my best friend's door a million times. I told the butterflies to simmer down and gave a hard rap on the wood, then waited. And waited. I shifted from foot to foot, listening for any sound of movement on the other side. None. I knocked again.

"You lookin' for Danny?"

I turned to find a woman with gray hair standing in a pink housecoat in the doorway next door. She had a fluffy white cat in her arms and was eyeing me suspiciously.

I nodded. "Uh, yeah, I'm a...friend of his."

She squinted at me, and I got the distinct impression she needed glasses. "Yeah," she finally answered, "I've seen you here before." Her face creased into a smile.

I smiled back. "Uh, do you know if Danny's home?"

She shook her head. "Nope. He's gone."

I felt those butterflies sink like a rock in my belly. "Oh." So much for my lunch-and-then-who-knows-what plans. "Uh, I don't suppose you know when he'll be back?"

She nodded. "Sure do. Six months."

I froze. "S-six months?"

"Yeah, he said he took some photography job. New Zealand. Though, I'll tell you, for someone goin' away to work in paradise for half the year, he didn't look all that happy."

That rock grew into a full-blown boulder as I digested her words. Danny wasn't just out to lunch. He was *gone* gone.

He'd told me he wouldn't wait forever, and he hadn't. He'd left, and now it was too late.

* * *

I snapped my fingers at the bartender and pointed to my empty glass. To heck with Zen. Jack Daniels was my new guru.

The bartender looked less than impressed at the way I'd reordered, but he went about pouring me another shot anyway.

The barstool beside me scraped against the dusty floor, as someone pulled it out. The old bar was far from crowded. Couldn't the guy find a spot that wasn't on top of me? I turned to give him or her the stink eye and did a double take.

It was Derek.

His brow was furrowed, and he looked annoyed. Then again, that could've been just his usual expression. He ordered a scotch neat from the bartender.

"What are you doing here?" I asked.

"I should be asking you the same. Isn't it a bit early in the day for you to be drinking?"

"No new cases or appointments today, so I gave the girls the day off." He didn't need to know everything about my life.

"Hmm," he muttered and set a twenty on the bar. "Don't you usually go to places with white tablecloths and various sizes of forks?"

I smirked. He knew me well. "Sometimes. Other times I like dives like this. It's quiet, and no one messes with you here."

Neither of us remarked on how we both enjoyed the same bar. Unlike Derek, I wasn't a regular here, but I enjoyed it.

"How are things with Elaine?" I asked.

The bartender set down Derek's drink and made change from the twenty.

Derek took a long sip. "Not good. She gave me the 'I need some space' line in Vegas and refused to ride home with me, as you well know."

I knew about the ride, since I'd driven, but not about the line. Of course, the irony of that line was not lost on me. I was definitely a Bond.

"I think I really screwed up this time. I showed up to her place this morning with a dozen roses. She took them, whacked me over the head, and told me where I could shove them." He pointed to a scratch on his forehead. It looked like it had been bleeding at some point. It was pink and not too pretty, but it wasn't in need of medical attention.

"From the roses?" I asked.

He nodded. "Damn stem. I guess I was lucky the florist doesn't sell them with thorns."

I snorted.

He took another sip of his drink. "So, why are you really drinking in the middle of the day?"

I sighed. "Because my love life sucks as badly as yours."

"Danny will come around," he said.

I shot him a hard look. "How did you know I was talking about Danny?"

"I'm a good investigator." He winked at me.

"*Retired* investigator," I mumbled into my glass.

He shrugged off that detail. "That is who you're broken up over, isn't it, kid?"

I started to say yes, but stopped. The truth was at that point I didn't really know. "I'm not totally sure."

Thankfully, he didn't push it.

"Don't worry," I said. "Elaine will come around too."

"Oh, I know she will. I've got a standing order for a dozen roses to be delivered to her place every day. No one can resist the charm of a Bond forever."

I couldn't help but smile. Sometimes the old geezer could be romantic. And I had a feeling he was right. From everything I'd seen, Elaine really did care for him. Though, in her place, I couldn't blame her for letting the old guy simmer in his own guilt for a bit. If I'd found him spying on me, I'd be tempted to do the same.

Then again, if some guy had stood me up and run off to Vegas to lip-lock with someone else, I'd probably let *him* simmer in guilt too.

That depressing thought must have shown on my face as Derek patted my hand on the bar. "And don't you worry. It's gonna work out, kid." He shot me a supportive smile.

"You think?"

"I *know*."

I smiled back. I had to admit, it was making me feel a little better. Either that or the Jack.

"Hey, I know what you need," he said.

I cocked my head at him. "Another shot?" Somehow my glass was empty again.

"No. A vacation."

I snorted. "Right. Like a road trip to Cabo would solve everything."

Derek shook his head. "No, I mean a real vacation. Away from work, the girls, me, everything. Some time to just relax. You've been too stressed lately, James," he said, wagging his finger at me for emphasis.

I couldn't argue with him there.

"Where would I go alone?" I asked.

Derek shrugged. "I don't know." He paused, staring at a point above the bar for a moment, as if thinking. "I hear New Zealand is lovely this time of year."

I raised an eyebrow his way. "Where on earth did you hear that?"

Derek shrugged again, blinking at me in mock innocence.

I glanced down at my empty glass, then back up at Derek's sympathetic smile and rose-scratched face. He might be a good *retired* investigator, but he was also pretty decent at the pep-talk thing. Maybe he was right. Maybe I did need some time to get away, clear my head, gain some perspective. Time to get my Zen back. And I did have a few frequent flier miles saved up. Maybe even enough to make it to New Zealand…

Derek pulled me out of my thoughts with a hand on my shoulder. "I promise you one thing, James."

"What's that, old man?" I asked.

He smiled, his eyes twinkling. "Women may come and women may go, but our *Bond*…now that's something that won't ever wane, kid." He gave me a wink and chuckled at his own pun.

I grinned and chuckled back. Derek was right. No one could resist the charm of a Bond forever.

Not even me.

ABOUT THE AUTHORS

Gemma Halliday is the #1 Amazon, *New York Times* & *USA Today* bestselling author of several mystery series. Gemma's books have received numerous awards, including a Golden Heart, two National Reader's Choice awards, three RITA nominations, a RONE award for best mystery, and two Killer Nashville Silver Falchion Awards for best cozy mystery and readers' choice. She currently lives in the San Francisco Bay Area with her large, loud, and loving family.

To learn more about Gemma, visit her online at www.GemmaHalliday.com

Jennifer Fischetto is the *USA Today* bestselling author of the Gianna Mancini paranormal cozy mystery series, as well as a dozen other titles. She writes family-centric murder mysteries and things that go bump in the night.

A lover of rainstorms and snow, she prefers fiction over reality and longs to live in a world where French fries grow on trees, chocolate appears whenever desired, and every day is October. She watches too much television and movies, which fuel her never-ending supply of plot ideas, and is a rabid fan of suspense, horror, and everything supernatural.

To learn more about Jennifer, visit her online at: jenniferfischetto.com

Made in United States
Troutdale, OR
05/18/2024

19975545R10133